Finding Us

*with Kimberley Woodhouse **with Karen Witemeyer, Regina Jennings, and Jen Turano
For a complete list of Tracie's books, visit traciepeterson.com.

Finding Us

TRACIE PETERSON

BETHANYHOUSE
a division of Baker Publishing Group
Minneapolis, Minnesota

© 2023 by Peterson Ink, Inc.

Published by Bethany House Publishers
Minneapolis, Minnesota
www.bethanyhouse.com

Bethany House Publishers is a division of
Baker Publishing Group, Grand Rapids, Michigan

Printed in the United States of America

Library of Congress Cataloging-in-Publication Data
Names: Peterson, Tracie, author.
Title: Finding us / Tracie Peterson.
Description: Minneapolis, Minnesota : Bethany House Publishers, a division of
    Baker Publishing Group, [2023] | Series: Pictures of the Heart ; 2
Identifiers: LCCN 2022053713 | ISBN 9780764237416 (trade paper) | ISBN
    9780764237423 (cloth) | ISBN 9780764237430 (large print) | ISBN 9781493442089
    (ebook)
Classification: LCC PS3566.E7717 F56 2023 | DDC 813/.54—dc23
LC record available at https://lccn.loc.gov/2022053713

Scripture quotations are from the King James Version of the Bible.

This is a work of historical reconstruction; the appearances of certain historical figures are therefore inevitable. All other characters, however, are products of the author's imagination, and any resemblance to actual persons, living or dead, is coincidental.

Cover design by LOOK Design Studio
Cover model by Dmitry Mosuzenko / Trevillion Images

Baker Publishing Group publications use paper produced from sustainable forestry practices and post-consumer waste whenever possible.

23 24 25 26 27 28 29   7 6 5 4 3 2 1

Prologue

William Reed, Bill to his friends and family, stood at the rail of the ship and watched the distant storm move in. He worried about his sister-in-law, Amelia, who was eight and a half months pregnant and sleeping soundly in her cabin below. She had struggled with nausea throughout her pregnancy, and the rocking motion made it all the worse. Thankfully, their trip was only another day, then they'd reach Seattle.

Bill's brother, Wallace, was somewhere on the ship, no doubt ministering to a lost soul. He had been beside himself as to how he might help Amelia. She had finally told him to do what he did best—go share the Gospel. Wallace hadn't hesitated.

Bill had to smile at the thought of his brother preaching to the customers of the *City of Canton*. They might very well have a full-on revival meeting before reaching Seattle.

When his brother had determined that God was calling him to minister to the people in Alaska, Bill had eagerly gone along. As a botanist, Bill knew Alaska would provide an entirely new classroom for him to explore. That had been nine years ago, and the experience had been marvelous. Bill had even managed to secure a contract to furnish a New York publisher with a book on Alaskan vegetation. That was the biggest reason Bill was returning to Seattle. He wanted to send his completed manuscript to the publisher and be able to more easily communicate with them regarding a new project he had in mind.

Wallace and Amelia were heading to Seattle to ensure Amelia had the best medical care possible for the delivery of her baby. The pregnancy had been difficult for her. After nine years of longing for a child, Amelia's pregnancy had been fraught with worries. The final straw that convinced them to go to Seattle was the worries of the midwife. The baby had still not turned. A breech delivery would be dangerous, and given Amelia's petite frame, the older woman wasn't even sure Amelia could pass a child safely. It had been a grave concern to all.

"I thought that was you," Wallace said, joining Bill at the rail.

"I was just watching the storm move in. I keep hoping it might shift to the far north and leave us and this part of the ocean undisturbed."

Wallace glanced in the direction of the dark, heavy line of clouds. "The waters are already picking up the effects. The waves are building higher."

"Victoria isn't that far off," Bill said. "I wonder if we might reroute to dock there for safety."

"I have no idea. I'm sure the captain must know what he's

doing," Wallace said, his face taking on a look of concern. "I don't suppose he would willingly risk our lives."

"No, I'm sure he wouldn't."

The ship lurched, and the waves seemed to grow almost instantly. Bill grabbed hold of the rail, as did Wallace. The storm front seemed to pick up speed and race toward them.

"I suppose I should get below and see how Amelia is doing," Wallace said. "I know the storm will scare her. She's been such a good sport about everything, but this will be a bit too much."

"She's a good woman, Wallace. You're blessed that God gave you such a wife. I wish He'd see fit to provide one for me."

"He will in time." Wallace reached out and touched Bill's shoulder. "I know He has someone special for you. Someone who will love the things you love and be a good helpmate for you."

"I pray you're right. This loneliness is starting to eat me alive. I can only bury myself in my studies for so long before the longing threatens to suffocate me."

A new voice interrupted their conversation. "Well, well. If it isn't the man who killed my brother."

Bill and Wallace turned to find Grady Masterson standing a few feet away. They'd been on this ship for days, but Bill hadn't known that Grady was on board too. This was a most unpleasant surprise.

Wallace released his hold on Bill and crossed his arms. "You know full well that your brother was responsible for his own hanging. Had he not killed that man, he would never have had to face his own demise."

"And had you not spoken up and told the court you witnessed him committing murder, he would have walked away unscathed," Masterson replied. He stepped closer to get right in Wallace's face.

Bill could smell the liquor on the man's breath and put his hand out to separate the two. "Come off it, Masterson. What's done is done, and as sorry as I am that you've lost someone dear to you, I won't stand here and let you pick a fight with my brother."

"He deserves to suffer like I have. Like my brother did. You both deserve to die."

The wind picked up, and a light rain began to fall. Bill noted that the storm was nearly upon them. "We should get inside. The seas are growing rougher, and the storm is only going to get worse."

"That's nothing to me. I'd just as soon the sea swallow you whole." Grady's eyes narrowed. "Somehow I'm going to make you suffer the same kind of pain I suffered as I watched poor Avery hang."

"Grady," Wallace began, "you need to turn your life over to God and trust that He will show you a better way. You and your brother too long relied upon anger and violence to resolve your problems. Threatening me isn't going to bring you any satisfaction. Revenge seldom ever serves a satisfying purpose, but putting your faith in God will make you whole. You'll know the peace that passeth understanding."

The rain came in a deluge, and Bill grabbed Wallace's arm. "Let's get inside. Amelia will need you."

The ship rose sharply as the wind blew stronger. The shoreline of tiny islands appeared dangerously close. Bill feared the ship might be tossed onto the land at any moment. He looked at Masterson. "Surely you must see the danger."

"I was born for danger," Grady yelled above the roar of the wind.

The ship was tossed back and forth as waves crashed over the railing. Bill pulled at Wallace's arm but lost his grip. Then Bill felt the ship hit something firm. He imagined rocks tearing at the hull and the ship filling with water.

Without warning the ship's whistle blew loud and steady, and everything seemed to happen at once. Several crew members appeared and yelled instructions. "Find your life vests. The ship is taking on water, and we must get everyone to the lifeboats."

Wallace and Bill pushed past Grady and headed below to their cabins. Bill grabbed his life vest and boxed manuscript and headed to Wallace and Amelia's cabin next door. Amelia was already trussed up in her vest, and Wallace was tying the straps over her expanded abdomen.

"Bill, get Amelia to the lifeboats and see that she's safe. I'm going to see if there are others who need help."

"No, Wallace, stay with me. I'm so scared," Amelia begged.

He took hold of her face and pressed a quick kiss on her lips. "Bill will see that you're safe. Now be brave. You have to do this for the protection of our unborn child. I'll join you as soon as possible."

She nodded, but Bill could see the fear in her eyes. "Come with me, Amelia." Bill put his arm around her. "Wait, where's your coat? It's quite cold outside, and the rain will only serve to make it colder."

Amelia pointed to where her coat lay atop the bed. Bill grabbed it. "We'll see you at the boats, Wallace."

"I'll be there." Wallace exited the cabin first.

Bill shifted the manuscript and then took hold of Amelia's arm. This way he'd have a solid grip. "Let's go."

They headed out of the cabin and into the chaos. People were yelling, some screaming. Many of the women were sobbing and clinging to whomever was closest. Bill knew it wasn't going to be easy to navigate through the mob, but he kept pushing forward with Amelia affixed to his side.

The ship was listing by the time they got on deck. It was easy to see that it was sinking fast. Bill directed Amelia to the nearest lifeboat and saw her safely seated despite the massive waves moving everything like toys.

A crewman took hold of Bill's arm. "It's women and children first. We'll board the men in a moment."

Bill nodded and fought against the wind. "Amelia, take this. It's my manuscript. Keep it safe for me."

"Where are you going?" she cried, her eyes wide in fear. "Come with me."

"I can't just yet. It's women and children first. Besides, I must try to help the others. There's a lot of confusion, and some of the people might not make it if someone doesn't intercede for them."

"But Wallace is already out there. Can't you stay and let him manage? I don't want to be alone."

Bill shook his head. "You're never alone, Amelia. God is with you, even now. You know that." He noted the number of the lifeboat. Number five.

She nodded and lowered her face. Bill wrapped her coat around her shoulders as the wind slammed icy rain against them. "Keep this on. I'll be back as soon as possible."

He didn't look back. He knew he'd never be able to leave

her if he did. She had become such a precious sister to him. It took everything he had to walk away.

Up ahead an elderly woman was knocked to the ground as the ship shifted again. Several people ran right over her as they hurried for the lifeboats. Bill reached her and helped her to her feet. "Let me help get you to the lifeboats."

She nodded, but the dazed look on her face left no doubt that she was more than a little confused. Bill helped her reach the boats, then handed her over to a crewmember who helped her from there.

"Women and children first," he told Bill.

"I understand. I'm just trying to help get them here."

He took off and hurried down the deck to find the next person who needed assistance.

The entire situation took less than twenty minutes. Bill was surprised at how quickly the ship lost buoyancy and how fierce the storm remained. The crew called for men to board the lifeboats just as Bill spotted Wallace. He grabbed his brother by the arm.

"Come on. The ship has only seconds left, and we need to get the lifeboats away from the ship."

Wallace nodded and joined Bill as they climbed into the nearest lifeboat. "Where's Amelia? Why didn't you stay with her?"

"I couldn't. It was just women and children at that point. Besides, I had to help—just as you were doing."

"Yes, but you left her alone? What boat is she in? Where are they?"

"She is in boat five. I'm not sure where they are, but they are likely already in the water."

Wallace nodded as they moved away from the *City of*

Canton. The moonless night offered no comfort as the lights went out on the ship and she slipped beneath the black roiling water.

It was the next morning before they were picked up by other ships. An American ship picked up some of the survivors, including Bill and Wallace. A Canadian ship picked up some of the remaining lifeboats.

Bill and Wallace searched among the survivors for Amelia, but she was nowhere to be found.

"What boat was she on?" a crew member asked, checking a clipboard of names.

"Boat five," Bill replied before his brother could speak.

The crewman looked up. His expression was grim. "I'm sorry. I hate to be the one to tell you this, but that boat and two others rolled over, and the people were lost."

Wallace grabbed the man. "What did you say?"

"I said that boat five and its passengers were lost in the storm. We might never recover the bodies, but if your wife was on that boat . . . I'm afraid she's dead."

1

I don't know why you think being a Camera Girl is such
a great job," Rosemary Connors told Eleanor. "You
have to walk miles and miles every day—rain or shine,
not to mention be in the middle of that deafening expo."

Outside, the morning traffic was starting to get noisy.
Given their little apartment was in one of the busiest areas,
it sometimes seemed as if the entire city was suddenly in
their front room.

Eleanor Bennett laughed and closed the living room's
single window. "But I love the expo. The Alaska-Yukon-
Pacific Exposition has so many great exhibits. I doubt I'll
ever get through all of them, but it's a wonderful place
to be. And I love being outside and meeting new people.
But best of all, they have the most extraordinary flower
arrangements. They've planted hundreds of thousands of
plants, and it's beautiful. I've taken so many pictures of
them for myself that I have to be careful not to spend more
than I earn."

Her roommate shook her head. "I still think you'd be happier working in an office like I do. You already know how to type, and I could get you a job where you could sit instead of walk."

"But I love walking. I'm not like you, Rosemary. I love being outside and walking. I'm not happy cooped up inside. And don't worry. I wasn't serious about spending more than I earn. I get a huge discount for the film I use. You know I'm saving everything I can for my fall classes at the University of Washington."

"That's another thing. Why are you bothering to go to college? Why not just go to work for a nursery or botanist if you want to study flowers and such? I'm sure someone would hire you to work with them, especially since you can type." Rosemary studied the stocking she'd been working to mend, then resumed her stitching.

"I know I can't afford to go to college full-time, but if I just take a few classes, then I would be even more valuable to someone hiring me on. Besides, attending the university sounds like fun. Maybe I'll even meet a botanist there."

"I suppose it's possible." Rosemary finished her sewing and rose. "I need to hurry, or I'll be late to work."

"Me too," Eleanor said, shoving the last bits of toast into her mouth. "I'll see you tonight." She grabbed up her satchel and headed for the door. "Have a great time typing."

"Have fun walking," Rosemary giggled and called back.

Eleanor chuckled and headed down the flight of stairs to the building's outside door. She really liked Rosemary. From the moment Eleanor had answered her ad in the newspaper for a roommate, Eleanor had enjoyed Rosemary's no-nonsense attitude. All her life Eleanor had enjoyed a sort of discernment about people who let her know up front if they were friend or foe, and Rosemary was definitely a friend.

Outside, the sunshine brought an immediate smile to Eleanor's face. It might rain this afternoon, as it often did, but for now everything was beautiful and bright. She prayed it would remain that way. It was hard to explore around the lake when it was pouring rain.

Making her way to the trolley, Eleanor hummed her favorite hymn, "What a Friend We Have in Jesus." It always made her smile to think of Jesus not only as her savior but also her friend. She boarded the trolley and continued humming softly as they made their way to the expo.

How blessed I am. I have this wonderful opportunity to work at an international fair and meet new people, plus get paid for it. Eleanor giggled, and the man sitting next to her looked over and smiled. She returned his smile. "It's a beautiful day, isn't it?"

The man nodded. "It is that. Are you heading out to see the exposition?"

"I work there as a Camera Girl," Eleanor replied. "We take photographs of the people attending the fair, and if they like them, they buy them as a souvenir. Are you going to the fair as well?"

"After a fashion. I'm one of the doctors who works there. We handle those who get sick or injured at the fair."

"Oh, that's wonderful. God bless you in your work. You are a very important part of the exposition. People should be very grateful for you."

"Fortunately, most do not even know I exist unless they have problems. It's probably best that way." He smiled. "I'll have to consider having my picture taken."

"Or buying a camera. The new Brownie cameras are quite a good deal. They take wonderful pictures and are very easy to operate. We're selling them at Fisher Photography. You should stop in. Just tell them Eleanor sent you. We get a commission on each camera we sell."

He chuckled. "Very well, Miss Eleanor. If I manage to make it over, I'll be sure they know you sent me."

Eleanor smiled and nodded enthusiastically before she turned her attention to the passing scenery. It was going to be a wonderful day. She just knew it.

At the gate, large crowds were already gathered to gain entrance as soon as the expo opened at eight o'clock. Eleanor presented her badge and was admitted without difficulty, although a few people called out protests.

"It's the same every morning, eh?" she mentioned to one of the gate guards.

Most of the gate people recognized her long red curls flowing out from under her Camera Girl straw boater. She wore the regular uniform of a black skirt and long-sleeved white blouse with the high neckline. It definitely identified her as being a Camera Girl, even without her camera.

Fisher Photography was her first stop. She stepped inside to find several of her coworkers already preparing for the day.

"Hello all," she said, smiling. "It's a beautiful day for taking pictures."

"That's certainly true," Pearl Fisher commented. "How are you today, Eleanor?"

"Very good. It's just so pretty. As we made our way here on the trolley, I couldn't help but thank God for my blessings. Flowers are blooming, and the berries are ripening. It's all just about perfect."

"I thought so too," Mary Appleton replied. "I love the summer here."

Bertha Michaels agreed. "It's the best of times. Great for getting on the water. We were invited to go boating with some friends last night. It was such a grand time."

"How are you feeling, Mrs. Fisher?" Mary asked the expectant mother.

"I'm doing very well, thank you. The baby should join us toward the end of September and can't come soon enough for me. We've long anticipated being parents, and here I am at forty-five, and finally it's coming true."

"You'll make a great mother," Bertha said, picking up one of the cameras. "You mother all of us perfectly."

The girls laughed and grabbed the Fisher Photography cards to give to potential customers. On one side was the official seal of the expo—three women representing Alaska, the Yukon, and the Pacific—which made a nice souvenir. The other side advertised the Fishers' at the expo, as well as their downtown shop address. Eleanor tucked a bunch of these in her satchel and grabbed a camera that had been loaded with new film. She couldn't help but think about the way the flowers would look in the sunshine. Hopefully she'd get some time to snap a few pictures of them.

A couple of other girls arrived, and Pearl went around the room speaking to each one until she was finally back at Eleanor.

"I trust you're set for the day?"

"Oh yes." Eleanor gave an enthusiastic nod, sending her curls bouncing. "I'm quite excited to get out there."

"Just don't make the vegetation your only subject matter," Pearl said, smiling. "Although you have taken some amazing photos of the flowers. If they were in color, I think we could sell them for quite a bit."

"Maybe we should try having May Parker paint a few." The young lady in question had been brought on to highlight personal postcards with color should the customer want to pay the extra fee. It was becoming quite the popular thing to do.

"We could at that. Do you have some particular photographs that you would like her to paint?"

"I'll take a few new ones and note the colors, then let her know the details."

"Sounds good."

Eleanor smiled and headed for the door. "Oh, Mrs. Fisher, I rode the trolley with one of the doctors who works here at the expo. He was very kind. I think if you should need medical help, he will be quite a blessing to you."

"Well, thank you for letting me know. I hadn't really even thought about needing help here at the exposition. I plan to quit before I get so far along that the baby might come, so hopefully I won't have any need of him."

"I hope not, but it's nice to know just in case." Eleanor all but danced out the door. She was always a more positive than negative person, but today it just seemed so easy to be happy.

"Thank You, God, for all of this." She gazed at the exposition buildings and the crowds of people pushing past her in a swell of bodies. "Well, You know what I mean." She laughed and put her camera around her neck. "I'm quite blessed to be here."

Bill put the coffee on and then sat down to read through the newspaper. It had been two months since the sinking of their ship and Amelia's death.

And the loss of his manuscript.

After three years of intense and sometimes life-threatening work, to have lost his manuscript in the sinking of the *City of Canton* was almost more than Bill could bear. Of course, the loss of human life was much worse, and he mourned his pregnant sister-in-law more than his book, but it was still a loss that went deep. Nothing seemed right anymore.

A noise to his left momentarily caught Bill's attention. He lowered the paper and watched as Wallace moved around the room in an absent-minded manner. Since losing Amelia, Wallace had lost all sense of purpose. His anger at God had driven him from the pulpit and even his church attendance was forsaken. Bill hadn't known a time in their lives when they hadn't both attended church. They'd practically been born on the pew, given their mother was the organist and their father a trustee and elder. Now Mother was gone. Their father was living in the family house in Chicago. And Bill was attending church alone.

"You know, we ought to write to Father and let him know we're in Seattle."

"Why?" Wallace asked. "We didn't send letters that often from Alaska. For all he knows, we're still there, and he's not anticipating any news."

Bill didn't want to fight, so he said nothing but made a mental note to drop a letter off to their father. Though Bill had no plans to remain in Seattle much longer. He was just waiting long enough to hear back from the publisher. If they would grant him an extension to return to Alaska and remake his manuscript, then Bill would leave immediately. If not, he wasn't sure what he'd do. Alaska was the only place that felt like home.

Seattle was definitely not where he wanted to remain. The big city was far too noisy and busy. Of course, the Alaska-Yukon-Pacific Exposition didn't help matters. That was bringing people in from all over the world, and the population of Seattle seemed to swell every day to new exaggerated numbers.

When they'd first arrived, finding a place to live had been almost impossible. Many of the regular apartments were now being rented out by the day for those coming to attend the expo. Bill had found a little church to attend, and while being introduced around, he mentioned their need of a place to stay. Thankfully, one of the elders had a place and agreed to rent it to them cheaply until they could figure out what they were going to do.

Of course, money had been something of an issue. Bill had been given an advance on the book, and although he'd been frugal with it over the years, it was nearly gone. They'd used the last of it for the ship tickets south.

Wallace had some money, but with that too dwindling, both men had sought jobs. Bill had approached the expo exhibit authorities, particularly those managing the Alaska exhibits. He got part-time work there leading tours and explaining the nature of Alaska's weather, vegetation, and native people. Wallace had surprised them both by taking a job at one of the local fish canneries. It was nothing that Bill would have ever expected his seminary-educated brother to do, but at least it got him out of the house and kept him from moping around and pacing in an endless fashion.

Bill gazed back at the newspaper. He spied the advertisement for passenger liners. There was one ship headed to Seward in two days. That was too soon, but just seeing the advertisement gave him a feeling of hope.

"As soon as I hear back from the publisher, I'd like to arrange to head back to Alaska. We need to save up enough to pay for the passage and some things we'll need. Our friends up there will have kept our things in good order, so we won't need much."

Wallace gave him a hard look. "I'm never going back. Alaska killed Amelia."

"You know that isn't true. Alaska wasn't to blame—it was a storm. Alaska is the one place she loved and the one place you are sure to feel her presence. Our friends there will make certain of that."

"I already feel her presence, and it drives me mad. I'm consumed with guilt. I can still hear her begging me not to leave her." Wallace put his hands to his ears. "I just want to forget everything."

"No, you don't." Bill got up to pour himself a cup of coffee. "We're brothers, and I know you better than you think. You're afraid you will forget. You can't bear the idea that you might lose the details of what you had with Amelia."

Wallace lowered his hands and met Bill's gaze as he returned to the table. "I can't bear that she's gone. Every morning when I wake up, I lie there with my eyes closed and pretend she's beside me. I pray for it all to be a bad dream, but God has truly forsaken me and no longer listens to my prayers."

"You know that isn't true. God is still with us. We have

no way of understanding why things have happened this way. I'm as grieved and guilt-ridden as you are, but I know that God's purposes will be known in time. We must trust Him."

"I won't," Wallace said, pounding his fist into his hand. "I want nothing to do with Him."

"And what is the alternative? To put faith in yourself? In the devil? Instead of blaming God, we ought to recognize that the devil is the one to blame for interfering in our plans."

"But God could have stopped him." Wallace's words were matter-of-fact.

"Yes, He could have, but He didn't. Now what do we do with that?"

Wallace's eyes narrowed. "I'll tell you what I'm going to do. I'm going to forsake Him, just as He's forsaken me."

Bill shook his head. "I'm confident that will get you nowhere. Wallace, I remember you counseling people who went through bad things like this. You encouraged them not to try to figure out the hows and whys but to just rest in the Lord. You assured them that in time God would reveal to them what He wanted them to know. You must now trust that He will do the same for you."

"Enough. I don't want to hear any more. I'm going to work."

Bill shook his head. His own sorrow over losing Amelia and the baby was great, but at least they were in a better place. Wallace, however, was a whole different kind of loss, and he was definitely not in a better place.

That afternoon as Bill led a group of visitors around the Alaska building, he couldn't help but feel an increased longing to return to what had become his home

"Alaska is quite diverse. You have islands and mountains, vast forests, volcanic activity, shorelines that seem endless, and miles and miles of land where you could walk for weeks, months even, and never meet another human being."

He pointed to one of Frank Nowell's photographs of Nome. Bill had met Frank in Nome, where the man had a photography shop. He was now the official photographer for the expo.

"As you can see here in this photograph, the Nome harbor freezes over every winter. Ships can only come in or go out from about late May to early October. In this photograph, which was taken May fifteenth, the first ship of the year has arrived, but the ice is still in place. So they will sled the goods and people from the ship into Nome. It's not an easy situation to be sure because ocean ice is uneven, and a path had to be created to bring folks through safely."

A well-dressed woman in the front raised her hand, and Bill gave her a nod. "How thick is the ice?"

"On average four to six feet is normal with hummocks—raised areas—that can be as high as one hundred feet." The crowd gasped as he knew they would.

Bill continued to the next photo, smiling. Alaska was a place of wonder, and the people were right to be impressed. "Here we have a photograph from another part of the district."

"Why isn't it yet a territory?" a man asked.

"That's a good question. The District of Alaska would very much like to become a territory. I suppose it's just a matter of time before it will be, but for now they remain a district, with limited rights."

The rest of the tour went on in a similar fashion with Bill pointing out interesting facts about the artifacts and photographs. He was quite happy to share what he knew about the place he'd like to call his permanent home. The place he and Wallace had once said they'd like to grow old.

If only he could get Wallace to snap out of his mourning. It wasn't that Amelia didn't deserve their mourning. Bill was still very saddened at her loss, and the guilt he bore for having left her alone was acute. He doubted he would ever stop feeling guilt and sorrow for her loss. However, Alaska was the only place they really belonged. Their friends were there, as well as their work, and there was nowhere as beautiful.

When his tours were over, Bill headed to the lake. He walked along the shoreline and tried to figure out what, if anything, he could do to lift his brother's spirits. He'd never expected this dynamic man of God to lose his faith so easily. Bill was certain it was still there, just buried deep beneath the anger and pain. Perhaps they should take a trip home to Chicago. Seeing their father might be of help to Wallace. After all, he knew what it was to lose the love of his life in death.

"I don't know how to help him, Lord, but I know You do." Bill murmured the prayer as he studied the vegetation. "Please show me what to do. If we should go to Chicago, make that clear. If we should stay put for a time, then help me to see the value of it. I want to go home, and I want Wallace to come too. Alaska is where we belong."

2

Toward the end of the week, Addie Hanson dropped into the office. Addie was on medical leave due to having been severely beaten by her oldest brother. Eleanor heard about the entire affair from Mrs. Fisher and found herself glad to be an only child. Apparently, Addie's brothers, Hiram and Shep, had always been a problem for her. They believed she possessed a vast amount of gold and, after serving time in prison for robbery, came to demand that gold from their sister. When she wasn't forthcoming in giving it to them, Hiram beat her so badly she nearly died. They even showed up at the hospital to force her to go with them but instead had a battle with police and were now dead. Despite all of that, Addie seemed to be healing well and her demeanor was very positive.

"I was getting stir-crazy, so when Isaac said he needed to deliver something to the college, I begged him to let me come along," Addie told Mrs. Fisher.

"I'm glad you came to see us. How's the arm?"

"It's much better. My ribs too. Everything is healing nicely.

The bruises are nearly gone on my face, but thank you for the face powder to help that along."

"Of course."

"How are you feeling?" Addie asked. She and Mrs. Fisher were dear friends, and Eleanor could see how much they cared for each other.

"I'm doing quite well." She touched her rounded abdomen. "Here I thought I was just getting fat. It's like a dream come true. I never thought I'd be able to have a child, and this little one is such a surprise."

Eleanor was busy picking out some newer painted postcards to show off to her customers. The popularity of the painted cards was really taking off. She turned to May, who was working in the window where passersby could stop and watch her work.

"May, these are amazing. Folks are really loving what you've done."

"Thank you," May replied. She was a rather shy and quiet young woman. The complete opposite of Eleanor's vivacious personality.

"I'm going to take some photographs of flowers, and I'll detail the colors for you so you can paint them. Mrs. Fisher and I think we can sell them to folks."

"She mentioned that to me. I think it will be fun. She said I could even take them home with me if I liked to work on them there."

Eleanor smiled. The young woman had elegant facial features. It was said she was half Japanese, which was probably why her hair was black. But her eyes were a striking green, and she'd overheard May mention that her father had the same color eyes.

"Addie, will you be coming back to work any time soon?" Eleanor asked as she packed the last of her supplies into the satchel around her neck.

"Isaac doesn't want me to work, but I told him as soon as I was healed up, I wanted to come back and finish out the expo since Pearl will be quitting to have her baby. After that, I know Otis intends to move to a new location, and they'll need extra help, so I want to assist with that too."

"First we have to get you healed up," Mrs. Fisher reminded her friend.

Eleanor gave them a wave. "I'm off."

Pay Streak, the main thoroughfare, was already filled with people, despite it only being nine thirty in the morning. The Ferris wheel and other rides were already eliciting cries of exhilaration from the children. The energy of the place excited Eleanor. It was unlike anything she'd ever known. When she'd first arrived in Seattle from Kansas, the large city fascinated and amazed her. There were people everywhere, and the noise was almost overwhelming. It had been noisy at times in her small Kansas town of Salina, but nothing like Seattle.

Her mother had nearly been beside herself when Eleanor had announced that she wanted to go to Seattle to experience the Alaska-Yukon-Pacific Exposition by working as a Camera Girl. Her father had understood, however. He was the one who had stirred her interest after telling her about the World's Fair he'd attended in Chicago in 1883. After that, Eleanor was determined to make her way to the exposition, or AYP as most were now calling it.

It was only after arriving that Eleanor had learned the AYP was on the same site as the University of Washington. There had been an agreement struck between the expo committee and the university. The college would provide the land for the fair to use, and the expo would make improvements. There were vast gardens and buildings put up all along the way. Of course, most of the buildings weren't to be permanent, but several were and would become classrooms for the college and various departments of study, including botany. The idea of attending classes had intrigued Eleanor, and she began saving her money.

Esther, one of the other Camera Girls, passed her in the crowd. Eleanor beamed her a smile, and Esther nodded. She wasn't a very happy person. It was said among the Camera Girls that Esther had been involved with one of Addie's brothers, and some blamed her for Addie's injuries as much as they did Hiram. Eleanor was determined to be kind to her and even be a friend, if Esther wanted one. After all, everyone made mistakes.

The day wore on, and Eleanor took several family photos, as well as those of individuals. She reminded the people where they could pick up the picture postcards and how much they'd cost before moving on to find someone else who wanted to see what the new Kodak Brownie camera could do. When her lunchtime came, Eleanor didn't bother to return to the camera shop. She took her camera and headed to a place down by the lake where she'd spotted some yellow flowering plants in the water a few days back.

There were even more blossoms now than there had been when she'd first spied them. Eleanor took a couple of pictures from a standing position, then discarded her satchel and straw hat and flattened herself out on the bank overlooking the floating flowers.

The blooms were round to heart-shaped and grew on short stalks above the water with one to five blooms on each. Below was a thick mat of floating leaves that reminded Eleanor of waterlilies. Come to think of it, so did the scent.

She stretched as close as possible without sliding off the bank and snapped one final picture. They were so striking.

"Ah, I see you've found the *Nymphoides peltata*."

Eleanor startled at the man's voice and jumped to her feet. She nearly lost her balance, and as her body shifted toward the water, she was grateful the gentleman reached out and steadied her.

"Thank you. I might have gone for a swim had you not been here."

He dropped his hold and laughed. "Had I not startled you, you wouldn't have lost your balance."

"True enough. What did you call those flowers?"

"*Nymphoides peltata* is their scientific name. Most folks call them yellow floating hearts."

Eleanor got out a little notebook and pencil and jotted down the information. "They're quite lovely. Do they always bloom like this?"

"No, they bloom mostly June through August."

Eleanor looked up and smiled at the handsome man. "You seem to know a lot about them."

"I've studied such things for years."

"Are you a botanist?" she asked, unable to contain her excitement.

He grinned, and it lit up his entire face. "I am. Are you?"

"Goodness no, but I'd like to be. I'm hoping to attend a few classes in the fall here at the University of Washington.

I've been fascinated with plants since I was a little girl back in Kansas."

He extended his hand. "The name is William Reed, but my friends call me Bill. You may call me that as well."

"Bill." She shook his hand. "I'm Eleanor Bennett."

"I see you're working as one of the Camera Girls at the expo."

Eleanor took up her satchel and put it on over her head. "Yes, I take pictures all day long. It's been quite the deal."

"Is that what brought you here from Kansas?"

"It is. Well, the expo itself brought me, but I saw an advertisement for Camera Girls, and since my father owned a photography shop and I've helped him from the time I was little, I thought it would be the perfect way for me to see the expo." Eleanor talked so fast she almost didn't draw breath. She was always like that when nervous or excited. The handsome man made her feel a little of both. It would be quite easy to lose herself in those beautiful blue eyes.

She set aside her pencil and notebook to take up her hat. She secured the straw boater over her curly red hair and carefully pinned it in place. "I would really like to become a botanist. I want to photograph plants and study them. I think it's wonderful to know all about them. Can you tell me any more about the *Nymphoides peltata*?"

He chuckled. "I've seldom found a woman who was interested in such things. Does my heart good to have met one so pretty."

Eleanor wasn't going to allow her nerves to get the best of her just because he made such a bold comment. Instead, she swallowed the lump in her throat. "Thank you, but seriously, what else can you tell me about these?"

Bill folded his arms against his chest. "Well, let me see. The key identification factors are the small floating leaves with the slit in them and the five-petal flowers. Sometimes they are mistakenly taken for the *Brasenia schreberi*, or watershield. Their leaves have no slits, and they commonly have a red flower, but it can be yellow."

"How interesting." Eleanor picked up her notebook and pencil again. "I love learning such things."

"Well, I'm out here quite often. I do tours through the Alaska building a few times each morning, but then I like to explore. I could teach you more."

Eleanor could feel her eyes widen just at the thought of such a thing. "You'd do that?"

Bill laughed. "Let me see, I'd get the company of a pretty and intelligent young woman who shares my interest in vegetation and flowers. I believe I can make that sacrifice."

Eleanor smiled. "You're very kind, and I would enjoy learning more about the plant life here around the expo and lake. They've done such an incredible job with the landscaping, but I really do prefer the wilds."

"As do I."

"Do you live around here?"

"Temporarily," Bill replied. "I'm down here with my brother. I was supposed to send in a manuscript to be published, but it was lost when our ship went down."

"How awful. What was the manuscript about?"

"The vegetation in Alaska. That's where I lived the last nine years. I've had the opportunity to live in several areas of that vast wilderness. It's an amazing place."

"I'd like to learn more about that as well. Perhaps we can discuss it in between the vegetation you show me."

"I'd enjoy that very much, Eleanor." He smiled. "It is all right if I call you Eleanor, isn't it?"

"Absolutely, Bill. But I'm afraid for now I must get back to work. When would you like to start our exploration?"

"Why not tomorrow? I finish up at noon and have my afternoons free. I could come by the photography shop if you like."

"No, tomorrow's my day off. I'd just as soon meet you by the lake. We could meet shortly after noon down by the boat ramp."

"Sounds good. I'll be there."

"Wonderful. I'm so excited. I'll bring my notebook, pencil, and camera." Her anxious feelings faded away.

"Does it cost much to operate that camera?"

"Actually, it's not as bad as it might be. Photography has never been an inexpensive hobby, but the Brownie camera can be purchased for as little as ten dollars. Of course, that's without its accessories. Film is seventy cents for ten exposures, and they make large picture postcards for the prints. Thankfully, the Fishers have offered me a discount on the cost of film and the camera. I'm saving up to buy one."

"I was thinking it might be a good thing for me as well. I use charcoals and watercolors for my manuscript pictures, but an occasional photograph might be something else to incorporate into the book. I'll have to discuss it with the publisher."

"Well, if you decide to buy one, would you tell them that I was the one who told you about it? We get credit for the cameras we sell and earn an extra commission."

He smiled. "I'd be happy to do that."

They began walking back toward the expo, and Eleanor

had never known a time when she'd enjoyed someone's company more than she did Bill's. The closer they drew to the fair, the louder the noise and the harder it was to hear each other.

"Thank you for what you taught me today. I'll cherish it," Eleanor said, smiling.

Bill gave her a little bow. "Until tomorrow."

Eleanor watched him walk away and couldn't help but giggle. It was like a fairy-tale encounter. She had met a prince at the lake, and he was handsome and smart. All the things that made for a great storybook hero. The day couldn't have been any more perfect.

"So you're just going to go off into the wilderness with a total stranger?" Rosemary asked as they fixed supper that evening.

"He's not a total stranger. Goodness, we talk so easily, and I've learned a great deal. We are just very comfortable with each other."

"But you just met. You don't even know someone who can vouch for him." Rosemary held up the knife she'd been using to cut apples. "He could be trouble."

"You're the one who looks like trouble, waving your knife all over the kitchen." Eleanor laughed and went to fetch some bowls.

Rosemary gave an exasperated sigh. "There are dangerous men all over the city who want only to kill and destroy."

"I seriously doubt that they're botanists." Eleanor smiled at her friend. "Honestly, Rosemary. Can't you just be happy for me? This man has studied the very topic I'm fascinated with and want to study for myself. He was pleasant to look at and very much a gentleman. I do wish you wouldn't worry for me."

"Well, at least find out if he goes to church. Your folks would want to know that much. If he goes to church regularly, then he might not be a problem."

"I'll be sure and ask him," Eleanor promised. She put a bowl down for each of them, then went to retrieve the ham and beans from the stove.

The kitchen was what Eleanor's mother called a turn-around. Once you entered it, there was just room to turn around and head back out. But, Rosemary had made the best off it. She was quite talented when it came to arranging a room. Not that she had been able to arrange much in the kitchen, with its fixed counter, sink, stove, and icebox. A row of three cabinets was lined up over the sink and counter area, and under the sink Rosemary had set up two crates to act as additional storage. Eleanor thought it all quite smart.

Bringing the beans to the table, Eleanor spooned a generous portion for each of them, then took the pot back to the stove and grabbed the plate with corn bread. "This is definitely a Kansas meal tonight. I'm sure glad you decided to like ham and beans. It's so inexpensive to make and goes a long way."

"Yes, but I wish you wouldn't make so much at one time. I get tired of eating ham and beans for a week." Rosemary finished cutting the apples and brought them to the table.

"That reminds me, we're going to need another block of ice for the icebox." Eleanor set the corn bread in the center of the table.

"This room is so hot and stuffy after cooking. It'd be nice

to put a big block of ice right in the middle of the room. I'm going to open the window for a while, even though it's probably still quite noisy outside," she said after depositing the fruit on the table. Rosemary went to the window in the living room and opened it. She leaned out just a bit and drew in a breath. "It's much nicer outside than in. Perhaps we should take a walk after dinner."

"That would be all right with me." Eleanor took her place at the table.

"Are you sure?" Rosemary came to join her and pulled back her chair. "I mean, you do walk around outside all day." She sat and took up her napkin. "I wouldn't want to impose more of it on you."

"I like to walk outside." Eleanor bowed her head. "Let's pray so we can eat. I didn't have lunch today, and I'm starved."

She blessed the food and then dug right in as Rosemary began telling her a story of something that happened at the office. But all Eleanor could think about was Bill and those *Nymphoides peltata*. That moment had seemed almost magical, and she couldn't shake the thought that something extremely important had just happened in her life.

"You aren't even listening."

Eleanor looked up and found Rosemary's expression all dejected. "I'm sorry, Rosemary. I didn't mean to get preoccupied."

"Oh, it wasn't all that important. I just thought it was funny."

"Well, tell me again. I promise to listen this time." Eleanor put down her spoon and folded her hands. "I swear."

"No, it really wasn't anything, and now that I think of retelling it, well, it doesn't seem that special at all."

"Did you have a good day at work?"

35

"I did, but the place was very stuffy, and the fans weren't working properly. Of course, Mrs. Grimes said she was chilly when the girls asked the supervisor to put the fans on high."

"I suppose that means they were left on low."

"Medium, actually. I found myself thankful for that at least."

"Aren't you fortunate to work in a building with electricity?"

"I couldn't work in anything else. I'm much too delicate. The heat makes me crazy."

"It's good then that Seattle is generally very temperate. Although this summer has been quite warm. That's probably good for the exposition."

Rosemary nodded and picked up her corn bread. She cut it in half, then buttered it before taking a bite.

"However, if you worked outside, you would have had a nice breeze. That's a fortunate thing for being out of doors."

"Only if the breeze is blowing."

Eleanor laughed. "Well put. In Kansas the wind blew incessantly. I sometimes wondered if it would ever stop, and then when it did, we all looked around as if something had gone terribly wrong."

Rosemary gave a shiver. "Or you had those tornadoes. I'm so glad I have never had to experience one. Your stories still give me nightmares."

"You learn to adapt and respond in a proper manner befitting the situation. Just as I imagine you would here if there was an earthquake."

"I'd rather not have to endure either one."

Eleanor reached for a piece of apple. "This makes a great dessert." She popped the piece in her mouth and smiled. It was the perfect balance of sweet and tart. "I sometimes forget just how perfect an apple can be."

When supper was finished and the dishes done, Eleanor took up her regular hat, a wide-brimmed straw hat devoid of finishings. She had put her hair up into a loose bun upon coming home, and now it nicely served as an anchor for her hatpin.

Rosemary had a new hat, something that seemed to happen with a bit of regularity. She had once told Eleanor that she had to keep up with proper fashions, as it was expected by her employer. Eleanor wasn't sure why an insurance company cared about new hats, but so long as Rosemary was happy, it really wasn't any of her concern.

She smiled at her roommate and asked the question she knew Rosemary was dying for her to ask. "Is that a new hat?"

3

B ill watched his brother stare out the window. Wallace had been sitting like that for the last hour. No doubt he was reliving the accident—going over each detail in his mind—wondering if he might have done something different. Every night Wallace had hideous nightmares, and he always shot up out of bed calling Amelia's name.

It was horrible to watch his brother die in bits and pieces. He had lost all interest in life without Amelia. Wallace was a mere shadow of the man he'd once been, and it saddened Bill more than he could say. Wallace was always the encourager—the one whose faith was strong enough for all of them. Bill had never seen Wallace defeated like this.

"Let's go out and get something to eat. I'm starved. Charlie's down the street has their fish special tonight. I'll buy."

Wallace looked at him for a moment. "I deal with fish all day."

"All right, I'll buy you a steak." Bill smiled and got to his feet. "Come on. I want to enjoy a nice dinner."

"I don't feel like I'll ever enjoy anything again," Wallace answered. He looked back out the window. "When Amelia died, I died as well. My soul feels completely dead. I have absolutely nothing to live for."

"That's not true, Wallace. Think of the people waiting for you to return to Alaska. Think of the children who believe in Jesus now because you and Amelia shared the Gospel. You have to return and carry on the work. Amelia would want you to do that."

"I suppose she would, but I haven't got it in me. I don't even know if I believe in God anymore. At least not the God I thought I knew."

"Wallace, you need to take your own medicine. I've heard you speak many times to people who have lost loved ones. Death is a natural part of life, and way too often it comes earlier than we feel it should. Infants, children, and young adults all die as a part of this fallen world. It will never be easy to face, and I'm certainly not suggesting you should put aside your mourning and forget about Amelia. That would be impossible and cruel."

"I'll never forget her nor the baby she carried."

"And I would never suggest you should. But I know my sister-in-law would be appalled to hear that you were contemplating putting God aside. She would be so upset to know that her death caused you to walk away from your ministry work—work, I might add, that you loved as much as she did."

"But that was before God let her die. Why should I work for Him when He did that?"

"Why is it God's fault? As I recall, Satan was given dominion over this world for a time. He could have brought on that storm with the very idea of getting rid of one of God's most powerful ministers—you. Only Satan benefits from you walking away from God."

Wallace looked at him for a long time, then got to his feet. "Let's go get something to eat at Charlie's."

They walked to the little restaurant in silence, but Bill was praying most fervently. His brother had suffered such a terrible loss, and even now after two months, he was still blaming God and refusing to return to his ministry work. Wallace was nothing like the happy-go-lucky man he'd once been.

They took a seat close to the door and waited for someone to serve them. A young man appeared soon enough and told them of the specials. Bill ordered the fried fish and steamed vegetables, while Wallace settled on a pork chop smothered in gravy and potatoes. Hot coffee rounded out the meal.

"I met an interesting young woman today," Bill said, desperate to fill the silence. "She's a Camera Girl and takes pictures of expo attendees. I found her down by the lake taking pictures of some flowers. Come to find out she loves botany and wants to learn more. I promised to take her around tomorrow afternoon and show her some of the places I've already explored."

Wallace drank his coffee but said nothing. When the waiter brought their food, he ate in silence. Bill kept trying to find ways to engage him, but Wallace had absolutely no interest, so Bill returned to his previous thoughts on Alaska.

"I figure we can save up enough money by late August, maybe early September at the latest, to buy our passage to Alaska. That will put us back in the village by the end of September. It's perfect timing. Once I hear from the publisher, I'll know better what we should do and when. Maybe we could even go see Father before we head to Alaska."

"I told you I'm not going back to Alaska."

"But you must. People are counting on you. Besides, you need to let them know what happened."

"You can do that, Bill. I don't need to be there."

Wallace's voice was filled with a weariness Bill had never heard. His brother was usually so energetic. He was a powerful speaker and teacher, but none of that was evident in Wallace these days.

"It will help you to heal, Wallace. You know it will."

"I'm sitting in my sorrow here, and it's doing nothing to help," Wallace replied.

"But don't you see, in Alaska you'll have others to come alongside you. Our friends there will be ever so supportive. And you can use the situation to help them through their losses."

Wallace slammed his fist on the table. "I don't want to help anyone else through their losses. I'm completely lost in mine. How could I be of help to anyone ever again?"

People at the tables around them turned to see what the problem was. Bill gave them a smile, then turned his attention back to Wallace. He reached out to cover his brother's hand.

"In time, you will be. I know it. Just don't turn away from God. He promised to never leave nor forsake us. He hasn't gone anywhere, and we can trust Him to help us through this."

Wallace pulled back his hand and went back to eating in silence. Bill could feel the wall he'd put up and decided maybe it wasn't the time to try to rally his brother's spirit. After all, there was no sense in the other customers having to deal with Wallace's anger and sorrow.

While he ate, Bill thought of the young woman he'd met

TRACIE PETERSON

earlier. Eleanor Bennett. She was such a lovely young woman. Pleasant and spirited. He had to admit she was just the kind of woman he had hoped to one day meet and marry. Could she be the one?

He smiled to himself. There was no sense asking such questions when they had just met. For all he knew, Eleanor already had someone special in her life.

They finished the meal, and Bill paid as he'd promised. Wallace still had nothing to say as they began to walk back to the apartment. Bill tried to figure out something to say that might comfort his brother. Nothing came to mind, however. If he wasn't going to find comfort in God, what else was there? To his surprise, it was Wallace who began to talk.

"I still remember her begging me not to leave her. But I was so sure I was supposed to help other people. I left her alone. I gave her to you to take care of."

"And I did my best. They weren't allowing men to board the boats yet anyway. You know it was women and children first," Bill replied, uncertain that he should have said anything.

"That's true enough, but I could have stood by. I could have stayed right there and helped others while keeping my eyes on Amelia. I knew she was scared. I expected so much of her."

"She was a very strong woman. Capable and full of energy. She would have been helping others herself had she not been expecting a baby."

"It's true. She would have."

The last vestiges of light faded from the sky, making the air seem quite chilly. Bill pulled up his coat collar.

"Then there was Grady Masterson. He'd upset me more

43

than I wanted anyone to know. I wasn't at all happy to find him on our ship."

"No, nor me. The man was full of hate and bitterness, and I truly feared what he was capable of, especially since he vowed revenge." Bill had never really talked with Wallace about his feelings, but he had been relieved to hear it suggested that perhaps Grady had been among those who had died.

The aftermath of the ship sinking had been a mass of confusion. The two ships that came to the rescue were from America and Canada, and each took passengers to different ports. The Americans came to Seattle, while the Canadians went to Victoria. The sinking was thoroughly investigated even though it was clearly the fault of the storm, but there was great confusion on the number of dead and who had gone to which port.

When Bill and Wallace had tried to find Amelia, the news of her death was given to them so matter-of-factly that the clerk had moved on before either brother could pose a question. The man had simply checked his list and stated her lifeboat had been among the ones lost in the storm and all souls on board had perished. He offered little in the way of condolences. Not that Wallace or Bill would have been comforted.

"I know what you're thinking, Bill," Wallace began as they neared the apartment. "You think that the pain of loss is robbing me of my ability to reason and understand." He stopped, and so Bill did the same. "It's not that at all. I'm truly torn in regard to my faith. I think about others in the Bible who faced great loss and sorrow. Job and David come to mind most often. They stood fast in the Lord. They honored

God even when things were at their worst. I don't have that in me, Bill. I feel hopeless. As if I'm in that black, icy water fighting to get a hold on something, but nothing is there."

"You can't give up, Wally." Bill used his brother's childhood nickname. "These are bleak times, and the pain is still fresh and raw. But God is there for you to take hold of."

"But He's the one responsible. Even if Satan did send the storm and cause the sinking, God allowed it to happen. Just as He allowed Satan to torment Job. How can I trust Him after that? It hurts too much to even consider it. My one constant—my rock—my hope. It's gone. He left me to face it all alone."

"No, Wallace, you know that isn't true."

"No." Wallace shook his head. "No, Bill. I don't know that. I don't know anything anymore. I feel completely alone—as if someone has walled me in a cell. I know you care, but it's as if you stand with everyone else on the other side, and I cannot reach anyone."

Bill thought his heart might well break. His brother was so lost and wounded. He reached out and gave Wallace a hug. "I wish I could make it better. I wish I could help you to see that God is still here for you."

He pulled back and looked Wallace in the eye. "But even if you refuse to trust God right now, you can trust me. I'm here for you."

"But in time you'll go away. You're already planning to return to Alaska. I have no constant in my life."

"That's not true." Bill started to argue the point all over again, then decided it would do no good. "But I know your pain is telling you otherwise. In time, however, you will know the truth again. I believe it."

They made their way to the apartment and had only just entered the foyer when the man who lived in the first apartment opened the door.

"Good evening, Mr. Emory," Bill said, giving the man a nod.

"Oh good, it's you, Bill. I have a package for you. Wait right here."

The man disappeared into his apartment and returned with a brown paper-wrapped package tied with string. "This came in the post earlier. I meant to leave it outside your apartment, but then thought better of it. I didn't want anyone to steal it."

Bill frowned and took the package. "That's strange, I'm not expecting anything." He looked down at the return address. It was from New York. "It's from my publisher. By the heavy feel and size, it appears they sent me a book."

The older man nodded. "I suppose a publisher would have a lot of them to send out."

"Indeed." Bill tucked the package under his arm. "Thank you for guarding it."

Wallace had already started up the stairs to the second floor, so Bill gave Mr. Emory a nod and followed his brother. He hoped and prayed that the publisher had also sent a letter of extension on his manuscript rather than a request that he return the advance.

Inside the apartment, Wallace went to the bedroom and closed the door. Bill knew he would ready himself for bed and be asleep long before Bill had interest in retiring. That had been the routine since coming to Seattle.

Bill took up a knife and cut the string in such a fashion to save the better part of it. He unwrapped the package and found another wrapped package inside. The letter on top drew his immediate attention, and Bill opened it.

Dear Mr. Reed,

As we were preparing to write to you after receipt of your letter dated June eighth, we received this in the mail. Apparently, a man in Canada found it washed ashore and forwarded it to us since you had the address already listed on the package. We were preparing our letter to you to encourage you to remake the book after it was lost at sea, so imagine our surprise to find your manuscript enclosed. It is quite water damaged, but perhaps this will allow you to remake it more quickly and still have it to us in the next month. We were quite impressed by what we saw and want to move forward with your book as soon as possible.

Bill didn't bother to read anything else. He dropped the letter and tore off the wrapping around what he'd thought was a book. There, just as the letter said, was his very water-damaged manuscript. Without thinking, he let out a yell of victory.

"Thank You, God!"

His yell brought Wallace to the bedroom door. "What's going on?"

"My manuscript!" Bill held it up. "The publisher received my manuscript and sent it back to me. Apparently, it washed up on shore, and someone found it. He sent it to the publisher since I had addressed it to them. They were preparing to write to me about the terms of our arrangement when it showed up. Look, Wallace! It's all here. Damaged, yes, but now I won't have to think it all up again or pull it together from my notes. I just need to retype it and redo the images. Oh, this is answered prayer."

"If Amelia wasn't already resting in a cold, watery grave, we might hope for her to come ashore and be returned to us as well." Wallace's voice was heavy with bitterness. He closed the door to the bedroom before Bill could reply.

For a moment Bill stared at the closed door, then he shook his head and looked back at the manuscript. The lost had been found, and as sorry as he was that it wasn't Amelia who had been returned to them, Bill was overwhelmed with joy to have the manuscript back in hand. It was a miracle, and he could only praise God for it.

Father, You are so good to me. Thank You for this gift. I won't take it lightly nor forget that You have provided it.

⁂

Despite it being her day off, Eleanor had come into the photography shop this morning to help sort postcards for mailing. When she'd returned to work after meeting Bill yesterday, Mrs. Fisher had mentioned how far behind they'd gotten with the mailings. Lately there had been more and more people who wanted their postcards sent, despite the extra charge to cover the stamp. It was quite a meticulous project to match the postcards with their assigned addresses, and accuracy was demanded for each and every card.

"Sometimes I worry that this will all go horribly wrong," Mary said as she helped Eleanor with the sorting. "I imagine some family father mistakenly receiving a postcard of a pretty young woman, and his wife taking it the wrong way and thinking her husband unfaithful."

"I hadn't considered that possibility, but I have worried about getting the wrong address on the wrong card. I'm glad Mr. Fisher is so careful with the rolls of film he develops. He clips up the handwritten lists we give him with the numbers and addresses and is faithful to do only one roll at a time and then move to a separate area to complete each one. Still, I know myself to be completely capable of mistakes and worry that I shall be the cause of a great catastrophe."

Mary laughed. "I can see it being front-page news."

"With a picture of me amidst hundreds of postcards and my hands up in the air in confusion." Eleanor laughed as well.

"Mrs. Fisher is smart to keep the addresses. She marks by each one if they bought a camera or not, as well. She said once the expo is completed and things return to normal, she plans to create a letter to send out to each address to advertise their new shop and the prices and such for the film and other things that go with the camera. I think that's very smart, don't you?"

"I do," Eleanor replied. "My father was good to keep track of his customers, and it benefited him greatly. Sometimes people just need a little reminder, and a letter like that will entice them to come to the shop and purchase additional film, if nothing else."

Mary nodded and refocused on the postcards at hand. "I think ten cents for a postcard isn't bad, especially since people are so willing to give twenty-five cents to ride the Ferris wheel."

"Oh, I quite agree. Although when you consider a loaf

of bread is just five cents and can feed a family, spending twenty-five cents on a five-minute ride seems quite silly. But I suppose some people just have money burning holes in their pockets." Eleanor addressed one of the postcards and checked it off the list.

"Well, well," Mr. Fisher said as he came into the back. "I told Pearl that I was certain I heard talking back here as we entered the shop."

At one time the couple had slept in the back room, but with Mrs. Fisher's advancing pregnancy, they were usually more inclined to return to their apartment. Eleanor couldn't help but wonder if the trips back and forth on the trolley weren't just as difficult as sleeping on a cot.

"We wanted to help get the postcards mailed out," Mary said, "so Eleanor and I agreed to come early."

"I'm so glad you girls care so much about the customers and their photographs." Mr. Fisher helped his wife with her shawl. "Good service will keep them coming back and hopefully lead them to our new store downtown once the expo is gone."

"Isn't it your day off, young lady?" Mrs. Fisher asked, looking at Eleanor.

"It is, but I was coming here anyway. I'm meeting a young man at noon. He's a botanist and promises to show me some of the wonderful plants he's found while walking about on his time off."

"Do you know this man?" Mrs. Fisher asked.

"His name is William Reed, and he works giving tours in the Alaska building," Eleanor replied. "But I know very little else."

Mrs. Fisher frowned. "I don't like the idea of our girls

meeting up with strange men. Otis, perhaps you could go over to the Alaska building and check up on him?"

"Sure, I can do that. You start setting up my darkroom, and I'll run over there right now."

"Oh, I don't know," Eleanor began to protest. "He might be embarrassed by that, and then I wouldn't get to see the plants."

"It's better to be safe," Mrs. Fisher declared. "You don't know him, and he could be trouble."

She sounded like Rosemary. Well, at least if Mr. Fisher was able to speak to Bill's superiors, they would have some idea of his character. She gave a nod.

"I suppose it couldn't hurt." She whispered a prayer that Bill wouldn't find out that people were checking up on him.

4

"So may I presume I passed inspection?" Bill asked as Eleanor joined him for their outing.

She felt her cheeks heat up. "It wasn't my idea to send Mr. Fisher to check up on you. I hoped you might not even find out. In fact, I prayed you wouldn't, as I didn't wish to cause you any embarrassment or offense."

He chuckled. "I'm not offended. In fact, I find it touching that the Fishers were concerned about you. That speaks highly of their character."

"They are good people. I've enjoyed working with them. They're kind and not overly demanding. They expect an honest day's work, but then they pay a good wage."

"I've already decided that before I return to Alaska, I'm going to buy a camera and as much film as I can afford. I won't be able to get my photographs developed until I come back to Seattle, I suppose, but at least I'll have them."

"You could learn how to develop them."

"I suppose I could." He smiled.

"And remember to buy the camera from me. We're paid commission." She hoped that wasn't too forward.

"I remember, and I'll be glad to help you out." He motioned to the area around them. "Are you ready to see some of the fascinating plant life?"

Eleanor nodded. "I am. I'm quite excited. As you see, I've borrowed a camera and bought a brand-new roll of film. There are only ten shots, of course, but I intend to make them all count."

They began to walk toward one of the more wooded areas. "Seattle is a very complex area because you have saltwater and freshwater so nearby. You have the mountains as well. It's an interesting combination to be sure. We have that in Alaska too."

"I love hearing about Alaska. It sounds quite amazing."

"It is. I had heard stories before going there, but they couldn't do it justice. The place is massive and changeable and unforgiving." He frowned and looked away.

Eleanor had no idea what bad memory had come to mind, but it seemed to momentarily put a damper on the man's spirits. She gave him a few moments and then asked, "What was the most intriguing thing to you about Alaska?"

He glanced back at her. "The vastness of it all. It's so big. These mammoth mountains seem to just rise out of the sea. You can walk for miles and miles and still not even put a dent in the number you'd need to cross the district from one side to the other. Of course, if I am being honest, I have to say that the people are even more amazing. There are numerous tribes of native peoples, and they're all very similar to each other and yet so very different."

"What about the cold and snow? Is it as bad as I've heard people say?"

"There are a lot more months of winter to be sure, and

. . . well, it's deadly. A blizzard can whip up out of nowhere and rage for days, even weeks. Then you have the lack of sun to contend with. At the lower end of the district, on the last day of December, the sun doesn't fully rise until around ten and then it sets again by four. Farther north there's even less sun, and at the top of the district, there's no sun at all for a time. In the summer, it's exactly opposite. The sun shines around the clock."

"What a place. I can't imagine. I was looking at Mr. Nowell's photographs of the snow and how it was ten feet deep in one place. I can't imagine snow like that. In Kansas we have snow and ice storms, but while it might drift to a depth of ten feet, I never saw it actually snow that much all over."

"Yes, it can be quite daunting. When my brother and I lived in Nome, we had some fierce blizzards and fogs that left us completely disoriented. But we saw truly deep snows in the area of the High One."

"The High One?"

"The mountain that the native people call Denali. You might have heard it called Mount McKinley after President McKinley. The snows are always quite deep in that area, but it's an awe-inspiring place to be sure."

"You make me want to go there."

"Our summer camp isn't far from there. In fact, you can see the mountain from our place on the Susitna River. It's some of the most beautiful, untouched scenery you could ever experience. And it's full of wild animals. You must always be careful and carry a firearm when you go out away from the village."

"Are there very many flowers?"

"Hundreds of different species. There are areas where it's

a riot of color, and many of the plants are useful for food or medicine."

"I would love to see it."

He looked at her oddly. "Aren't you afraid of the isolation? Once you're up there, it's not that easy to get back here, and there aren't any stores or easy means of transportation. Walking is the main way we get around."

"Well, it sounds like you'd need a very long time to explore it all, so maybe it's good that you can't easily come and go. No, I don't think the isolation would bother me at all."

She could tell that her answer surprised him, but she let him think on it for a time. When they reached a little opening in the forest, Bill paused and pointed out a flowering bush.

"This is *Gaultheria shallon*, or more commonly, salal. It's actually part of the evergreen family, and the leaves will remain green year-round. This is a great time to view it because the time for flowering is just about done, but you can still see some of the blossoms."

Eleanor noted the pink-and-white flowers. "They're like little bells or pendants hanging along the tiny stem. So delicate."

"They are, aren't they? I thought you might enjoy seeing it. Now note the dark blue-black berries that are taking the place of the flowers. They won't be ripe until August, but they're quite delicious. You can make jams out of them."

"I've never seen these plants before. How wonderful." Eleanor got her camera out and focused in on an area that showed both flowers and berries. She framed it just so, then checked the lighting before snapping the picture.

Bill continued walking as soon as she was done and came to stand by another bush that looked much like the last.

"Are these also salal?"

"No, but they're often thought to be the same. They're also in the evergreen family. These, however, are evergreen huckleberries, or *Vaccinium ovatum*. Note the tighter clusters of berries and flowers."

"Yes, I see it now. They are very similar to the salal though."

"Yes. The native people of the Pacific Northwest rely heavily on these, as well as other berries."

Eleanor got out her notebook and jotted notes regarding the salal and huckleberries. When that was complete, she took a photograph of the plant. "There's just so much to learn. What are the most important things to look for in identification of plants?"

Bill smiled. "Observation is everything. You need to note what type of a plant it is. Is it a tree or shrub? Vine or flower? What shape are the leaves?" Eleanor retrieved her notebook and pencil and started writing as fast as she could. It was hard to keep up with Bill's narrative, as he was quite well versed in the topic.

"You look at the bark or stems, the structure of the plant. Are there flowers or fruit? If so, note what you see, the shapes, colors, the way they are positioned. There's just so many features to each individual plant. It's quite wonderful and always reminds me of the detail God put into all of creation."

"Yes, I've thought that too," Eleanor said, stopping her writing momentarily. "It's always so fascinating to see how intricately it is all designed."

"My brother is a pastor . . . well, he was. I hope he still will be. He has often preached on God's attention to detail—how nothing was too small or unworthy of His attention and neither are we."

"That's a comforting thought." Eleanor wrote that down at the bottom of the page.

"It's something most people never consider, and some simply refuse to believe. They look at the world around them and believe it just somehow sprang into order." He looked around the forest. "But how could such intricate creations just happen?"

"They couldn't. There clearly was a Creator. A very attentive Creator."

Bill turned back to her and nodded. "Exactly. There is a reason one plant can be useful for medical problems, while another is good for food. There are telltale signs that reveal plants that can benefit us and plants that can cause us harm. It's all a matter of observation. I once had a professor who said that speaking was totally optional in the study of botany."

Eleanor laughed. "I have to admit that I've always marveled at the variety and beauty. Plants and trees in Kansas are so different from what we have here, and I'm sure these are different from what folks enjoy back east. Well, I know some plants and trees are in multiple places and can be found all over, but I think you understand what I'm saying. It's the variety that amazes me."

"Exactly. It amazes me as well." He shook his head and smiled. "I've never met a woman quite like you. Although I've wanted to. I've always wanted to find someone who shared my interest in botany."

"Well, I do. I'll probably drive you to distraction with all my questions and demands on your time."

Bill's expression grew thoughtful. "You definitely distract, but not at all in a bad way."

For a moment neither one said anything. Eleanor had never known anyone like Bill. He was thoughtful, intelligent, handsome, and a perfect gentleman. She felt her heart beat a little faster. It would be very easy to fall in love with this man.

Bill knew without any doubt in his mind that Eleanor was the woman he'd searched for. She shared all of his interests, at least the ones that mattered. She loved God and believed strongly in His participation in creation and the lives of His children. She loved botany and desired to study and gain knowledge, just as he did. A thought came to mind.

"Eleanor, do you by any chance type?"

She looked at him oddly and put away her pencil and little notebook. "I do. Why do you ask?"

"I wrote a book on the vegetation in Alaska, remember?"

"Of course."

"Well, I thought it was lost, but it turns out someone found it."

"How did you lose it?"

"It's a long story, but in coming to Seattle from Alaska, our ship ran aground and sank. We had to evacuate to the lifeboats, and I left my manuscript in the care of my sister-in-law. Unfortunately, she perished. Everyone in her lifeboat was lost, and I assumed my manuscript was also lost. But someone found it and sent it to my publisher, and they returned it to me. It's in very bad shape, but good enough to use for retyping. I need someone to type it for me while I redraw the pictures."

"That's a very sad story, but also miraculous that your

work was located. I'd be happy to help you with the retyping, but I haven't got a typewriter."

"I think I can probably work out something with the university. I've become friends with many of the faculty and even the president. I'm sure they would let me use a typewriter in the evening when it wouldn't interfere with their regular business. School won't start for several weeks, so I don't think we'd be in the way."

"Then I'd be happy to do it. I could start right after I finish work for the Fishers. Just let me know where to go."

"Well, you'd have to have some supper and a little rest, wouldn't you? I wouldn't dream of making you give up your meals."

"I could stop by the YMCA restaurant at the expo. Their prices are very reasonable, and I get a discount." She smiled.

"I would, of course, pay for your meal."

"Oh, that isn't necessary."

"I believe it is. I can't pay much for your typing, so the least I can do is include your supper. Perhaps I could even join you, and we could discuss what work was needed that evening."

Eleanor's smile broadened. "I'd like that."

He could see in her expression and hear in her voice that she was most sincere. He couldn't imagine her being any other way.

"Good. Then I'll speak to the university president and let you know tomorrow morning. I'll come to the photography shop before I start work at the Alaska building."

"This is so exciting. I'll get to learn so much by typing your work. I can't imagine anything being more fulfilling."

"Nor I," he said, but his mind wasn't at all on typing or botany.

Rosemary looked at Eleanor as if she'd lost her mind. "You can't be serious. You can't spend your evenings alone with a stranger." She was ever the voice of reason.

"Oh, Rosemary, Bill is not a stranger. Not anymore. I feel like I've known him for a very long time." Eleanor continued tidying up the tiny living room.

"But you haven't, and that's what has me worried. Not only that, but have you considered that you'll be coming home very late in the evening? You'll have to be sure and catch the trolley before it stops running, or you'll be stuck without a place to stay. It just sounds like the kind of thing someone might do to take advantage of a young, helpless woman."

"You are worse than my mother when it comes to worrying. Mr. Fisher went to the Alaska building and spoke to Bill's supervisor. The man goes to church and has been very faithful to work his assigned duties. He's never given any sign of being anything but polite and genteel. Besides, maybe I can stay with someone who lives close to the university. It's just for a short time."

"You'd leave me?" Rosemary planted her hands on her hips. "You'd desert me just like that?"

Eleanor laughed. "Listen to you. You sound like a frightened child. Goodness. Like I said, it would only be for a short time. I asked him about the length of the manuscript. It's about three hundred pages, and some of those are drawings. I don't know how many pages I can type in an evening's time, but I can't see it taking more than a few weeks at the most. So stop your fretting. If I can get back at night, I'll be here. If it proves to be too much, then I'll have to give some thought into what other options might present themselves. I seem to recall that my supervisor, Mrs. Hanson, has a little house near the expo. I don't know if she's rented it out yet, but perhaps she'd let me stay there."

"I think this is madness."

Eleanor shrugged. "I'm hungry, so why don't we fix something to eat and talk about something else?"

Rosemary's eyes widened. "That's another thing. You won't be able to have supper."

"It's all accounted for. Bill is going to buy me supper at the YMCA restaurant at the expo. It'll be part of my pay." Eleanor dusted off the side table near the well-worn sofa. How they had ever managed to get a sofa to fit in the small living room was a mystery. Just beyond the sofa was a tiny table with two chairs. It made up their dining area, although there was no real separation from the rest of the front room.

"So he's actually going to pay you?"

"As I said, he's a good man." She didn't want to explain that her meals would probably be the only pay she'd get. The pay didn't matter compared to the education she was going to get. Eleanor thought of all that she could learn from Bill. It would be even better than attending college, because this way she would have the teacher to herself for hours on end.

Her friend's gaze rolled heavenward. "I just find all of this much too disturbing."

"Maybe I could have him stop by so you could meet him. Perhaps that would put your mind at ease. You could ask him a few questions and get to know him for yourself."

Rosemary shook her head. "No, I wouldn't want him knowing where you live. Just imagine if he turned out to be some sort of cad. He might be stopping by all the time. We'd never get rid of him."

The idea of Bill coming by on a regular basis sounded perfectly lovely, but clearly Rosemary thought otherwise. Eleanor put the dusting cloth under the sink with the other cleaning things, then went to the icebox and pulled out a bowl of boiled potatoes. "Shall I fry some of these up with eggs?"

"I suppose so." Rosemary's tone was one of defeat, and yet Eleanor knew the matter was far from over. She appreciated Rosemary's concern, but this was one battle the young woman was not going to win. Bill was becoming far too important to Eleanor, even if they had only just met.

She'd never believed in love at first sight, but this wasn't first sight. She'd seen him twice, and she was generally a most discerning person. Nothing about Bill's demeanor or character put her off or warned of problems. She would, of course, commit the entire matter to prayer, but she was convinced that God had sent Bill into her life for a reason—a very good reason. And her discernment was never wrong.

5

E leanor got to work early and was pleasantly surprised to find Addie Hanson there. Mrs. Fisher wasn't sure she should be back on her feet already, but Addie assured her she was ready, and idleness was driving her mad. Even Isaac, her husband, agreed something should be done.

With Addie available to talk to, Eleanor wasted no time. "I wonder if I could ask you a question."

Addie looked up and smiled. "Of course, Eleanor. What is it?"

"Well, you see . . . Oh, I don't know where to start. I met a man who gives tours at the Alaska building. He's a botanist who lived in Alaska and wrote a book. It's going to be published and everything. But the manuscript was lost at sea when his ship sank. Then it was found and sent to the publisher." Eleanor could see by the look on Addie's face that she was doing a poor job of explaining.

"Oh good grief, have you rented your cottage out? I remember you saying that you were thinking you might. I don't have much money, and I would only need to stay there at night for about a month."

Addie laughed. "I have to admit, I'm completely baffled. You start with talk about a man and his book, and now you want to stay in my cottage."

Eleanor sighed. "I know. I'm making a complete mess of things. Bill Reed is the man's name. He has the manuscript back in hand, and it's a mess. Horribly water damaged and such. It needs to be retyped, and he asked me to help. He plans to speak to the university and see if we might use one of their typewriters in the evening hours. Since I can type, I told him I'd love to help. Mainly because I love botany and have a great interest in this project and in . . ." She let her words trail off.

"In him?" Addie asked with a raised brow.

"Yes, but don't say anything. It's all very new to me. The thing is that typing each evening will mean having to catch the last trolley back to the city, and it will be very late. I just thought if I could maybe stay at your cottage for the time it takes to type the manuscript, then I wouldn't be so tired or have to risk the streets at night."

"Of course. I don't see a problem. I haven't rented the place out yet. You could stay there, and you wouldn't have to pay rent so long as you took good care of the place."

Just then Mary and Bertha came into the shop to start their day. Addie smiled. "In fact, maybe Mary and Bertha would like to stay with you for the month. Then you wouldn't have to be alone."

Eleanor looked at Mary and then Bertha. They had all become fast friends, and she couldn't imagine a more suitable arrangement. Even Rosemary would have to concede it was a safe option.

"What are you talking about, Addie?" Mary asked.

"Eleanor has need to stay close by for a month and asked to use my cottage. I thought if you and Bertha wanted to join her there it would be safer and more pleasant for everyone. You wouldn't need to pay rent, just take care of the place. I have a man already arranged who cuts the grass and tends to the flowers, so all you would have to do is tend to the inside."

"That would be a lot of fun," Bertha admitted. "Living on the lake for a month would be like a vacation."

"Count me in," Mary said. "I love that cottage."

Eleanor couldn't have planned it better. "I think this is answered prayer, girls. I wanted very much to help Mr. Reed, and this will allow me to do it with the least amount of trouble."

"Who is Mr. Reed?" Mary asked.

Just then Bill walked into the shop. He took off his hat and nodded to all the ladies. "Good morning."

"This," Eleanor said, going to stand beside Bill, "is Mr. Reed. He's a botanist and has asked me to help him by typing up his manuscript. You know about my interest in botany, and this will be a real opportunity for me to learn about the various vegetation in Alaska."

"Mr. Reed, it's very nice to meet you," Addie said, coming forward. "Eleanor tells me you are checking with the university about using one of their typewriters. My husband, Isaac Hanson, is one of the new instructors there."

"I've met him. He's been quite amiable."

Addie laughed. "Yes, that's definitely one way to describe him."

"We talked about living up north. I believe you and he both lived in the Yukon during the gold rush."

"We did." She added nothing more, so Eleanor jumped back in.

"Bill, Addie said that I could stay at her cottage near here for the month or so it will take for me to type up your manuscript. That way I won't have to worry about getting back to town really late or even having to buy my supper out. I could just swing over there before coming to whatever building we're working in and grab a bite."

"But I was looking forward to sharing supper with you." His voice betrayed disappointment.

"Well, perhaps we can do that from time to time, but we won't have to do it all the time because it will be costly."

Bill smiled. "So long as we can do it once in a while."

"I suggested Mary and Bertha could join her there, so she won't be staying alone," Addie said, nodding at the other girls.

"That sounds like the perfect arrangement," Bill replied. "I won't be worried about her being there by herself on my account."

"Well, I need to get to work. Mr. and Mrs. Fisher will be here momentarily, and they like to see that we're out doing our jobs," Mary declared. Bertha nodded and followed suit. They took up cameras and headed for the door.

"It was nice to meet you, ladies," Bill called after them.

"Nice to meet you too," Mary and Bertha replied in unison.

"Well, I need to follow their example," Eleanor said, turning to him. "I take it you managed to arrange the situation at the university?"

"Huh? Oh, yes," he said, nodding. "We are able to use a typewriter in the history department. It will be perfect. I have a key for the room and a filing cabinet where I can store my things. We can start tonight."

"Wonderful. I don't know exactly where the history department is, but if you could meet me by the gates tonight, you could show me the way."

"That will be perfect." Bill turned for the door. "Now I must dash, or I'll be late for my job."

"See you this evening." Eleanor watched him go. When she turned back, she could see Addie grinning.

"You like him very much, don't you?" she asked.

Eleanor felt her face flush. It was a problem many redheads had with their fair skin and embarrassment. "I do. I just feel like God has put him in my life for a very special reason."

"I know how that is," Addie said, slipping behind the counter.

Eleanor loaded her satchel and grabbed a camera. "It's like every day is suddenly Christmas."

Outside the crowds were already growing in number. The exposition had become very popular. Eleanor had heard there was some talk of extending it past the October ending date, but no one had said if that would happen.

The day was perfect for photography. There were a few clouds overhead, but they weren't a problem. There was no sign of rain, and that was good. Eleanor found a lovely family right off the bat and talked them into posing for a picture in the sunken gardens just south of the Geyser Basin pond. It was one of Eleanor's favorite spots at the expo with its beautiful walkways surrounded by flowers and plenty of benches to sit and rest.

"This is the best way to commemorate your day here," she

told the parents as they struggled to manage their three small children. "Here, let me help." She took hold of the littlest girl and lifted her up. The child seemed quite fascinated by Eleanor's satchel.

"You sit right here, Mom and Dad, and I'll put her right between you." They did as she instructed, and Eleanor placed the child very carefully. "Just hold the boys on your laps." The little girl got to her feet almost the instant Eleanor let go of her.

"Oh, that's even better." Eleanor went to the little girl. "Put your hands here and here," she said, placing the child's hands on her parents' shoulders. "Perfect. Now everyone hold very still."

She took the picture before anyone moved and felt confident it would be a great shot. Eleanor took a notebook out of her satchel along with a pencil. "If you would be so kind as to write down your name and address, we can mail the postcard to you. You just need to prepay the ten cents. Or—"

"What if we don't like the picture?" the mother interrupted.

The father agreed. "Yes, couldn't we stop in and see it before agreeing to buy it?"

"Of course, I was just getting ready to explain that," Eleanor replied, holding back on handing him the notebook and pencil. "You can stop by Fisher Photography on Pay Streak this afternoon before five." She jotted down the information they would need, then pulled out the page and gave it to the man. "Give this to the person who waits on you. This will tell them which group of photos to search for yours."

The father nodded. "We'll do that, thank you."

"And should you decide you like the photograph enough to purchase the camera, be sure and remind them that Eleanor took the picture."

"Oh, I don't think we'd ever be interested in purchasing one for ourselves. We aren't rich," the father replied.

"The cameras have been priced for the average person at just ten dollars," Eleanor countered with a smile. "However, I understand that is still a lot of money to some. If you should decide to take a look, just let them know that Eleanor was the one who suggested you check it out."

Eleanor put her things away and headed off for the next customer. By ten o'clock, she only had one last picture to take. She felt confident that three of the customers she'd taken photos of were going to buy cameras, and that felt very good. The commission money was generous, and she knew she could use it, especially now that she would be sharing time between two houses.

As she turned back toward the shop, Eleanor spied a young woman dressed all in black. She wore a mourning veil and held an infant. It was hard to see her face through the veil, but just the figure of her sitting there, babe in arms, was haunting. People seemed to avoid her and made wide circles around her as they passed by. Reminders of death were never welcome.

Eleanor couldn't explain it, but she couldn't look away. For several minutes, she continued to watch the woman, wondering what in the world she was doing at the expo. People in mourning didn't generally come to public places like fairs. Society would frown upon that, but also the person in mourning would have no desire to be around such revelry. She might have come with someone. Maybe someone she was staying with had insisted she come along, and now they'd gone elsewhere to enjoy a ride or get food.

Normally Eleanor wouldn't have bothered someone who was obviously in mourning, but for reasons she couldn't explain, she felt like she should take this woman's picture. She approached the woman and smiled.

"Hello, I'm Eleanor, and I work for Fisher Photography. We're taking photographs for fairgoers so that they will have a memorial of the day. The photographs are prepared as a postcard and cost only ten cents. Could I take your picture with the baby?"

The woman looked up and met Eleanor's gaze through the black veil. "I suppose so. I haven't had a picture taken yet of the baby."

"Perhaps you could push back the veil so that we could see your face and then hold the baby a little higher." The woman complied with Eleanor's instructions.

"Like this?" she asked.

"Perfect. Let me take the picture before the baby wakes up."

Eleanor positioned herself a little to the side and captured the woman looking past her. It was as if she were looking for someone—perhaps her lost loved one. There was just something so haunting about the woman that even after she took the picture, Eleanor just stood watching her.

"Are you finished?" the woman asked.

"Yes, I am." Eleanor hurried forward with her notebook and pencil. She put the number ten at the top of the page since the photo was the last on the reel. "If you would just write down your name and address, we can have the postcard mailed to you. As I said, it's just ten cents plus the cost of the stamp. You would pay me, and when the photo is processed, we will put it in the mail. Unless you'd rather wait for it today. You can go to the shop before five and pick it up."

"No, I'd rather you mail it." She shifted the sleeping baby and took the notebook and pencil.

Eleanor wanted to offer to help her but wasn't sure it was appropriate. The woman seemed very guarded of her child. Almost fearful. By the time Eleanor worked up her nerve to ask, the woman had managed it all. She handed the closed notebook back to Eleanor.

"Thank you. I hadn't intended to do such a thing, but I'm glad you asked." She pulled a little coin purse from her waistband and fished out the necessary payment. She handed the coins to Eleanor.

Eleanor nodded. "You looked so very sad sitting here. I know you've obviously suffered loss, and for that I'm very sorry."

The woman got to her feet. "Yes, my husband died before the baby was born. He never got to see him or even know he had a son. I was just thinking about that when you came to me."

"That is very sad indeed." Eleanor glanced at the baby. "He's quite beautiful. I'm sure his papa would be proud."

"Yes." The woman gave Eleanor a nod. "I shall look forward to seeing the photograph."

Eleanor watched her walk away. A part of her wanted to run after the woman just to offer companionship. She seemed so very alone. Instead, Eleanor made her way back to the shop to get another camera and continue her work.

She entered the shop and found Mrs. Fisher busy with the postcard mailings. She looked up and smiled. "You girls put a real dent in these. I appreciate you helping us to get caught up, especially since you weren't even expected to work that day."

"I didn't mind at all." Eleanor held up her camera. "Is Mr. Fisher in the darkroom?"

"Yes, but he's not developing just now."

Eleanor was glad for that. She wanted to see him and talk to him about the woman's photograph. She made her way to the darkroom and knocked on the open door.

"May I come in for a moment?"

Mr. Fisher straightened from his task of cleaning. "Yes, come in."

She held out her camera. "The film has been used, but on the last photo I wanted to make a special request. I'd like you to make two copies of the picture. I'll pay for the second one. I was just really captivated by the woman and her baby. She was in mourning, and her image isn't one I'm likely to forget. I don't know why, but she really touched me."

"Of course, we can make two."

Eleanor handed him the camera, then tore out the pages of names and addresses from her notebook to give him as well. "All but one wanted to have them mailed. The other plans to come in later today."

Mr. Fisher took the information and camera. "I'll let you know when it's ready."

"Thank you." Eleanor made her way back out front and picked up another preloaded camera. "I'm heading out again. It's such a lovely day. My roommate, Rosemary, works in an office and believes herself the luckier one, but I am so very blessed to be outside. It doesn't feel like work at all."

Mrs. Fisher smiled. "I know what you mean. I love taking

walks in the park. I think after the baby is born, I will buy one of those large baby buggies and go for long walks every day. At least until the weather turns too cold."

"That sounds like a wonderful way to enjoy the day. How fortunate too that you'll be able to take lots of pictures of the baby and mark the time and their growth."

"I know. I've already got plans to take at least one picture every week."

Eleanor opened the door. "Yours will be the most photographed baby in the world—or at least Seattle."

Outside she thought again of the woman in black and her baby. She said she hadn't a single photograph of the child. Eleanor was glad she had listened to her instincts and approached the woman. Now, no matter what happened in the future, the woman would have that memento of the day.

6

Grady Masterson knocked again at the window. There was still no answer, and he began to feel a slight sense of panic. Where was she? Hadn't he warned her to stay inside? He peered through the window but could see very little. Straightening, he began to pace back and forth on the porch. His hands were balled into fists, and he wanted to hit something or someone.

For two months, he'd hidden Amelia Reed and her child away like buried treasure. He had kept any and all news about the shipwreck from her, not that much information had been given.

When the *City of Canton* went down in May, Grady had cursed his bad fortune. It had been irritating enough to learn that Wallace Reed was on the same ship. Reed was responsible for the death of his brother. Oh, Avery had killed the man, but Reed didn't have to come forth as a witness. If he'd left well enough alone, Avery would have gotten away with the murder and still be alive to tell the tale.

Grady had never hated anyone as much as he did Wallace Reed, and he had figured out the perfect revenge on the man. He had made him believe his wife was dead—lost forever.

It had been no easy feat to arrange everything either. He had managed at the last minute to get into the same lifeboat as Amelia. He avoided her at first. The bad blood between him and her husband was well known, and there was no sense making a scene when they were all about to face the possibility of death. Then one of the ship's crewmen asked Grady and Amelia to move to another lifeboat to make space for another crew member, which each lifeboat was required to have. Grady helped Amelia from the boat, despite her looking rather worried. She had clutched a package, as well as a small bag, and allowed his assistance. In her condition, she had little choice.

The ship's crewman put them on lifeboat number ten, and once they were settled in, Grady could see this boat consisted of mostly men. It had been one of the last to be loaded. Everyone there had been very congenial toward Amelia, making sure she was warm enough and comfortable. But once they were released to the water, there was no comfort to be found. Grady had feared for his life, certain that they were doomed to overturn in the tumultuous sea. Amelia sat beside him in silence, her face white as a sheet.

At one point, the roughness of the storm tossed them about so violently that Amelia actually passed out. Grady took the opportunity to put his arm around her and pull her close while the other men worked frantically, trying their best to row to shore. When help finally arrived in the form of a Canadian freighter, there was great relief. Once on board, Amelia immediately began to search among the survivors for her husband and brother-in-law, but they were nowhere to be found.

Grady found out that an American ship had picked up some of the survivors. They would be taken to Seattle while the Canadian freighter was bringing its survivors to Victoria. It became difficult to know who went where and how many had actually survived. When word came that several lifeboats, including number five, had overturned and all passengers had been lost, Grady began to get an idea.

It was clear that the Reed brothers weren't on board the freighter. Grady could only hope they'd been among those who had perished, but even if they hadn't, he intended that Amelia would believe they had.

The freighter managed to get them all ashore in Victoria, and the injured were immediately sent to the hospital while the others were moved to a local church where they would be warmed and fed. Amelia almost immediately went into labor, and thankfully, a midwife was among the helping congregants. She told Grady she lived nearby and urged him to bring Amelia to her home. He did so and, with that one little act, managed to further his plan without even trying. Neither he nor Amelia were counted among the survivors. Grady couldn't have planned things any better.

Amelia developed a fever after the baby's difficult birth, and they remained at the house of the midwife for two weeks. The midwife, thinking he was the husband, told him that she wasn't sure if Amelia would make it, but the baby seemed strong. When Amelia did rally, she was surprised to find Grady by her side, but he was quick with a response.

"Your husband and I put our differences aside. I could finally see that the decision he made to testify against my brother was only right. Avery killed a man and deserved to pay the price." The words had threatened to stick in his throat, but they pleased Amelia, and she relaxed regarding his presence. After that it was just too easy.

The midwife suggested Amelia rest for at least another couple of weeks once her fever was gone. She faithfully tended to the baby as well as the mother and left Grady with little to do, so he went in search of some small job he could do to earn money. The midwife's husband suggested he try down at one of the sawmills. He suggested Grady give them his name as a reference. Having had experience in sawmill work, Grady did just that and managed to get the position. He earned enough money to pay the midwife for their room and board, as well as her care of Amelia, plus save some for passage to the United States when Amelia recovered.

When Grady heard a few of the bodies were recovered from the icy waters, he went to visit the makeshift morgue. He told the authorities he was certain that two of the men were Wallace and William Reed. The bodies had no identification, and so the authorities were glad for the help and information. Grady was unable to help them with next of kin or any addresses, so he lied and told them the two were alone in the world except for each other. This satisfied everyone enough that the two men were buried and quickly forgotten. Grady then had to break the news to Amelia.

Amelia. Where was she? It was getting late, and she knew nothing of Seattle. Grady paced all the faster. He had a key to the apartment but had left it at home since she was always here. He'd grown accustomed to coming to see her after work. They would often share a meal and talk about what was going on in the city. Amelia seldom had much to say, but she was at least accepting of his help. And well she should be. He was paying her rent in a decent apartment while he was staying in a hovel with ten other men.

"Well, Avery, what should I do?" he muttered, casting a glance around. Of late he had started talking to his dead brother. The strange thing was that at times it almost seemed that Avery answered. Grady could feel his sibling's presence, and why not? They'd always been very close.

He heard the approach of the trolley and paused to watch. It came to a stop, signaling to him that someone wanted off since there had been no one waiting to board. To his relief, Amelia, with the baby in her arms, stepped off with the help of a well-dressed gentleman. She made her way across the street and walked toward the apartment. When she caught sight of Grady, she gave a little wave.

He moved down the sidewalk to meet her as she approached. "Where have you been? I was so worried."

She shook her head. "You needn't be. I'm quite capable of functioning on my own."

"But I warned you that you shouldn't go out and about without me to protect you. It's a dangerous city, especially with the exposition in town."

"That's where I went," she said as she continued to walk toward the apartment. "I just needed to get out and do something different."

"You went to the expo?" He felt slightly sick at the thought that someone might have recognized her.

"I did." She climbed the steps to the porch and offered nothing more as she used her key to open the building's outer door and then her apartment door just inside.

Grady followed her into the apartment and took off his

hat. "You shouldn't have done that. It could have turned out tragic for you. Some very bad people in this world would see a young widow with a baby as the perfect target."

She placed the sleeping baby in the small crib on the far side of the room. The one large room was separated with a curtain to designate the sleeping quarters from the living area and tiny kitchen. Fortunately, the place had running water, and there was a bathroom down the hall to share with three other apartments.

Grady had thought it quite the find. The entire two-story building had once been a nice house but was now divided into apartments, and only women were allowed to rent them. It was the perfect setup for Amelia and for his purposes.

Amelia rid herself of her veil, hat, and gloves. She put them away and took up an apron. As she tied it around her waist, she looked to Grady. "Did you have a hard day? You seem out of sorts."

"I was worried about you. My workday went well enough. Picking up trash for the city of Seattle is laborious, but not difficult. Unless of course the wagon breaks down, and you have to transfer all of that garbage to another wagon."

She nodded and went to the icebox. "I can fix some ham and potatoes if that suits you."

Grady smiled. "Anything is fine."

A knock sounded on the door to Amelia's apartment. She went to see who it was and found her landlady, Mrs. Becker.

"Good evening, my dear. I heard you come in. I see your brother is here." She looked past Amelia to where Grady stood. "Good evening, Mr. Masterson."

"Evening." He had told the old woman that he was Amelia's brother and would often be by to check on her and his nephew. He figured that was the easiest way to avoid trouble since the woman forbade romantic visitors. Amelia had surprisingly gone along with it. Of course, when they'd first arrived, she'd said very little to anyone, just as he encouraged.

"Did you enjoy the expo?" Mrs. Becker asked, turning back to Amelia.

"Yes, it was very interesting. I can't say that I have any need to go back, but it was a pleasant enough outing, and I'm glad you recommended it."

Grady held his tongue. He would have liked to condemn the older woman for suggesting that a young mother without an escort board a trolley and go to the exposition. The fact was, he'd never cared for Mrs. Becker. She was opinionated and fixed on her beliefs. If she told you it was raining and you pointed out the falsehood of that, she would reiterate her belief and condemn you for not seeing the truth. Plus, she was nosy.

"There were people everywhere," Amelia added. "I'm definitely not used to that."

"No, I would imagine not. Well, I'm glad you were able to enjoy yourself."

Amelia glanced back at Grady. "I'm afraid I worried Grady."

"It's silly to worry. All is well." Mrs. Becker turned to go. "I'll speak with you more tomorrow, Amelia. I can see you're busy."

"Yes, I was just about to make dinner." Amelia followed Mrs. Becker to the door.

Once Mrs. Becker was gone, and Amelia was again in the kitchen, Grady began to relax a bit. He'd been thinking about his revenge—keeping Amelia and Wallace apart. He

knew the satisfaction of his deed, but it would be even better if Wallace knew it too. But how could he let him know?
He had no idea where the man and his brother had gone.
He knew from the information he'd gathered at the Seattle
newspaper office that they were listed among the American
survivors. He wondered if anyone had compared that list to
the Canadian list of the dead. If they had, no one seemed
to have brought up the fact. At least not in the newspapers.

They could still be here in Seattle, but he doubted it. Amelia had said they were only coming down for the birth of
the baby, then planned to return straightaway to continue
their ministry work. Upon learning Amelia was dead, Grady
guessed they returned to Alaska within a matter of weeks.

He sat down and watched Amelia peel potatoes and slice
them. Next, she put them in the skillet with a little lard. She
then cut up the ham into bite-size chunks and added that
to the potatoes as well. She really was a handsome woman
and much too young to be left alone in the world. Grady
had been thinking lately that an even more priceless revenge
would be to take her as his wife. Of course, it wouldn't be
legal, but he didn't care.

"I've really come to care for you and little Wally. You must
know that. No man would do the things I've done if he
didn't care."

Amelia stopped and fixed him with a look that suggested
concern. "Is something wrong?"

"No, not at all. In fact, just the opposite. I realize that I
want to keep taking care of you both. You're alone in the
world now, and I want to provide for you—give you a home
and safety."

"You've already done that. And I am very grateful. If I

don't say it enough, I'm sorry. My mind is still on my losses, and sometimes it's hard to see my benefits."

"And I understand that. I get a little sick inside when I imagine you trying to manage alone."

"Yes, that's true for me as well. I don't know what I would have done had you not taken us under your care."

"Well, I know it's too soon to suggest what I'm going to say, but I can't help myself. I want to marry you."

Grady had handled himself as a perfect gentleman and would continue to do so because he knew that's what this game required. But the thought of taking Amelia as his own was ever present these days. The more they were together, the more he wanted to possess her. The idea of causing further pain and damage to Wallace Reed, whether he knew about it or not, was something that filled Grady's days with pleasure.

"I will never marry again, Grady. I thought I made that clear."

"You have, but, well, you must know how I feel. How hard it is for me to see you like this and know your sadness. I believe I could make you happy."

"You're kind to suggest so, but no. I won't marry you or anyone else. I am going to devote myself to Wally and seeing him raised properly."

"And what are you going to do for money? I can hardly be expected to continue supporting you both." He hadn't meant to speak the words out loud, but now that he had, he couldn't help but wonder what her response would be.

She stopped what she was doing and looked at him for a long moment. "That's true. You have been most generous, and I will pay you back. I've already thought about this. I believe I will put an advertisement in the paper and take in sewing. I'm quite good, and even though I don't have a machine, Mrs. Becker does, and she offered to let me use it."

"No, you shouldn't work." He scrambled for what to say to convince her. He wanted her dependent on him, completely helpless and without money.

"But I should. If I can do something here that won't take me away from the baby, then I can get you paid back. I mended a few things for one of the ladies upstairs, and she was quite pleased. It gave me a little money, which is how I paid for the trolley and the expo ticket. I know I probably should have given it to you, but I just couldn't help myself."

"That doesn't matter. I just don't want you having to worry about it while the baby is so young and needs you so much."

"I know, but like you said, you can't be expected to keep supporting us." She went to the stove and stirred the potatoes-and-ham concoction. She added salt and pepper. "I think this is ready."

"Amelia, I never meant to worry you or say those things. I'm just tired. It was a long day hauling trash."

She plated some of the food for him and set it on the table. Next, she brought a fork and napkin. "Would you like some coffee? I don't have any made, but it won't take long."

"No, just come and eat with me."

She nodded and dished up her own plate of food. She brought it with a glass of water and sat down at the little two-seat table. "Shall I offer grace?"

Grady nodded. He had little interest in such things, but she was fanatical about it. After her prayer, he picked up his fork and dug in. He hated the way things had gone. Now instead of making her see how much she needed him, Amelia was trying to figure out how she could exist on her own. This wasn't at all how he wanted things to go.

The meal passed much too quickly, and Grady knew he had no real excuse for extending the evening. The baby awoke for a feeding, and Amelia went into the privacy of her little curtained-off bedroom to change and feed her son.

I need to figure out some way to convince her that marriage to me is a good thing—a needed thing. He toyed with his fork and considered the situation. If he could just get her to marry him, then his revenge would be complete. It would thoroughly satisfy him, and he could use her for as long as it suited him. Then one day he would tell her the truth. The whole truth about how he'd kept her apart from Wallace and made him believe she was dead, then tricked her into an illegal marriage.

Amelia returned after some time with the baby in her arms. Wally was wide awake and looking over his mother's shoulder as if trying to figure out his surroundings.

"He's sure growing fast."

Amelia smiled. Her only smiles these days were related to her son. "He is. He's going to be a fine young man someday."

Silence fell between them as Amelia took a seat near the window and placed the baby on her lap. Without any thought for Grady, she spoke to her son and gently touched his face. The tenderness of the moment left Grady no doubt he was intruding. Not that he should care, but strangely enough, he did.

"I suppose I should head out." Grady got to his feet. "Please promise me you won't go back to the expo. Or anywhere else for that matter. If you want to have an outing, I can take you on Saturday after work."

"I'll be fine. You just see to yourself." She paid little attention to Grady even as she answered him.

He nodded but knew she didn't see him. "I'll be back tomorrow."

"All right."

At the door, he glanced back. There was something about the moment—her sitting there all dressed in black with the baby on her lap. Grady frowned and opened the door. He refused to care about the wife of his enemy. He was there to cause her and her husband as much pain and misery as possible. He wouldn't yield that opportunity.

7

Eleanor's last duty of the day was helping Mr. Fisher develop the photographs. She had plenty of experience in this as she had helped her father on many occasions.

"I heard that you placed another order for cameras," Eleanor said as she moved a pan of chemicals to the opposite table.

"I did. We have sold so many that Kodak is sending a representative out here to speak with me and bring the new supply of cameras. I'm hopeful they'll leave me to continue as I have, but I suppose there's a possibility that they'll want to open their own little shop here."

"Hopefully not. I'll pray for them to have no desire for such things."

"It's been such a help to me. I've raised a good deal of money and have even found the right property downtown. I'm in the process of working out that arrangement and will soon be able to settle us in a much nicer building."

"Does it have an apartment upstairs for you and Mrs. Fisher to live in?" Eleanor asked.

"It does. It's much bigger than what we have. It will be perfect for us and is in a wonderful location with all sorts of other shops and businesses nearby."

"That sounds amazing. I'm very happy for you. Oh, and don't forget, I'd like to apply for a job with your shop. Although I have my heart set on college classes, I will still need to work. I'm really not sure how I can make it all come together since the classes will be in the daytime and most jobs I would qualify for would be as well."

"I'm sure we can figure something out," Mr. Fisher assured her. "Oh, I nearly forgot. I made the second photograph of that woman and her baby. It's over here." He went to the end of the table and reached under to pull out a box. The very top photograph was the one of the woman in mourning. He handed it to Eleanor.

"Isn't it haunting?" Eleanor studied the woman and child. There was such pain in the woman's eyes and her expression was one of such sorrow. "She lost her husband before the baby was born."

"I was very impressed with the photograph and would like to display it in the window if you don't mind. It draws attention, and once passersby stop to look, they might come in to see what else we have."

"That sounds like a great idea," Eleanor replied. She was more than a little pleased that someone like Mr. Fisher should be captivated by her photograph.

❧

"And I told him it was a great idea," Eleanor told her roommate as they walked to church for choir practice.

"I've seen some of the plant pictures you've taken. They are quite good. You definitely have an artistic eye," Rosemary answered.

"I have to admit, I can't get that woman and her baby out of my head. There was just something about her. Something that connected us. I wanted so much to just sit and hold her hand—assure her that God had not forgotten her. For whatever reason, however, I said nothing of the sort. I just let her walk away."

"I don't think God calls us to stick our noses in everyone's business, Eleanor. She was a widow. Her sadness touched you. That's all it was."

"I don't think so, Rosemary. I have even dreamed about her. I don't know her name, yet she's always there somewhere in my thoughts." Eleanor shook her head. "I think I might try to find her. Like I said, I feel that I should have done something more—perhaps offered some sort of help."

"And just how would you help her? You've barely got enough money to make ends meet and save for your classes."

They turned toward the little stone church, and Eleanor paused. "I don't know how I would help her, but I just feel that I'm supposed to."

"Maybe you should talk to the pastor and tell him your situation. I'm betting he'd suggest you pray, and if God wants you to do something more, He'll bring her around to you again." Rosemary put a hand to her hat. "Is this on straight?"

Eleanor glanced at her friend. "It is."

All through choir practice, Eleanor thought about her dilemma. It would surely be easy enough to look up the woman's name and address. She had paid for her photograph to be mailed, and Mrs. Fisher kept meticulous accounts.

Eleanor tried to imagine what she would say if she actually went to the woman's address. How could she explain the way she had touched Eleanor's heart? There was just something about the woman and baby that refused to leave her thoughts.

"Let's try that last part again. Eleanor, will you be joining us this time?" The choirmaster looked at her with a raised brow.

Eleanor's cheeks went hot. "Sorry. I've had a lot on my mind. I'll pay better attention, I promise."

She forced the woman and baby from her thoughts and concentrated instead on the music. When rehearsal concluded, she felt obliged to apologize to the director before hurrying to catch up with Rosemary at the door to the church.

"Do you want to stop with some of the others and have something to eat?" Rosemary asked, stopping in the vestibule to adjust her hat.

"No, I really can't afford to spend the money. You go ahead if you want to. I can see myself home. It's just a couple of blocks."

"Aren't you glad you don't have to go all the way back to the cottage on the lake tonight? Still, I wouldn't feel right about you walking to our apartment alone. At night we really need to stick together. You know it's the wise thing."

"I do, but I hate for you to miss out. Besides, it's not really dark yet." Eleanor glanced around to find the others were already starting out from the building. "I suppose I could go and just have a coffee. That doesn't cost all that much."

"No, let's just go home. I'm tired, and I know morning will come soon enough. I also need to write my mother."

"I should do that as well. I've not told her anything about my typing job."

Rosemary frowned. "I forgot to ask how that was going."

"Bill is the perfect gentleman. I love his wit and his wisdom. He's very intelligent, Rosemary. He knows all sorts of things, especially about plants and wildlife in Alaska. I'm completely captivated when he talks about his life there. I want so much to experience it for myself."

"Next thing you'll be telling me you plan to follow him north." They exited into the chilly night air.

Eleanor momentarily bit her lower lip and looked away.

"Eleanor! You can't be seriously considering such a thing." Rosemary's tone was indignant and the look on her face was one of complete shock.

"I don't think it would be such a terrible thing to do."

"It would be positively scandalous. As a single woman, you cannot travel with a single man into the wilds of Alaska. It's not appropriate. Think of the risk—the lack of protection."

"Bill would be my protection. He's a wonderful, godly man. His brother is a preacher—or he was. I don't know if he's going back to Alaska or not, but I could travel under their protection."

Rosemary shook her head and stomped off down the church steps. "I can't even believe I'm hearing this. I thought you had more sense."

Eleanor kept pace with her friend. "I have plenty of sense. I just want to study the things Bill studies. He's talking about making another book. This one would be on medicinal herbs and plants. Wouldn't that be amazing if I could help him with it? I could take photographs. Instead of going to college to learn what I need to know, I could actually be a part of learning as I live."

"You'd be learning all right—sad and unfortunate lessons, I'm afraid." Rosemary crossed her arms. "You'd probably end up killed."

"Oh, Bill would never do something so hideous! He's not at all that kind of man."

Rosemary kept walking but glanced at Eleanor. "You haven't known him long enough to know what kind of man he is, Eleanor. You've only known him a short time, and yet you're talking about running off with him to a place thousands of miles away. It frightens me when you talk that way."

Eleanor reached out and took hold of Rosemary's arm. "I didn't mean to cause you distress. I won't mention it again."

Rosemary stopped. "Even if you don't, I'll know that you're plotting and planning."

Laughing, Eleanor looped her arm with Rosemary's. "I'll probably be much too busy with school and work to plot and plan much. So stop fretting and just enjoy the fact that I'll be staying with you tonight instead of sleeping at Addie Hanson's cottage."

This seemed to cause Rosemary to relax a bit. "I am glad for that. I've missed you. It's lonely in the apartment by myself." She sighed. "Let's get home before we lose the light. How about I pop some corn for us?"

"Sounds perfect." Eleanor gave her an approving smile and started to walk.

She wasn't going to stop considering the possibility of going north when Bill headed home to Alaska, but she wasn't going to discuss it further with Rosemary. She was too much of a worrier.

Bill looked over the typed manuscript pages for any mistakes. Eleanor was quite good at typing, and there had only been a very few times when she'd transposed letters or forgotten a word. She was also very good at fixing her mistakes, which wasn't at all easy. She and Bill had agreed they needed to make a copy of the manuscript to keep, just in case something terrible should happen again. That required each page be typed with a sheet of carbon paper, so when the letter was struck and printed on the first page, the carbon copied it to the second page. When mistakes were made, it was necessary to take a special eraser and clear the mistake, then carefully line the pages up again and retype the information.

"These are great, Eleanor. I've proofed them, and they're perfect."

"I proofed them too. I wanted to make sure I did it exactly the way you had it. I held the pages side by side and went over each letter and space."

He chuckled. "I've never had so intense an assistant. You've done a wonderful job. Much better than I did myself. It took me a great many nights to type the original, and that was without a carbon copy."

"How are your drawings coming along?"

"Slow, but just fine. Even on the pages where the original is a mess, I've been able to remember the particulars, for which I'm very grateful. I have detailed notebooks in Alaska, but that doesn't do me much good here."

"No, and I don't suppose you could write and have them mailed here." Eleanor couldn't begin to imagine the amount of time that would take. It was a lengthy enough process just getting mail from one coast of the United States to the other.

"I'd be on my way back by the time they'd get here." Bill put down the typed pages and picked up the drawing he was working on.

"This devil's club plant—*Oplopanax horridus*—sounds alarming and fascinating all at the same time. Is it really used for so many medical purposes?"

"It is." Bill seemed to light up. "The Tlingit—one of the native groups—use it for a great many things. Coughs, ulcers. They even use it with tuberculosis and diabetes. They swear by it and use it all of the time to cure or heal."

"It sounds like a wretched plant with its spikes and stickers. It's fascinating that anyone even bothered to use it in the first place. Seems such painful complications would have influenced folks to stay away from it."

Bill chuckled. "It's true. It is a force to be reckoned with, but such a beneficial one. As I state in the manuscript, the Tlingit steep it, chew it, and mash it into salves. They even use it as a means to ward off evil. Although I'm not certain that works as well as the medicinal uses."

"Maybe they just wave the stickery stalks and evil flees." She smiled and looked back at the manuscript and began typing again. "I'm really learning a lot."

He couldn't help watching her for a moment. She was a hard worker, but not only that, she loved what she was reading. She had a passion for this work, just as he did.

God, is she the one You've sent me? Bill couldn't help but ask the question. He was terrified of missing the gift if she was indeed the woman God had sent to him to be his wife. She was pretty and smart and shared his love of plants.

Added to that, she was a godly woman. She read her Bible and prayed regularly. They had even discussed passages of Scripture when talking about all manner of things.

She had to be the one.

There were only a few weeks left before he would head back to Alaska. How could he possibly court and woo her in that time? He supposed if she was the one God had for him, then He could make it all come together. *This isn't about me making it happen. This is about resting in God and letting Him work.*

That was hard for someone who liked to plan and produce results on his own. Bill had always been the kind of man who meticulously worked out his agenda, then pressed forward with great gusto. It was hard to wait for God's timing.

He forced his attention back on the drawing he was making, but all he could think about was the young, redheaded woman typing his work.

Two hours later, they stopped for the night. Eleanor was exhausted. She'd worked a full day and now most of the evening.

"Thank you for this, Eleanor. I promise when I get my first royalty check, I'm paying you before buying anything else."

"I didn't ask for pay." Eleanor stretched her shoulders. "I am happy with the education I'm getting. I've learned so much. Much more than I would have learned at school. At least I think I've learned more. You had that wonderful introduction that spoke of all the ways to observe nature and why it's important. I've committed that to memory. I hope to memorize a lot more before we're done."

"You soak up knowledge like a sponge soaks up water."

He looked at her for a moment. "May I walk you to your cottage?"

"Yes, of course. That would be lovely. Mary and Bertha are there waiting for me, but it is rather shrouded along the way." She gathered her things as Bill put away his work. The head of the history department had given him an entire drawer to use in the filing cabinet, and he utilized this to store his drawing supplies. Once the drawer was locked, he turned to find Eleanor watching him.

"Is something wrong?"

"No." She smiled. "I know this may sound rather bold, but I'm just so fascinated with you."

He laughed out loud, and she smiled. "That is bold," he agreed. "But rather nice, for I find myself fascinated with you. As I've said before, I haven't known many women who wanted to learn the same things I have."

"Well, you needn't worry about that anymore. I want to know it all." She laughed. "I may be bold, but I feel like this time has been precious. Perhaps more so because I know it's short."

Bill took up his coat and put it on while walking toward her. "I don't know that it has to be short."

Her blue eyes widened slightly at his words. He said nothing more but took hold of her arm and led her toward the door.

They walked in silence to the cottage. Bill was actually surprised that Eleanor didn't make any comments. She was always quite talkative. He frowned. Had he upset her? She didn't seem upset. Should he ask? *Lord, I really don't know what I'm doing, but when I remember Wallace's stories about Amelia, I'm beginning to wonder if it isn't a little bit like falling in love.*

"Well, it looks like the girls are still up. Thanks for walking me home," Eleanor said, slipping her arm from his. "I have tomorrow off but wasn't sure if the university would allow us to come and work all day."

"I don't know. Let me ask. I'll come by the cottage around nine and let you know. Will that be all right?"

"Of course. I'll even get to sleep in." She held her hand up to cover her yawn. "I'm more than ready for sleep."

"You've been working very hard, and I appreciate you more than I can tell you."

For a moment they stood facing each other. Just inches apart. He could very easily bend forward and kiss her. He glanced at her lips, then back up at her eyes. Smiling, he backed up.

"Good night, Eleanor."

She smiled. "Good night, Bill."

8

T wo important pieces of mail arrived that day for Amelia Reed. They were the first she'd had since coming to Seattle. One was the postcard photograph of her and Wally. The photograph brought tears to her eyes as she truly saw herself for the first time as a widow. Somehow the postcard made it more real. Wallace was gone, and she and Wally were alone in the world. She couldn't help remembering the kind young woman who'd taken the photograph. Amelia was glad that she'd crossed the bounds of propriety to ask her about the picture.

The second piece of mail was from Wallace and Bill's lawyer back in Chicago. A couple of weeks ago, she had written to him to let him know that Wallace and Bill were dead. She told of the ship's sinking and how she and the baby were now on their own in Seattle but planned to return to Alaska. She had hoped the lawyer would share the death of the men with their father, as well as the birth of his grandson, Wallace Reed Junior.

However, the letter told of how her husband's father had died in early May. The lawyer had sent a letter to Alaska, not realizing the men were headed south. He thanked her for the information, then proceeded to tell Amelia that she was entitled to not only her husband's inheritance but William's as well.

She reread the paragraph.

You and your son are the sole survivors of Wallace and William Reed, and as such it has been designated that you will inherit the money their father left to them. I have contacted a local bank to set up an account for you. I will telegraph with the final details once they are set in place. This should see you and your son through life in comfort.

It was answered prayer. Amelia would have money enough to pay back Grady and get him out of her life once and for all. She was glad to know that he and her husband had made peace with each other, but the man was becoming more obvious in his intentions. He had spoken of marriage more than once. So far it had always been one of convenience that he suggested, but she couldn't help but wonder what his real plans were.

She folded the letter and put it in her pocket. The inheritance would change everything. She hadn't gotten to know Wallace's father very well. They had left for Alaska very soon after marrying. Wallace's mother was already dead, and Wallace, Bill, and their father had lived together in a small house near a lake. She had known there was money in the family. After all, Wallace's father had given them quite a stake for the move to Alaska. He had been proud of his son's desire to spread the Gospel to the people there.

Amelia, having no family of her own, had been happy to follow her husband anywhere. She longed for a place where she belonged, and Wallace had provided that in abundance. Bill too. Bill had treated her like a loving brother and was always mindful of her. She couldn't have had two better men to watch over her and provide for her. But now they were gone, and all of her family too. The only place that sounded like home was Alaska. She had friends there. Friends who had loved Wallace and Bill as well. They would welcome her back, and it was where she wanted to be.

Grady, of course, was going to be a problem. He had been more than a little perturbed at her venture to see the expo. What was he going to say when she explained that she was going home?

She didn't have long to wonder. The knock on her door came early that evening, just after she changed and fed Wally. Amelia picked up her son and cradled him close. He looked at her with wide blue eyes.

"Sounds like we have a visitor." She hoped it was Mrs. Becker but was fairly certain it would be Grady. She was right.

He smiled and held up a sack. "I've brought some groceries. Thought you were probably getting low."

"Come in." Amelia stepped back to let him enter.

He crossed the room and called back over his shoulder. "I have to admit I shopped rather selfishly. I bought a beef steak and some pork chops. I got some canned goods too, as well as flour, sugar, and coffee. I remember you saying you were nearly out of those."

"Yes." She closed the door as Grady took the sack to the tiny kitchen. "What would you like me to fix for you?"

"The steak, please. I've been thinking of nothing else. Steak and potatoes fried nice and crisp."

"All right." She glanced down at the baby, who was already falling back asleep. "Give me a moment to get Wally to bed." She headed for the crib. She wished Grady would just leave but knew that wasn't going to happen.

Should I tell him the news now or after he eats? Either way he isn't going to like it.

Amelia went to the kitchen and took the groceries in hand while Grady took a seat at the table. There was a strong odor of sweat and trash about him, as there often was.

"Maybe you could go wash up a bit while I get the food cooking," she suggested.

"Sure. Sorry I didn't clean up first. I was just too anxious about the food." He got back to his feet. "I'll be back in a quick minute."

She hurried to put lard in the cast-iron skillet, then cut up potatoes in thick slices just the way he liked them. She gave them a good dose of salt and focused on putting the groceries away while the potatoes cooked.

Grady wasn't gone long, just as he'd promised. "There, that does feel better, and I'm sure smells better too."

She said nothing as he reclaimed his seat. She pulled a newspaper out of the grocery bag and handed it to him.

Grady glanced at her before taking it. "You look worried. Is something wrong?"

"No, nothing is wrong." She turned back to tend to the potatoes. She turned them over, pleased that one side was already nice and brown. Thankfully Grady liked his steaks rare, and she'd soon have him fed and hopefully on his way. She went to slice the bread.

"You just seem . . . I don't know. Different."

Amelia knew she wasn't going to be able to keep from telling him about the letter if he pressed much more. She didn't want to ruin the poor man's supper, but she wasn't going to keep the news from him either.

"There are a few things I wish to discuss, but they'll wait until after you've had your steak."

"I intend for you to have a part of that steak too. Good red meat will keep you healthy. You still look very pale. Remember, the midwife said you needed to make sure you ate properly."

She glanced at the steak. "I'll cut a small piece for myself, but I'm not all that hungry." She finished putting away the groceries, then tended the potatoes again. They were just about ready. The steak was a quality piece and sliced very easily. She plopped both pieces down in the grease as soon as she'd pulled out the potatoes.

He put the paper aside. "So what do you want to talk about?"

"It will keep." She went for a couple of plates.

"Amelia, you're starting to worry me. It's not like you to keep secrets."

"It's no secret. I fully intend to talk to you about what's on my mind, but I think it would be best to eat first. Why don't you tell me about what's happening in the city? What news is in the paper?"

"Nothing of importance."

She hurried to dish up the potatoes and then turned the steaks. It wouldn't be much longer before they were ready. She grabbed silverware and glasses, then took them to the table. She avoided looking at Grady. She could tell he was watching her and most likely unhappy that she was being closemouthed. He was going to be even more unhappy when she told him her news.

"The baby is two months old. Time goes by so quickly." She took Grady's steak from the skillet and left hers to cook just a bit longer. "Before I know it, he'll be walking and talking."

"It'll be quite a while for those things," Grady replied.

Amelia placed the plate in front of him. "I have some cold lemonade, would you like some?"

He met her gaze and nodded. She could see the apprehension . . . maybe even fear in his eyes. She hurried to retrieve the pitcher of lemonade, as well as the bread and butter. She wasn't sure waiting to tell him her news was the best idea. Now he was suspicious and anxious.

"Here, I'll let you pour the drinks. I need to get my piece of steak out of the skillet." She hurried back to the stove and moved the pan from the burner. She put the steak on her plate, pushing aside the guilt she felt for having ruined Grady's fine dinner. She supposed it would be best to just tell him everything as they ate.

"Would you like to say grace?" she asked, knowing he wouldn't.

"No, you go ahead."

She bowed her head and offered a simple prayer of thanks. Silently she prayed for wisdom in dealing with Grady and all that she had planned.

They began to eat in silence, but the tension was enough that Amelia could no longer remain silent. "I had some interesting mail today."

"Mail? Who would send you mail? No one knows you're here."

"Well, the first piece of mail was a postcard photograph I had taken at the expo." She produced it and showed Grady. "It's Wally and me."

He looked at the photograph and frowned. "Why would you do that?"

She was surprised by his question. "Because I wanted a photograph of the baby while he was still very little." She put the photo aside. "The second piece of mail was a letter from our family attorney."

"What?" He nearly yelled the question.

Amelia was taken aback and must have looked as frightened as she felt because Grady was immediately apologetic.

"I'm sorry. I didn't mean to upset you. I just had no idea that you had a lawyer, much less that he knew where you were."

"I wrote him a couple of weeks ago. I thought I should let him know what had happened so that he could share the news with Wallace's father. However, Father Reed has passed away. That was one of the things the lawyer wrote to tell me."

Grady cut into the steak with a vengeance. "I see. What else did he have to say?"

"Well, that Father Reed left his sons an inheritance, and since they are dead, I am to inherit it instead."

Grady stopped eating. "What kind of inheritance?"

"Money, but I don't know how much. I am just hopeful that it will be enough to pay you back and . . . book passage back to Alaska for the baby and me."

"What?" This time he didn't yell. "Why would you want to return to that godforsaken place?"

"It's hardly godforsaken. I find God quite prevalent there. In fact, I've never felt His presence more clearly than in Alaska. But besides that, I feel that the people there are my only family. They love and care about me, and I know they will love and care about Wally as well."

"I care for you. Haven't I proved that? If all of this isn't love, what do you call it?"

Amelia dreaded the turn the conversation had taken. "I know that you care and that you felt obligated to help me after making your peace with my husband."

"It's more than that, and you know it. I've come to love you and want to marry you."

"I will never marry again. I've told you that." She stiffened and lost her appetite at the very thought of being intimate with someone other than Wallace. "I will never love another."

"You say that now, but it's only been two months. In time you will feel differently—you'll see." He tried to soften his tone. "These things take time to get over."

"I will never get over the loss of my husband—the father of my child. You need to understand this because as grateful as I am for what you've done . . . I will never love you."

Grady fell silent and stabbed a forkful of potatoes. He stuffed them in his mouth and chewed, all the while his gaze remained on Amelia. She didn't like the look in his eyes. He was angry. Very angry. She had expected disappointment but not this.

"I'm sorry. I wanted to wait to discuss it because I knew it would ruin your nice dinner. Please forgive me."

He chased down the potatoes with a liberal amount of lemonade and shook his head. "This isn't about forgiving. I just can't approve of your plans. You're very vulnerable, and for you to travel alone with a baby isn't at all wise or safe. I must forbid it."

This stirred anger in Amelia. She leaned back and crossed her arms. "You have no say in this."

Silence hung between them as they stared at each other for several long moments. Amelia hadn't meant to sound so harsh, but now that the words were out, she could scarcely take them back. Fortunately, Grady's anger seemed to calm. He picked up his fork and knife and cut into the steak once more.

"When will the money be available to you?"

"I don't know." She had no desire to tell him anything more. No doubt he was already plotting how to keep her from going. For the first time since having to depend on him, Amelia felt truly uneasy.

"Well, we can discuss this later, then. I think once you ponder the details, you'll be less likely to want to leave. Remember, it was a water passage that took the lives of your husband and brother-in-law. You could have another situation where a storm comes up, and this time you could lose your baby."

"What a horrible thing to say, and all to try to persuade me not to go." Amelia got up from the table. She took her plate to the counter and left it there. She had no desire to share this meal or any other with Grady Masterson.

"It's the truth," Grady said with a shrug. "As a new mother, I cannot imagine you would risk your baby's life that way."

"You brought us to Seattle by way of ship and said nothing of it being a risk. You knew I was nervous about the trip, but you convinced me that as American citizens, it was best we return to America. And you were also insistent upon visiting the shipping office to see if they were doing anything financially for the victims of the shipwreck."

"That was different. I knew the passage would be short and easy. You're talking about going all the way back to Alaska. You're not thinking straight. I suppose being a woman you don't see the seriousness."

"Please finish your meal and go. I have no desire to listen to your insults."

"Amelia," he said, looking up at her with what she recognized as his sympathetic expression, "I'm only trying to help you see reason. You just got this news, and it's propelling you to thoughts that go beyond your understanding. Once you take some time and calm down . . . well, you'll see what I mean."

She started to speak, then bit her tongue. She didn't want to fight with Grady, and she certainly didn't want to hear any more of his faulty logic.

"I'm sorry I've upset you, my dear. Here I thought we'd have a lovely dinner and be able to talk about our future."

"We have no future, Grady. You'd do well to remember that. Now please finish your dinner and go. I need to be alone."

Grady nodded and turned his attention in full to the steak and potatoes. Amelia couldn't shake the feeling that this wasn't over—that Grady would never accept her decision. Would he try to keep her from leaving? Would he use force? She swallowed the lump in her throat. What would she do if he tried to physically prevent her from leaving?

❧

Grady was a very unhappy soul. He walked the streets back downtown to where he shared a roughly furnished apartment with ten other city trash workers. They'd set up the large bedroom with cots in a dormitory fashion and shared the rent amongst themselves so that no one paid more than twenty-five cents a week. It was a wreck of a place in the worst part of town, but it was all he could afford while paying for Amelia's place.

And now she wanted to throw that in his face and walk away from him. Not only that, but she was to come into money. Money that should belong to Grady for all he'd done. Of course, she'd said she would repay him. That would give him a nice bit of money to move forward with. He had long contemplated getting out of Seattle. It had only been a short stop on his planned trip south. California was where he figured to take Amelia once they were married. Instead, she wanted to return to Alaska, where Grady was confident her husband would have gone after realizing she was dead. Everything would be for naught if that happened. She'd learn the truth, and the joke would no longer be on them but on Grady.

"She owes you big."

Grady's head snapped up. That sounded like Avery, but there wasn't anyone around. Was there?

He heard the voice again. *"She owes you big, and she's pushing you aside."*

He gritted his teeth and growled at the thought of her rejection. She was an ingrate to be sure. He'd done everything possible for her and that brat. For her to refuse him now was unthinkable. Even if she wasn't able to love him, she ought to be able to please him by doing his bidding.

He let out a yell, not caring at all who might hear. It wasn't likely in this neighborhood that anyone was going to care.

"You're right. She owes me," he said, lowering his voice. "She owes me plenty."

9

"Oh, May, these postcards are lovely." Eleanor looked over the various cards she'd left with May for her artistic touch. "You've captured the colors so nicely."

The dark-haired beauty smiled, lighting up her green eyes. "Thank you. I hope they'll sell."

Mrs. Fisher joined them and admired one postcard of pink roses. "You can almost smell the scent. This is very good, May. I'm sure that we'll be able to entice someone to purchase it. Perhaps a young suitor will buy it for his lady fair."

Eleanor smiled. "How are you feeling today, Mrs. Fisher? If my memory is right, the baby is due in just about two months."

"You're correct, and I'm feeling quite good. Mr. Fisher was able to purchase the new building where we'll have our shop and home. He's going to get some friends from church to help us set up our apartment. He wants everything in order before the baby comes."

"That's very wise." Eleanor had heard Mrs. Fisher and Addie Hanson discussing how older women had a bit more risk than younger women who were expecting.

"Yes, well, I'm quite ready for this little one to come," Mrs. Fisher declared. "And I would imagine you'd like to be finished with your typing job as well."

"Oh, I very much enjoy it. It does keep me busy to be sure, but I'm learning so much." Eleanor put the postcards back on the table. "I suppose for now I'd best get out there and do what I can to sell cameras and take photographs." She picked up a loaded Brownie and smiled. "I do love this job as well."

She started for the door just as Esther returned. She scooted past Eleanor in a hurry. "Mrs. Fisher, I have pictures in here of a large family. There are three different poses, and they want them all. They told me they'd be by to pick them up by five." She extended the camera out to the older woman.

"I'll make sure Mr. Fisher gets right on them," she said, taking the camera.

Eleanor heard nothing more as she stepped outside into the sunshine. The day was perfect, and she felt nothing but joy. Oh, if her time with Bill could just go on and on.

She worked through the day, approaching first one family and then another. Sometimes she stopped to suggest older folks have their picture taken for the sake of their younger family members. That seemed to appeal quite often. And as usual during her lunch hour, she found places to photograph the vegetation and write notes to herself as she observed the various plants.

Bill had taught her so much in such a very little time. Even though it was now nearly August and he was slated to leave toward the end of that month, Eleanor continued to enjoy her time with him. She tried not to think of him leaving. Tried her best to just live in the moment.

Still, there was that nagging voice that kept asking what she would do when he was gone. School no longer held the same appeal. How could she sit as a student in a stuffy classroom when she might be working with Bill in Alaska?

Of course, he hadn't asked her to join him, and it would be rather risqué for a single woman to undertake such a big journey. Women were doing more and more on their own, though. She knew her parents wouldn't be too excited for her to head to the isolated north. It had been hard enough to see her move to Seattle, but they were under the impression that she would return after the expo concluded.

Now, however, that wasn't at all on Eleanor's mind. She wanted to take the money she'd saved for school and go to Alaska with Bill. There just had to be a way to convince him that she could be a true asset.

"I thought I'd find you out here."

Eleanor looked up to find Bill watching her. She smiled. "I was just thinking of you."

"Me?" He sounded genuinely surprised. "Whatever for?"

She laughed. "If you must know, you come to mind quite often. You've changed my life with all that you've taught me. You've changed my thoughts and even my plans."

Bill shook his head. "I don't know how I could have done that." He smiled and seemed pleased.

"Well, be that as it may, it's true." Eleanor returned her observation to the small and delicate fern she'd been about to photograph.

She heard Bill chuckle. She loved the sound of his laugh. "So are we working tonight as usual?" she asked.

"Absolutely. I wondered though if you might let me take

you to dinner. I thought it might be nice to just have time to talk without having to focus on work."

Eleanor snapped her picture and straightened once again. "I'd like that very much."

"Good. I'll come by the shop, and we can walk together to the YMCA restaurant."

"Sounds good. Oh, do you have the time?"

He pulled out his pocket watch. "It's nearly one."

"I must get back to work. I tend to lose myself out here and forget the hour. I'm glad you happened along." She started toward him and kept thinking of how she might bring up the idea of going to Alaska with him. Just as she reached Bill's side, Eleanor took a misstep and started to fall. Bill easily righted her, and when she stood, she found herself very much in his arms.

She gazed up into his blue eyes. His arms felt strong and capable as he held her close. Eleanor wasn't sure, but she thought her heart had skipped a beat.

"Uh, thank you."

His gaze was fixed on her face. Bill gave the slightest nod. "No problem. I . . . well, I didn't want you to fall." Very slowly, he released her.

Eleanor didn't want to step away, but she knew she had to get back to work. "I should go," she murmured, but leaving was the last thing she wanted to do.

She forced her senses to return and stepped back. "Guess I need to be more careful. I'll see you at five." She didn't wait for his reply but hurried away. Had she remained, Eleanor was quite certain she would have kissed him.

Bill let out his breath and watched Eleanor as she headed back to the expo. He wasn't at all sure if the moment had affected her as it had him, but he could tell she felt something. Frankly, she was quickly consuming all of his thoughts. Even the idea of getting the manuscript completed was centered on the fact that he could work with Eleanor.

He stuffed his hands in his trouser pockets and began to walk toward the lake. He couldn't help but note the immediate feeling of loss in her absence.

"Bill, old boy, you've got it bad. I'm afraid you've lost your heart."

There it was. He was finally quite clear minded on the matter. He had fallen in love with Eleanor Bennett.

So what do I do about it? We've known each other only a few weeks, but already I know that I want to make her my wife. I can't leave Seattle without her.

He couldn't help but wonder what she might think of that. Bill contemplated what he should do about it all. Should he just tell her how he felt? Explain that somehow after years of praying for the right woman to come to him, she had appeared and fulfilled all his desires? She was beautiful, fun, intelligent, and loved the same things he did. She was also adventurous. She had come to Seattle to work at the Alaska-Yukon-Pacific Exposition without knowing a single soul in the city. That took a great deal of courage, and she would need that for Alaska.

Standing at the water's edge, Bill looked out, noting several small boats. Maybe he could rent one sometime and take Eleanor out on the water. It looked quite peaceful, and he was sure she would enjoy herself. Maybe he could even steer them into less-traveled coves where she could see species of plants she'd not yet viewed.

In the distance, two young boys were playing a game of tag. They squealed with delight when one caught the other, and the chase continued with a new pursuer. They seemed to be having so much fun.

Bill thought of Wallace. They had once played games like that. They had once been as close as two brothers could be. Now things were completely different.

Wallace was so discouraged—so hopeless. Bill wanted desperately to encourage him and bring him back to faith in the Lord. But nothing he said seemed to bring Wallace any comfort. No matter how Bill prayed, it seemed Wallace was lost to him.

He had tried to interest his brother in moving back to Alaska. Bill didn't want to give up on him and leave him to die in Seattle. And that was what Bill was convinced would happen if he went north without his brother.

Wallace told him last night there was absolutely no circumstance that would convince him to go back to the home he'd shared with Amelia. His anger at God continued, and there had been nothing Bill could do or say to dissuade him from blaming their heavenly Father for all the bad that had befallen them.

"So . . . I leave Wallace and take Eleanor with me to Alaska. I take her back as my wife." He murmured the statement. It didn't sit right. Taking Eleanor as his wife was quite fine, but leaving Wallace was something Bill couldn't quite settle in his mind.

Walking back to the building where the history department was housed, Bill felt at peace with his decision. Yes, he'd only known Eleanor for a few weeks, but he couldn't possibly be more certain of his feelings. He could only pray that she felt the same. Now he needed to figure out a good time to discuss the matter with her. Was supper too soon?

At five o'clock, Eleanor put away her things and checked her appearance in a backroom mirror. Her red curls were still pinned in place despite the very busy day she'd had. She deliberated over whether to resecure the straw boater in place, then decided against it. The hat suggested she was still working, and that was going to be furthest from her thoughts as she enjoyed supper with Bill Reed.

Ever since their chance encounter earlier in the day, Eleanor had been unable to think of anything but Bill. She hadn't even been able to keep her mind on work and had finally gone back to the shop hoping Mr. Fisher might need her help with developing. He had.

"Are you coming home or going straight to work with Mr. Reed?" Mary asked as she and Bertha headed for the door.

"Neither. Bill asked me to have supper with him, so we're going over to the YMCA restaurant."

"Seems you two are spending all your spare time together," Bertha said. The look on her face challenged Eleanor to deny it.

"It's true." She smiled and shrugged. "Seems God has put us together for a reason."

"I guess we will see you later tonight, then," Mary said, giving Bertha a jab with her elbow. "Come on. Let's get out of here. I'm tired of everything related to cameras, pictures, and film."

Eleanor laughed. She had to agree she felt the same way. She picked up her purse and drew in a deep breath. *Lord, I'm gonna need help in figuring out how to talk to Bill about my thoughts and feelings. Please, if this is Your will for me, show me what to do and say.*

Bill arrived just as she exited the shop. He tipped his hat to her and smiled. "You're quite prompt."

"And hungry. I skipped lunch today to take pictures."

"Yes, I remember." He extended his arm for her to take hold of and put his hand over her arm once she did. "Did the rest of your day go well?"

"Yes, I got to work a little in the darkroom. I always enjoy that."

"So you're able to completely run the shop?"

"I can run the counter, advise the customers, load the cameras, and develop pictures. I worked with my father back in Kansas for years before coming here. I've always enjoyed every aspect of photography."

"How did you develop the love of botany?"

She thought about it a moment. "I suppose it was always there. I remember being completely enthralled with flowers from the time I was little, but I was also interested in strange plants. You know the type that aren't typical. I've just always found it fun to note the differences. I never even realized it was part of a botanist's observation."

"Do your folks still live in Kansas?"

"They do. They live in a town called Salina."

"And do you have brothers and sisters living there as well?"

Eleanor shook her head. "I'm an only child. I always

wanted a brother or sister, but it was just never meant to be. Sometimes that made me lonely, but then again, I had my parents to myself. I never had to share." She laughed. "And since I could be quite demanding with their time, it was probably for the best."

"I can't imagine you being demanding of anyone." Bill looked at her and shook his head. "You don't strike me that way at all."

"Well, I can be quite demanding. You already know I can be quite outspoken and bold. I suppose growing up as an only child I learned to speak up and do so often."

They reached the restaurant and found it packed with a long line of people waiting to get inside. Bill frowned and wondered what a better solution might be.

"Why don't you just come with me to the cottage? Mary and Bertha are there, and we can put something together for dinner."

"I wouldn't want to impose."

"It's not an imposition. We just got groceries, so I know there's plenty of food. Come on."

They headed to the cottage and indeed found Mary and Bertha just contemplating what to have for supper.

"I hope you don't mind, but I've invited Bill to join us. We were going to go to the YMCA restaurant, but it was very busy, and the wait would have been much too long."

"I don't mind," Mary replied. "How about you, Bertha?"

"That's fine. I have three brothers. It'll be nice to have some male company at the meal."

Eleanor turned to Bill. "Why don't you sit here in the living room area, and I'll help the girls get supper. It shouldn't be too long."

Bill seemed content to do as she directed, and Eleanor hurried to take up her apron. "Why don't we heat up that meatloaf Bertha made and open a couple cans of vegetables? Corn and green beans?"

"That sounds good," Mary said. "I'll slice some bread."

"Sounds perfect. Simple and won't take too long. Bill and I have quite a bit of work ahead of us tonight."

"How's the typing coming along?" Mary asked.

"We're over halfway done. It won't take much time at all to finish with that. The drawings are taking a little longer, but Bill has that under control."

"Too bad he didn't have a Brownie up in Alaska. He could have had some great pictures," Bertha declared.

"I plan to take one with me when I return," Bill said from the living room. The cottage was small enough to make his comment easy to hear.

"That's a smart idea," Mary said. "I don't know how hard it would be for the publisher to put them in a book, but I always enjoy good photographs when I'm reading about something unfamiliar."

"That was the idea with the drawings," Bill replied. "If the publisher can't use photographs, at least I'll have them to make my drawings at leisure."

"Bill is very good at drawing with charcoals and water-colors. He has a natural talent," Eleanor added to the conversation.

They chatted on in a casual manner, and eventually Bill came to stand near the kitchen table rather than sit in the living room. Eleanor liked the way he made himself at home. It seemed like she'd known him for years instead of a few weeks.

When they sat to eat dinner, Bill offered to say grace, and Eleanor couldn't help but smile. She ducked her head and closed her eyes, hoping no one had noticed. It pleased her more than she could say that Bill was close to God.

"So tell us about yourself, Bill. We really know very little about you," Bertha said, passing him the platter of meatloaf.

Bill helped himself to a healthy portion and held the platter so that Eleanor could take what she wanted, then he passed it back to Bertha.

"I was born and raised in Chicago," he began. "I have one older brother, Wallace. He's a preacher. Well, he was. It's a long story, but he recently lost his wife, who was expecting their first baby. It's soured him on God."

"That must be very difficult to deal with—to not only lose a wife but also a child," Mary said as she slathered butter on her bread. "His grief must run deep."

"It does, and he seems inconsolable most of the time. He's taken a job at a fish cannery, mostly because I think it's where he feels the farthest from God. The men there are rough and crude. Wallace wants to harden himself against further pain, and I think he looks to them for examples."

"That is very sad." Eleanor's sorrow was evident in her tone. "Poor man. You know, I took a photograph of a widow and her new baby a while back. She had such sorrow in her eyes that it touched my heart. I found myself wishing I could have done something for her. I still think of her often."

"There doesn't seem to be much we can do but give them time and love. I try my best to get Wallace to come out with me for dinner and such, but he wants little to do with the living."

Bertha spoke up at this. "When my little sister died, I thought my mama was likely to die as well. We were all heartbroken to lose her, but Mama couldn't bear the sorrow. She cried day and night."

"Death is difficult, even when we know that person is heaven bound," Bill replied. "I mistakenly thought Wallace would take comfort in the fact that he would one day see her again, but instead, it only caused him to be even more upset. He told me God was cruel to do such a thing—to take the only woman he would ever love. And his child . . . his unborn baby. It was just devastating."

The girls nodded. Eleanor could only imagine his pain, but her imagination was quite vivid.

"What about you, Bill, have you ever had a wife?" Mary asked.

Bill shook his head. "No, I've never had the occasion to fall in love or marry. I was always so busy with my studies and then with my work." He looked at Eleanor and smiled. "But I've been praying God would send the right woman into my life. Someone who would share my passions."

Eleanor felt a strange tingle go through her. *Let me be that woman*, she prayed.

The food and conversation continued for the next half hour when Bill finally put an end to it. "Eleanor, we really need to get back to our work. This meal was wonderful. Best I've had since coming to Seattle, and the company has been perfect. Thank you for having me."

Mary and Bertha smiled. Eleanor started to gather some dishes, but they shooed her away.

"Go on now, and get your typing done. You'll be exhausted by the time you get back. We can take care of this."

"Thank you, girls. I appreciate that so much. I'll make it up to you." Eleanor got to her feet and headed to the bedroom for her shawl. When she returned with it, Bill was already at the front door.

"Ready?" he asked.

Eleanor smiled and nodded. "I am." If only he knew the full meaning of her words. She wished there was a simple way to tell him. Usually her boldness served her well, but this time Eleanor felt rather overwhelmed by the thought of confessing her heart. Hopefully God would speak on her behalf in some way.

10

The more Bill prayed about Eleanor, the more at peace he became. He knew that she was the one for him—the woman he had prayed for. As he finished cooking breakfast, he decided to mention her and his intentions to Wallace.

When his brother sat down to the table, Bill put a plate of eggs and bacon in front of him, then retrieved the coffeepot and his own plate. He joined Wallace at the table and, without asking, bowed his head in prayer. "Lord, we thank You for this food and for the new day You've given us. Make us worthy of Your blessings and send good things our way. Amen."

He glanced up and met Wallace's gaze. "How did you sleep last night? You didn't seem as restless, and I didn't hear any nightmares."

"I was pretty exhausted from the double shift I worked."

"I can well imagine. I have some interesting news to share and hoped you might advise me," Bill continued. "I met the woman I believe God wants me to marry."

Wallace's expression never changed. "Save yourself the heartache and forget about her."

"Would you forget Amelia?"

"Yes. If I could." He lowered his head and started to eat.

Bill knew he didn't mean it. His brother's pain was overtaking his reason and logic, not to mention his emotions. How he wished Wallace could find a way through the darkness.

"Her name is Eleanor Bennett. She's a sweet woman with a mop of curly red hair and the prettiest blue eyes I've ever seen. She loves what I love—she's the one retyping my manuscript. We've made wonderful progress, and by the end of the month, I intend to have the manuscript turned in to the publisher and then return to Alaska, hopefully with Eleanor as my bride."

"You'd do better to stick to your studies and forget about a wife. She will only complicate your life."

"Like Amelia complicated yours? Be reasonable, Wally, she made your life better."

"It's not better now."

Bill watched his brother mechanically shovel food into his mouth. He doubted Wallace even tasted it. He was rather pathetic in appearance. Before losing Amelia, Wallace had taken care with his grooming and dress. Even in Alaska where such things were of little importance, Wallace had always taken pride in his looks.

"So your only recommendation to me is to avoid taking a wife, even though yours gave you the best years of your life?"

Wallace finally looked up. "She did that, but to lose her is too great a pain. It's a never-ending grief to know that she and our baby are never again to be mine. I wish it had been me who died in those icy waters."

"Dying all at once would have been preferable to seeing

you die a little bit day after day," Bill admitted, hoping his statement would jar Wallace into better thinking.

"Yes."

That was all he had to say on the matter before picking up his coffee cup. Bill watched as his brother took a long drink of the hot liquid. He thought of Eleanor and wondered if he would grieve losing her in the same way his brother grieved Amelia's loss. It was such a consuming and complete pain that engulfed Wallace, and each day it hardened him all the more.

"I intend to marry Eleanor, so you might as well get used to the idea. I haven't yet proposed, but I will. I had rather hoped you might offer words of wisdom about marrying, but I can see you've put your mind against such things. Seems sad that you would deem those years of happiness with Amelia to be such a waste. I would think that having at least a few years of such deep love and devotion would be better than having had none at all."

"You can think what you like," Wallace replied. "I cannot produce feelings that no longer exist. The past is gone."

"Your faith in God as well?"

"Yes." He said it so matter-of-factly that Bill was momentarily stunned. He could scarcely believe his brother would so blatantly abandon his faith.

"You don't mean that. I know better. Wallace, you know deep within your soul that the same God is in charge now that was in charge a year ago. The same God you praised and taught others to trust is still worthy of that action from you. You've given the devil too much room to wreak havoc in your soul, and it must stop. You must flee the devil. He has no place here. Imagine what Amelia would say."

Wallace shook his head. "She would say nothing. She's dead."

"She's not. She accepted Christ as her Savior long ago. She put her faith in Jesus as her advocate and the forgiver of her sins. She will never die."

Wallace's eyes narrowed slightly as a pained expression crossed his face. He got to his feet. "I'm gonna be late for work if I don't get out of here."

"Wally, don't let go of God's hope. We both know that He's the only one to see you through this time of pain. Don't separate yourself from the consolation He offers. Please hear me. God is there for you in this. Don't abandon hope."

Wallace looked at him for a moment. "Maybe you should take my place as a preacher. You seem to have all the answers."

Bill watched him gather his things and leave. He wanted to say so much more—to encourage him with the love he bore him as a brother. To share with him the hope that could still be found in God. But instead, he remained silent.

Finishing his breakfast, Bill tried to imagine how he could change Wallace's heart. There had to be a way. He didn't want to give up on him. Bill remembered his mother saying on many occasions to give someone over to God to be dealt with. Was that all that was left now with Wallace? Should he abandon his attempts to bring Wallace back into hope?

He washed up the dishes and made sure the food was put away before pulling on his suit coat. At the door, he took his hat down from the peg and gave the room one last glance. Everything he needed for work was safely secured at the university, so there was nothing to take with him. With a sigh, he secured his hat and headed out into the world. His heart was so heavy for Wallace that he wasn't even sure he could find joy in seeing Eleanor today.

Please, Father, help my brother. His pain is so intense, and he feels there is nothing left. I give him to You, knowing that I can do nothing, but You can do all things. Help us both to make it through this difficult time. Give me wisdom to deal with the matter. In Jesus's name, amen.

Bill arrived at the expo and university grounds quite early. The expo hadn't yet opened, but already people were standing in line awaiting the opportunity to enter. Bill had a special pass that got him on the grounds since he gave lectures at the Alaska Building. He ignored the sights and sounds of the exposition and, without really thinking about it, made his way to Eleanor's cottage near the lake's edge. He felt compelled to greet her that morning—perhaps even discuss his feelings. Time was passing much too quickly, and even with Wallace's negativity about taking a wife, Bill felt he mustn't waste time now that God had given him the right woman.

Mary and Bertha were just leaving when Bill arrived at the cottage. He smiled and tipped his hat.

"Good morning, ladies. Is Eleanor still here?"

"She's right behind us," Mary replied. On cue, Eleanor appeared in the doorway.

"Bill, I wasn't expecting you this morning. Is something wrong?"

He smiled and tipped his hat again. "Not a thing in the world. I just felt compelled to come by and walk you to work."

She pulled the door shut and locked it. "That's very nice of you."

"We'll see you at work, Eleanor," Bertha called as she and Mary headed toward the expo.

Eleanor joined Bill and smiled. "It's nice to see you, although I suppose we were just together no more than ten or so hours ago."

"I couldn't help myself. Eleanor, these past few weeks have proven something to me that I feel compelled to share with you." They began a slow walk toward the exposition.

Eleanor smiled and took hold of Bill's offered arm. "I'm glad you feel comfortable enough to share."

"You may think otherwise once I tell you, but it's important to me. I've really come to enjoy being with you, Eleanor. I've looked forward to our working together and to our chance encounters. I feel so much better when I'm with you than when we're apart. I hope I'm not putting you off by declaring such feelings."

"Not at all." She glanced at his face. "I feel the same way and wasn't at all sure what to say or do. My roommate back in the city feels I'm being silly—that it's much too soon to have such feelings."

Bill stopped and turned her to face him. "I challenged myself with those same thoughts, but frankly, I believe in love at first sight."

Eleanor dropped her hold and took a step back. "Bill . . . are you telling me that you're in love with me?"

He looked at her for a second, knowing this was a critical moment. He wondered if he would regret his answer. "I . . . well . . . yes. I guess I am." He waited for her to respond, but for a long beat, she did nothing but look at him.

"I was certain that I must be immature or silly," she finally said, "because I feel the same way."

Bill took hold of her hands. "It's neither immature nor silly to love someone. I believe God put us together because that's where we belong."

Eleanor nodded. "Goodness, what a lot to take in this early in the morning."

Laughing, Bill couldn't believe he'd just confessed his heart to her. He was even more amazed that she felt the same way he did. He wanted to give out a yell but knew it would probably send Eleanor running. It was clear she was stunned by this entire situation. He would tread carefully and resist pulling her into his arms as he longed to do.

"I know I've shocked you, but I hope you'll forgive me. We haven't a lot of time. Just a few more weeks and it will be time to leave for Alaska, and I want you to come with me." He let go of her hands, and to his surprise, Eleanor began to walk. He kept pace at her side.

"You're right. There isn't a lot of time." She seemed completely lost in her thoughts. "There's so much to do."

They entered the expo grounds and found there were already hundreds, if not thousands, of attendees. Music was playing from a variety of locations as they made their way to the photography shop.

"I hope you know it wasn't my plan to just blurt all of this out. I know it wasn't done in a very romantic way."

She looked at him oddly. "It was completely perfect. I cannot imagine hearing such news in a better manner. It's the perfect birthday present." She smiled.

"Birthday present? Is today your birthday?"

Eleanor laughed. "It is. I'm twenty-one."

"Then we definitely should celebrate. I think a nice dinner is in order."

They reached the shop, and Bill glanced up at the display window. There were several photographs of the flowers Eleanor had taken as well as pictures of families and individuals. He was about to look back at Eleanor when one postcard in particular caught his eye. He gasped and put his hand to his chest.

"Where . . . how . . ." He pointed to the portrait of the black-clad woman and her baby. "That's my sister-in-law."

Eleanor looked at the photo, then back to Bill. "I thought you said she was dead."

"I thought she was. I must talk to whoever took that picture."

"I did." Eleanor put her hand on his arm. "Bill, are you certain it's her?"

"I'd know her anywhere. Eleanor, you must tell me where you took the picture and how it came about. The baby . . . she has a baby."

"Yes, he was just a few weeks old."

"He? She had a boy." Bill was dumbfounded. He felt as if he might pass out. "I need to sit."

Eleanor led him to a bench and joined him on it. "Bill, I had no idea. This was the woman I mentioned at dinner. The one who said her husband had died before the baby was born."

"My brother didn't die. We were told she had died. Oh, this is beyond belief. First my manuscript comes back to us and now Amelia. Do you have any idea how we can find her?"

"I do." Eleanor edged up on the seat of the bench. "She wanted us to mail the postcard to her and left her address."

"So you haven't sent it yet? That's wonderful."

"No, it was sent. This is a second copy. I asked for it because she so haunted me. I can't stop thinking about her. I found myself wishing I had done more to offer her comfort. She was so devastated and sad. It was clear that her husband had been her whole world."

"He was. Just as she was his. You have no idea how my brother is suffering. I've worried that he might even take his own life. Oh, Eleanor, we have to put them back together."

She nodded. "It might take a while to find the address. We have mailed a lot of photographs, but I know we'll find it. She would have put her full name on it. I'll talk to Mrs. Fisher, and we'll start going through the addresses immediately."

Bill was beyond shocked by the turn of events. Gone was his own joy at having confided his love to Eleanor. Amelia was alive, and she'd given birth to his brother's son. This was a miracle, and Bill knew that they had to find her.

"I'll speak to her myself as well." He got up, and Eleanor rose beside him.

She took hold of his arm. "Are you all right? Can you make it? I'll see to it that Mrs. Fisher gives me the day off, and we'll find that address. I promise we will."

He looked at her. "I'm so glad you took that photograph, Eleanor. Imagine if you hadn't. We would have gone on believing Amelia dead." He hugged her close. "Thank you! A million times, thank you!" He glanced heavenward. "And thank You, Lord!"

❧

"Oh my!" Mrs. Fisher said, looking from Eleanor to Bill.

Bill had retrieved the postcard from the window and showed it to her. "Do you remember where she lived?"

"I know it was here in Seattle. I remember the photo because, as Eleanor said, it was completely captivating."

"I told Bill we should be able to go through the addresses and find where she lives," Eleanor added. "I know you keep all the records."

"Yes, we would have it. It'll just be a matter of looking through the records to find it."

"I wondered if you would give me the day off so I can sit with Bill and go through the addresses," Eleanor said.

"Of course," Mrs. Fisher declared. "We have plenty of people working. I'll even help you when I can." Just then a customer came into the shop, and Mrs. Fisher excused herself.

"You see, Bill? We'll soon have the address and find where your sister-in-law and nephew have been living."

"Nephew." He had a nephew who was healthy and safe. The very thought was almost more than he could comprehend.

Tears came to his eyes. How was he to break the news to Wallace? This was an answered prayer that no one had even had the courage to pray. Amelia was alive. The baby was alive.

"Come on, Bill. We'll go in the back room and get started," Eleanor said, taking his hand. She looked up into his eyes. "This is the most wonderful day of my life."

"Mine too," he whispered, knowing that now things could be set in order.

⟳

"Mrs. Reed, I'm glad you could come to tea. Mrs. Becker told us yesterday after services that you're alone in the world," Pastor Harris said as he helped Amelia with her chair.

Joanna Harris came in carrying a platter of small sandwiches, while Mrs. Becker followed with a fruit salad. "Yes, Hazel told us all about your predicament."

The pastor took the platter from his wife and put it on the table. Next, he helped her into her chair, then claimed his own. Mrs. Becker was already seated when he straightened. "Shall I offer grace?"

The ladies nodded. Amelia wasn't entirely sure what this meeting was about. She'd only been to church twice with Mrs. Becker and didn't know the pastor and his wife well. Last night, only a day after her confession to Mrs. Becker that Grady wasn't her brother and that she was rather desperate to leave his company, the old woman told Amelia she absolutely had to come to tea at the pastor's house.

Once the prayer concluded and the food was passed, Amelia decided to just pose the question. "If I might be so bold, why did you ask me here today?"

The pastor looked to his wife, then back to Amelia. "Well, as Joanna said, Mrs. Becker told us that your husband was killed when the *City of Canton* sank back in May, and you and your young son are alone in the world."

"Yes, that's true. I was rescued by one of the men in my lifeboat and went into labor almost immediately. He got me help and later identified my husband and brother-in-law among the dead. He and my husband were at odds up until that trip. My husband had testified against the man's brother, and it resulted in his brother being hanged. But in the months following the sinking of the ship, he has provided for the baby and me while pretending to be my brother."

"Well, that is quite a lot to have dealt with." Pastor Harris took a moment to drink from the cup of tea. He made a face. "Goodness, Joanna, you know I don't like tea. Perhaps you could get me some lemonade?"

She smiled. "Of course." While she fetched the cold drink, Mrs. Becker chimed in.

"I knew something wasn't quite right with the situation. Poor Amelia has been under the man's thumb for all these months. As I told Joanna, she's most desperate to be rid of his influence, but we both fear he will be angry—if not dangerous."

"I plan to head to Alaska as soon as possible, but it would be nice to be able to make my plans without worrying about Grady trying to put an end to it." Amelia had been quite concerned about this since finding out that she had her own money and could return to Alaska. "I think he means well enough, but he hates Alaska and doesn't think I should even consider it. However, I have many people who care for me there. More so than I have here, although Mrs. Becker cares a great deal for the baby and me."

He nodded. "Well, that's why we asked you here today. We care too." Joanna returned with his lemonade, and he paused to have a drink. He smiled in approval and placed the glass on the table. "We have a little house here on the parsonage grounds. It's just a tiny place that the last pastor built for his aging father. But we'd like to offer it to you rent free so that you won't be under obligation to anyone."

Amelia sat back, rather surprised by their offer. "I must say, I'm deeply touched. In order to make my plans to leave, I feel I must be rid of Mr. Masterson. It's not that I don't appreciate what he's done, but it is an uncomfortable situation. He's fallen in love with me. He doesn't understand my heart is forever broken and I will not marry again, but he asks all the same."

"Well, it seems this would be a perfect answer to your problem. The little house is scarcely more than a couple of rooms, but it's furnished with everything you'll need. We can even provide a crib."

Joanna handed Amelia the fruit bowl. "We have a carriage too and can help you get to the shipping office for your tickets to Alaska. And when the day comes to leave, we can take you there."

Amelia couldn't begin to believe her good fortune. Leaving the apartment Grady had provided would send a clear message. She wouldn't tell anyone where she was going, and hopefully that would prove to him once and for all that she wanted nothing more to do with him.

"I recently learned I've come into a small inheritance. The lawyer has arranged an account at a bank here in Seattle. I could pay you rent. I also intend to leave for Alaska at the end of the month. I want the baby to be a little bit older. I worry about the voyage being too hard on him."

"Why Alaska, Mrs. Reed?" Joanna asked.

"My only home and friends are there. I have no other family. I won't need the apartment for very long, and as I said, I can pay."

"That's quite all right. We do not want rent for the place," Pastor Harris said. "We see it as a part of our ministry to help those in need. This will provide you safety while you're waiting to go back to Alaska. The city can be a difficult place for a young woman on her own, especially one with a baby."

"Yes, I've found that to be true. I haven't really anything

to bring with me save a few items of clothing for myself and the baby. When could I move in?"

"The sooner the better," Pastor Harris replied. "I could come tomorrow with the carriage."

Amelia smiled. "That would be perfect. Thank you both." She turned to Hazel Becker. "And thank you. You've been a good friend to me."

"I'm glad I could help. No woman should have to feel so put upon. We'll make sure Grady Masterson is completely unaware of your whereabouts."

11

Bill hadn't wanted to return home until he had Amelia's address, but the search was proving more difficult than they'd first anticipated. So many postcards had been mailed, and it wasn't as if the addresses were listed in alphabetical order. When it came time to close up the shop, Bill and Eleanor remained, poring through the pages of addresses until nearly eight o'clock. They had forgotten all about the manuscript work.

It was Mrs. Fisher who insisted they go home and get some rest. She promised they could come as early as seven and start again, but for now she felt Bill should go home and tell his brother what they'd learned. She even had Eleanor give him the photograph to take with him as proof.

When Bill arrived, he'd expected Wallace to be there, but he wasn't. This gave some concern, as Wallace had always returned promptly after his shift. Perhaps he'd taken a second shift. If that was the case, he'd be home at midnight.

Waiting for his brother, Bill couldn't help but look at the postcard photograph of Amelia and her baby. How could it have happened that she was reported dead? Worse still, according to Eleanor, Wallace was reported dead to her. She was convinced that her husband had been lost. Her widow's weeds were proof of that. How could such a mix-up have happened?

There was of course the fact that two different ships from two different countries had rescued the survivors. And there had been those who'd been lost and accounted for as best they could be. Bill and Wallace were recorded as survivors in Seattle, but perhaps Amelia hadn't been recorded. Maybe something had prevented her being counted.

He paced the room with the picture in hand and was still doing that when Wallace came through the door. He looked wretched and smelled even worse, but Bill didn't care.

"Sit down. I have incredible news."

Wallace shook his head. "I just want to get cleaned up and go to bed."

"You need to do as I say." Bill pointed to the chair. "You'll need to be sitting for this."

"I'm tired, Bill. I have no interest in whatever has you so over the moon. I suppose you proposed to that young woman. Frankly, I don't care."

Bill smiled. "You'll care about this. God has once again returned the lost. Please humor me and sit."

With a sigh, his older brother crossed the room to sit on a wooden chair at the table. "Very well. Tell me what you must."

"I want you to get a hold of yourself. This will come as a shock, but it's a good thing. It's the best of things. Amelia and the baby are alive."

Wallace's head snapped up, but the look on his face wasn't

one of joy. He looked angry. "How dare you torment me this way?"

Bill stuck the photograph in front of him. "Look for yourself. Eleanor took this just a few weeks ago. The woman said she was in mourning for the loss of her husband, who died just before their son was born."

Wallace looked at the photograph and promptly turned as white as a sheet. He grabbed the picture and drew it closer to the lamplight. "How can this be?"

"We don't know. Apparently, she was rescued by someone and didn't get recorded as having survived. Somehow, she believed us to be dead too. Wallace, she's alive and so is your son."

"My son." Tears streamed down Wallace's cheeks. "This cannot be."

"But it is. God has answered our unspoken prayers. He has taken the bad and hopelessness and made beauty out of it. Amelia is somewhere here in Seattle."

"Where? Where is she? We have to go to her now." Wallace was up on his feet. "I want to see my wife and son."

Bill nodded. "I know you do, but we haven't found the address yet. Eleanor and I spent all day and evening looking for it. You see, Eleanor took her picture and had her write down her name and address because Amelia wanted to have the postcard mailed to her. A lot of people prefer that to waiting around for it to be developed, so there are a great many addresses to go through."

"Then let's get back to it. I'll come and help. We can't just sit here and do nothing."

"The shop is closed and so are the expo grounds. It will have to wait until morning." He grinned. "We'll find it tomorrow, and then we'll go straightaway to wherever Amelia is living."

"I can't wait until morning. I must find her now. This is a miracle—a miracle that I had no courage to believe in. Oh, God, forgive me."

"Of course He does, Wally." Bill went to his brother's side. "You go get a bath, and we'll have a good night's sleep, and tomorrow . . . tomorrow we'll find her."

"How could I ever sleep?" Wallace looked at the picture again. "I won't rest until she's back in my arms."

⁂

"Thank you so much for the help, Mrs. Becker. You certainly didn't owe me anything after all the lies." Amelia held Wally as they waited for the pastor to show up with his carriage.

"Sometimes we are trapped into doing things that we don't want to do. With Mr. Masterson's suggestion that you lie, you should have known he was up to no good. That man had too much interest in you. I've never seen a brother care for a sister quite like that." The older woman took the key Amelia offered. "I presume he has the other one."

"Yes. I hate to leave you to ask for it back, but I don't want to see him again. Something changed when I told him I was going to be self-sufficient."

"Not to worry, deary. I'll get the key back. He's sure to come to see you and when he does, I'll simply demand he give it to me."

"I don't like to think of him as a bad man, but despite how he looked after Wally and me, I can't help remembering

144

how he once treated us—especially my husband. There was a time I feared he might even kill Wallace."

"Well, you needn't stick around to see what will happen. I'm glad we could get you away from him. He'll simply have to accept things the way they are."

Amelia nodded. "I just pray he doesn't give you any trouble. I left him an envelope with a letter to explain and money to repay his generosity. Hopefully that will keep him from losing his temper."

"Does he know about the church you're attending? Might he seek you out there?"

"No. As you well know, I've only just started to attend, and I haven't said a word to him about it. Thankfully he sleeps late Sunday mornings and doesn't come to pester me until the afternoon."

Mrs. Becker shook her head. "Well, I'm just glad I could help. I shall miss you. You and this sweet little babe." She gently touched Wally's face. "You were some of my best tenants."

"I appreciate all that you did for us. I just ask that you don't tell Grady where we've gone. I know I'll have others there to help in dealing with him should he find me, but I'd rather he not know where we're at."

"I won't tell a soul." She smiled and touched Amelia's arm.

"That's good, because I wouldn't put it past Grady to have someone else try to get my address out of you once he realizes you won't tell him. He's tricky that way."

"Your secret is safe, my dear. Hopefully I can come and see you after you're settled. If not, then I will see you at church. I do wish you well. I hope you can find happiness in returning to Alaska. I'm sure it would be an adventure well beyond my abilities, but you speak of that place with such fondness that I know you'll be happy there."

"As happy as I can be without my husband."

Just then Pastor Harris arrived in his carriage. Amelia had already set her single trunk at the end of the drive.

"Thank you for the trunk. I'd be happy to pay you for it."

Mrs. Becker smiled and shook her head. "I like knowing that it helped you in some small way. You've endured so much, and I will be praying for you on your journey."

Amelia nodded. "Thank you for everything."

Pastor Harris had already loaded the trunk by the time Amelia and Wally reached the carriage. The day was beautiful, and Amelia couldn't help but feel that God had provided the sunshine just to encourage her that she was doing the right thing.

"Let me take the baby while you climb aboard," the pastor said, reaching out for Wally.

Amelia reluctantly passed the baby to him, then quickly took her seat and reached out to have Wally returned. The pastor seemed to understand her anxiety and quickly complied. He said nothing about the situation, for which Amelia was grateful.

"It's such a nice day," she murmured, hoping to put the matter behind them.

"It is indeed. Joanna is tending her flowers and garden. I'd guess by the time we have you settled in, she'll be bringing you fresh vegetables from the garden."

"I do so appreciate what you've done for us. My story is complicated, but not so my heart. I'm looking forward to returning to Alaska."

"Will you not find it painful to do so without your husband?"

"Yes, I'm sure it will be. But . . . it's also where I can remember him best. I want to remember him—every detail. I want to be able to tell Wally about him and be with others who can also tell him of their memories. A boy should know his father, and I have hundreds of stories to tell Wally. I know they'll be more vivid when I'm there."

"And you have people there who will care for you? I've long heard that Alaska is a hard place to live."

"Yes, I have friends who are like family. Good people who are kind and considerate. I will be blessed to be back amongst them."

"I'm glad to hear it, Mrs. Reed."

She looked out at the passing houses. "It's nothing like Seattle. It's really nothing like any place else in the world, but it is dear to me, and I want it to become dear to Wally. I want him to know why his father felt so compelled to spend his life ministering there."

"I didn't realize your husband was a pastor."

Amelia smiled. "Yes, he had such a passion for the people of Alaska. He said the States had all sorts of preachers and teachers and different denominations and churches, but he was quite certain there were very few opportunities to hear the Gospel message in the wilds of Alaska."

"Well, until just ten or eleven years ago, folks hardly knew much about Alaska. When gold was found, suddenly everyone wanted to venture north."

"Yes, we were in Nome for a time when their gold rush was going strong. The natives were amazed at the way the people practically sold their souls for that yellow rock. They thought us all quite mad."

"I can imagine that. Did you stay in Nome for long?"

"We were there a couple of years. We met Frank Nowell, the exposition's official photographer. He had a shop there. We traveled to various parts of the district. We found our real home among the Athabaskans in a most beautiful and mountainous area. That's where I hope to return. That's where I call home."

After another day spent looking for Amelia's address, Bill and Wallace were more than a little frustrated. The Fishers were kind and encouraging, but there were thousands of addresses to go through, or at least it seemed that way.

"We will find it," Eleanor encouraged. "I'm sure it won't be long now. Don't give up hope."

Bill couldn't help but love her enthusiasm and encouragement. She was such a joy to be with and so uplifting in her attitude. She had been there every step of the way, and Bill couldn't help but love her all the more for the way she treated his brother.

"She will be so excited to have you returned to her," Eleanor told Wallace. "Her every thought was of you and the baby."

Wallace smiled, and to Bill it was like balm to his soul. He'd not seen Wallace smile in months. Just knowing Amelia and his son were alive brought Wallace back among the living.

"She seemed well, didn't she?" Wallace asked.

Eleanor nodded with great enthusiasm. "With exception to her heartbreak, she was quite well. I believe the baby had given her the will to go on. She was clearly very much in love with him."

"Of course she would be. We were anxious to be parents, and it had taken her a long time to . . . conceive. We weren't even sure we could have children."

"He is a beautiful boy. So sweet, and he has lots of dark hair. I know you couldn't see him well in the photograph, but he's quite perfect."

Wallace smiled at that and gazed off as if trying to imagine it. Bill met Eleanor's eyes and smiled as well. She was doing such a grand thing for his brother.

The clock in the shop chimed eight times, and still they hadn't found the address. Eleanor looked completely done in, as did the Fishers. It wasn't going to be easy to drag Wallace away from the shop, but Bill knew they would have to let the matter wait.

"Otis, do you imagine the address could be with those boxes of addresses and receipts we took to the new shop?" Mrs. Fisher spoke up.

Everyone stopped what they were doing and looked at the woman. She seemed to realize this news might have been better discussed earlier in the day. "I'm sorry," she said, "I only just thought of it. I don't know if it would be among those things. I can't remember exactly when we moved that stuff, but I suppose it is possible. Addie Hanson has been working to put some of it to rights."

"We can bring the boxes back here tomorrow," Mr. Fisher said. "But for now, you are exhausted, and for the sake of your health and our own baby, you must rest. I'm sorry, folks, but we must stop for the night."

Wallace opened his mouth as if to protest but then closed

it again. Bill knew it was taking all his patience to endure the search. The night would stretch out long ahead of them once again.

As they walked to the trolley stop, Bill wanted only to encourage his brother. "We're so close. I'm sure we'll find the address tomorrow."

"It's so hard knowing she's out there—that they're out there—and I'm not with them," Wallace replied. "How could I have not known she was alive? How could I have so readily given up?"

"Death is a hard thing to argue with. People told you she was dead, and you had no reason to think otherwise. It was a horrendous accident, and many lives were lost. It seemed completely logical that she had been among their number. Her lifeboat was even one of the boats that overturned in the storm."

"I just keep thinking that I should have known. Something in my heart should have told me. But I was so far gone in my grief that I couldn't hear anything. Not even God."

"You were pretty lost there for a time, but now you've come back to us."

The trolley arrived, and they climbed on board. Several other people joined them, and soon the trolley was headed downtown. Bill closed his eyes. Everything had happened so quickly regarding Amelia that he hadn't had time to properly ask Eleanor for her hand. He knew it didn't matter. He knew she was already his, but he thought it only right that he at least make it official.

"Do you suppose once we find her that you'll return to Alaska and take up ministering again?" Bill opened his eyes and turned to Wallace.

His brother nodded. "I owe the Lord that and so much more. I want to return to Alaska with Amelia and the baby and never leave again. I want to share how my faith was weak—how I blamed God for all that happened and how wrong I was. Now I have living examples of difficulties and ways that even strong Christians can fail. I will use that to teach about God's forgiveness and the fact that He never fails us."

"But life still produces death. One day it will come to us all."

"Yes, I must accept that and learn how to deal with it for myself. I can see now how easily I was deceived into thinking that death was the end. Bill, I must thank you for never giving up on me. It is as if I can see God's own heart through your actions. I can see that He never gives up on us."

"No, and He never will. No matter what death takes from us, it cannot take away our relationship with Him."

"Unless we let it," Wallace replied. "I've learned a most difficult lesson in this, but I am steady once again. I will stand on the promises that God has given and trust Him for the future."

12

Wednesday morning dawned bright and clear. Grady had planned to sleep in, given he'd quit his job with the refuse service, but his body wouldn't cooperate. He was used to the early morning habit of rising before dawn. Besides, the other men who were still working for the trash company were getting dressed and making enough noise to wake the dead. Grady had no choice but to join them.

"When are you leaving us, Masterson?" one of the men asked.

"Day or two. I have to make arrangements for travel." Grady had all sorts of plans.

Now that Amelia had inherited money, he intended to see to it that she allow him to manage it for her. He also intended that they move to California.

He had it all figured out. They would just pick up and go. Neither one had much of anything. A change of clothes and little else. It would be easy to board the train and head south. He figured San Francisco or Sacramento would suit them. He was told by one of the men he'd worked with that the weather was temperate in those locations. The scenery was also quite beautiful and jobs plentiful. It sounded a little like paradise, if such a place could exist on earth.

One by one, the men left for the day. Grady drank a cup of strong coffee and dreamed of the future. He hoped Amelia had inherited an outrageous fortune. With the right amount of money, he'd never have to work again. He could just manage the money, learning how to invest. Such things had always fascinated him, but he'd never had a stake to start. Now he would, and it could very well make him a rich man on his own.

He finished dressing, and even though it wasn't yet six o'clock, he decided to leave and walk around the city until he could pop in on Amelia and the baby. He hadn't been able to see them for three days given the trash routes had gone extra long. They had been charged with helping pick up some of the exposition trash, and that kept them out well after normal hours. He'd had no chance to tell Amelia what he was up to but knew she wouldn't care. She was so caught up with that brat of hers she hardly noticed anything else. Grady intended to change that soon enough. One day she would be glad to focus her attention on him.

The city was gradually coming awake. He made his way to where vendors were already setting up for the morning market at Pike Place. That area always generated a lot of pedestrian traffic and trash. Grady gave a nod to one of the farmers who was even now unloading his wagon. The man had crate after crate of blackberries and fresh vegetables. There were at least twenty similar wagons with other farmers coming to sell their goods. Along with this were fishermen with fresh catches and bakers who had some of the most tempting treats. Grady gave in and bought a loaf of rye bread.

Finally, it was eight o'clock, and Grady felt more than confident that Amelia would be up. He headed to her apartment feeling quite positive about the day. He knew she might not be too excited about moving, but he was going to point out the benefits of California's weather for the baby. Here it was always damp, and surely that couldn't be good. Knowing her worried nature for the child, Grady was certain he could sell her on the move.

He reached the apartment steps just twenty minutes later. On the porch he paused to look into Amelia's apartment window. He saw nothing of her. Perhaps she was down the hall using the facilities.

Fishing in his pocket, Grady produced the extra keys and let himself into the building. He was just about to knock on Amelia's door as a courtesy when Mrs. Becker's door opened and the nosy old lady stepped into the hall.

"She's not there."

Grady frowned. He'd admonished Amelia over and over not to go out on her own. No doubt Mrs. Becker had encouraged her to return to the fair.

"I suppose she's gone to the exposition again."

"No, she's moved out altogether." Mrs. Becker seemed pleased to be able to give him this information. "And before you go on about your poor sister, I know the truth about it all and would appreciate the return of my keys." She nodded toward his hand, then reached out and took them.

Grady was so stunned by the news of Amelia moving that he could do nothing but let her take the keys. Amelia had moved? It made no sense. Why would she do such a thing?

"Where did she go?"

"I wouldn't tell you under any circumstances. She asked me to say nothing."

"I don't understand. Why this sudden hostility toward me? I've done nothing wrong." He was livid that Amelia had made such a request. How could she cut him out of her life? After all he'd done?

"I told you she didn't appreciate you." Avery's voice rang in his ears.

"Nothing but cause that poor woman to be stuck here with her child while you try to woo her," Mrs. Becker said. "Good grief, man, she's just lost her husband and yet you hound her for marriage."

"She said that?" Grady tried to act innocent. "I only wanted to make sure she was cared for. I felt I owed it to her husband." It was a lie, but it made sense to Grady. Even Avery would have approved. Did approve. No doubt he was watching over Grady in death, as he had in life.

"Be that as it may, she's gone now, and you don't owe anybody anything except me for the rent. However, I'll forgo it and keep your deposit. We'll be even."

Grady shook his head. "She is hardly capable of caring for herself. And added to it, she has the baby. What was she thinking?"

"She was thinking that she wanted her freedom. I know that much. She left you a letter, and I'm sure she'll explain her feelings." Mrs. Becker fished the letter from her pocket. "Take it and go. As you know, this is a building for women only. I only tolerated you because I thought you were her brother and I felt sorry for her newly widowed position."

Taking the envelope, Grady stood momentarily confused.

Mrs. Becker opened the outside door and waited for him to leave, but Grady found it almost impossible to move.

"I . . . wish you would just be honest with me. I need to find her."

"I am being completely honest with you, Mr. Masterson. She doesn't want you to know where she's gone. Now please go."

Grady stepped outside onto the porch. Mrs. Becker immediately closed and locked the door behind him. The action of her locking the door seemed to bring him out of his stunned silence. He looked back at the door. It wouldn't take that much to knock it in. He wanted to strangle the old woman. She was so happy—so smug—at this turn of events.

He tucked the bread under his arm, then opened the letter. Amelia thanked him for his help but explained that she and Wally needed to be on their own and return to Alaska. She had been able to get money from the bank to leave for him and hoped it would be enough to cover all that he had spent on her over the last few months. To Grady's surprise, it was nearly double what he'd put out. It made a nice amount of money for him to use in starting over.

A slight breeze tugged at the brim of his hat and ruffled the single-page letter. Maybe it was best this way. He had accomplished what he'd set out to do—keep Amelia separated from her husband and brother-in-law. He had denied Wallace Reed the right to his newborn son and had been able to fill in as the only father figure the infant knew. That pleased him immensely.

So why couldn't he just walk away?

The money. Knowing she had all that money was more than he could just walk away from. He had struggled all of his life, and she was sitting on a fortune. A fortune he should be entitled to share.

It wasn't right, and he couldn't just let it go. He had to find her and take her in hand. He had to make it clear to her that she needed him. That she should marry him. Besides, if she headed back to Alaska and Wallace was there, then all he'd done would be for naught. The temporary pain he'd caused would be forgotten in light of their reunion.

"But how do I find her?"

Mrs. Becker knew where she'd gone. He looked at the money in the envelope. Perhaps he could bribe her. It was possible she would appreciate a little more money.

He glanced back at the house. No. Mrs. Becker seemed the type to keep the information to herself just for the purpose of defeating him. She wouldn't say anything unless her life was threatened. Perhaps he could return later when all of her renters were at work. He could pretend Amelia referenced something of his still in the apartment and he needed to get it. That seemed more than reasonable. Once he was inside, he could take the old woman in hand—beat her if necessary until she told him the truth.

It was possible she might ask why he didn't just come back immediately to retrieve it, but he could make up something about needing to be elsewhere.

Grady tucked the money in his trouser pocket and put the letter in his coat pocket. He needed to think this all through, and since he hadn't had breakfast, he figured to stop at a little café he favored. He cradled the rye bread and started on his way, confident that he could make this all work out.

Eleanor was waiting for Bill and Wallace when they showed up. She had found the address after going through one of the boxes Mr. Fisher had brought from downtown. It was one of the most exciting things that had ever happened to Eleanor. She knew this was the missing key for the reunion of Wallace and Amelia. This was the happy ending to their tragic story.

"Here it is," she said, holding up the paper. "I found the address."

Wallace came to her, and Eleanor put the paper in his hands. He glanced at the address and nodded. "That's her handwriting." He traced the writing with his finger.

"Now you can be reunited with her. I wish I could come with you, but I have a manuscript to type since this is my day off, and I've already missed typing two nights in a row."

Bill smiled at her, and Eleanor felt her knees go weak. Goodness, but he had such a handsome face. "Thank you, Eleanor. This is wonderful news. We could hardly sleep last night." He reached into his pocket and produced a key. "You'll need this for the filing cabinet."

Eleanor nodded and took it. "I'll do my best to get as many pages completed as possible."

Mrs. Fisher stepped into the room and noted the men. "I suppose you heard the news. I'm surprised you're still here."

Bill laughed, and Wallace gave a nod. "Thank you, ma'am. We're just heading out."

"I'll catch up with you after we find her," Bill told Eleanor as he followed Wallace out of the shop. "I have something special to discuss, so don't go anywhere else."

"I won't." Eleanor turned to her boss. "It's such a wonderful day for miracles. I'm so happy for them."

Mrs. Fisher patted Eleanor on the shoulder. "It is a miracle to be sure. How awful for two people to be thought dead and separated during such an important part of their lives. I thank God you took that picture, Eleanor."

"I do too." Eleanor gave a little clap. "It's such a wonderful day."

She headed out across the expo grounds. Around her, children and adults made their way from exhibit to exhibit. Eleanor couldn't help but wonder if anyone else had an interesting story to tell. Surely none were as exciting and intriguing as that of the Reed family.

"Where are you headed?" Mary asked, coming up to her from the crowds.

"To type Bill's manuscript."

"I thought you were searching for his sister-in-law's address." She shifted her satchel and caught the brim of her straw hat. "Oh bother."

Eleanor reached up to help her straighten things out. "I found the address. Bill and his brother are on their way. I'm so excited for them I can hardly stand it. I wanted to go with them, but it really is a very private matter. I know there will be buckets of tears shed and such great happiness to be had. Bill will tell me all about it when he joins me to work on the manuscript." Eleanor stepped back. "There. You're all properly arranged."

"That is wonderful news. About the address, not my arrangement, although I'm happy for that as well." Mary smiled. "I can hardly imagine finding someone I thought was dead. That would be . . . well, unnerving and wonderful at the same time. At least if it was someone you wanted to be back from the dead."

Eleanor nodded. "No man has ever wanted that more than Mr. Wallace Reed. Bill said he has died a little every day since losing his wife. He even lost his faith in God, poor man. Now he's restored, and his faith is too. Nothing could be more perfect."

"No, I don't suppose so." Mary held up her camera. "I guess I need to get back to work. Folks aren't all that excited to have their pictures taken this morning. They're more interested in the amusement rides."

"Everyone's looking for a thrill. Some sort of excitement." Eleanor glanced down the Pay Streak toward the Ferris wheel. "I'm finding real life to be much more thrilling. I think Bill intends to ask me to marry him when he joins me later today. This day couldn't be any more perfect."

"Oh, Eleanor, do you really think he will?" Mary looked as excited as Eleanor felt.

"I do. My heart is about to leap out of my chest. I need to write to my parents, but I wanted to wait until he made it official. I hope today's the day."

"I do too. I'll be praying." She gave Eleanor a brief hug. "Now I must be off."

Eleanor watched her go, then turned to head back on her way. She couldn't help but be happy. Even if Bill didn't propose today, she knew he would soon. After all, they could hardly travel to Alaska without marrying first. The thought of that made Eleanor all the happier. She couldn't help but giggle. Things had certainly changed since she'd first come to Seattle.

13

"I can hardly believe we're finally going to see her again," Wallace said as the trolley came to a stop. He hurried to step off with Bill right behind him.

"I know. I'm beyond happy." Bill looked at the street signs and noted the house numbers. "It's down that way." He pointed to the left.

They hurried across the street after the trolley departed and checked each address as they went. "This is it," Bill said when they arrived in front of the two-story brick house.

They hurried up the walkway to the small porch. Wallace pounded on the front door. It was far from a polite knock.

An older woman opened the door and looked quizzically from man to man. "Yes?"

"I'm Wallace Reed. I've come to see my wife, Amelia."

The woman looked at him for a long moment. "Who are you really? Mrs. Reed's husband is dead."

Wallace shook his head. "No, she was mistakenly told that. I'm not dead. My brother isn't either. This is him, William Reed."

"What a grand scheme. I'm sure Mr. Masterson put you up to this, but it won't work. Amelia no longer lives here, and I will not divulge where she has gone. The poor woman and her babe deserve to live in peace."

"Masterson?" Wallace's eyes narrowed. "Grady Masterson?"

"Of course. No doubt he's hired you to come here and ferret out the information I wouldn't give him. Well, it won't work." She stepped back and started to close the door, but Wallace put out his hand.

"Please, listen to me. Grady Masterson is a foul character. He was my enemy because I testified against his brother, and it resulted in his death. I would never be associated with him, and I am shocked to find out that my wife would allow his company."

"Bah, you can't fool me with this act. I know that you're working for him. He's sent you here to get me to believe Amelia's husband is alive. I'll tell you where she's gone, and you'll give the information to Grady, and Amelia will once again be under his thumb."

"No, I'm her husband. I swear it's true." Wallace was nearly beside himself.

Bill stepped forward. "Mrs. . . . ?"

"Becker. Hazel Becker. I own this building and rent apartments to proper young ladies. Grady Masterson told me he was Amelia's brother, and for a time I believed him for her sake. But the fact is, as you well know, he's a schemer and plotter. He thinks he'll marry poor Amelia, but she will not have him."

"I should hope not since her husband is alive and well," Bill replied. "Mrs. Becker, how can we possibly prove that we're telling the truth?"

"You can't as far as I'm concerned."

"But there must be a way. My poor brother has been grief-stricken since the ship went down and he was told Amelia was dead. We recently saw a photograph of her and the baby and realized she was alive. Since then we've worked with the photography studio to find her whereabouts." Bill fished something out of his pocket. "This is one of my business cards. It clearly gives my box number in Alaska, but I've handwritten down our address here as well. Would I have something like this if we were working for Mr. Masterson?"

She took the card. "You might. That man is crafty." Mrs. Becker shook her head. "I just don't believe you, even with this." She held up the card. "I won't risk that girl's life. She's gone through way too much, and now that she has her inheritance she can finally be rid of Masterson. Leave her be. She deserves to return to the land she loves."

"Return to the land she loves?" Wallace asked. "Alaska?"

Mrs. Becker paled. "I've said too much." She took advantage of the moment and slammed the door closed.

Bill heard her turn the lock and knew they'd get nothing more out of the woman. "So she's gone back to Alaska. That's perfect. We can follow her there. We know where she'll be, Wallace."

Wallace stood staring at the door. "But she was here. Right here. I can feel her presence. Why can't I be with her?"

"You will be. Have faith, brother. You know as well as I do that she is smart. Mrs. Becker said she had an inheritance. Where might that have come from? Do you suppose she contacted our lawyer in Chicago?"

"She might have, but there was no inheritance to be had," Wallace replied.

Bill shook his head. "Unless Father has died."

"Oh my word, he very well may have." Wallace's expression turned even sadder. "Do you suppose he has?"

"We must get in touch with Mr. Potts. Maybe he'll know where Amelia has gone since she's obviously been in touch. After all, there is no other family. She couldn't have inherited in any other way. She thought us both dead. It's possible she wrote to tell him and learned Father was dead and had left us money."

"This gets more complicated by the minute." Wallace finally turned to walk down the porch steps. "Our poor father. I grieve to think he's passed on. I grieve to have come so close to Amelia and my son only to be thwarted by the likes of Grady Masterson."

Bill walked alongside his brother as they made their way back to the trolley. "Grady must have done all of this to get his revenge on you. He told Amelia we were dead."

"And arranged for others to tell us she was dead." Wallace shook his head vehemently. "How could that have happened?"

"I don't know." Bill was truly baffled by the turn of events.

They reached the trolley stop, but Wallace was looking only to the house from where they'd just come.

"She was there. She was there, and so was my son. And now they're gone, and that old woman knows where they are, and she won't tell me. And all of this is Grady Masterson's fault. I'd like to kill him for the pain he's caused me."

Bill put his hand on Wallace's arm. "That won't find Amelia for you. Look, if she's determined to move back to Alaska, then we know where to find her. It'll just take a little longer. You can't give up."

"I'm not giving up, brother. I would never give up now. But I am so full of rage that Masterson would do such a thing."

"I am too."

The trolley approached, and Bill let go of Wallace. He knew this wasn't going to be easy no matter how they dealt with it. Grady Masterson had created a nightmare for them.

"We should have asked how to find Masterson," Bill muttered.

The trolley stopped, and before Bill and Wallace could climb aboard, a man stepped down and stopped dead in his tracks.

"Masterson." Wallace barely breathed the name.

The trolley waited for them to board, but Bill waved them on. Once the trolley was down the street, Wallace managed to speak again. "You scum."

Grady had the audacity to laugh. "So you know. I had always hoped to find you one day and tell you how I got my revenge."

"You knew we were alive?" Bill asked.

"Of course. I saw the survivor list printed in the Seattle paper. But I kept it from Amelia. I certainly didn't want her to know. It would have ruined my plans."

"You let her suffer," Wallace stated more than asked.

Grady shrugged. "Of course. I wanted you all to suffer just as I had. You took my brother from me, so I took your wife and son from you. And he's a sweet little boy. I was the only father he knew."

Wallace's hands went into fists, and Bill put his hand again on his brother. "Don't let him get the best of you. He's obviously demented."

"I'm not demented at all. In fact, I'm quite brilliant and fully logical. Your wife and I ended up on the same lifeboat. Number five—the one that was overturned, and the people drowned. But we'd been moved to another boat before that disaster. I told Amelia that you and I had resolved our differences. That you had forgiven me, and I you. She seemed pleased, even mentioned that it was an answered prayer.

"We were taken to Victoria, where your wife went into labor almost immediately. Thankfully it happened before we could be counted as survivors." He laughed. "That's when I got my idea of how I could repay you for the misery you'd caused."

He crossed his arms and sobered. "A midwife presumed I was Amelia's husband and took us to her house. I was there when your son, Wallace Junior, was born. She calls him Wally."

"Wally." Wallace smiled. "We had planned to call him Isaac."

"She thought you were dead," Bill interjected. "She wanted to name him for you."

"Yes, I suppose she thought it was to honor you," Grady continued. "You know, it was me who broke the news that you were dead. I went down to the morgue and saw a couple of deadbeats who would never be missed. I told the authorities that it was Wallace and William Reed. Then I told Amelia that you were both dead. Of course she was devastated."

Wallace struck without warning, punching Grady square in the nose and knocking him onto his backside. Blood streamed down Grady's face as he struggled to his feet. Wallace reared back to hit him a second time. Bill stopped him before he could strike again.

"Wallace, it won't change a thing."

"Maybe not, but the man is devious and cruel and deserves to be beaten for what he did to Amelia."

"I agree," Bill said, glancing at Grady, who was already reaching for his handkerchief.

"I got you all but good. You have no idea the great satisfaction I took from my schemes. This punch is nothing. I'd endure it and a hundred more just for the knowledge that I made you suffer. That you're still suffering."

Wallace was obviously livid, and Bill knew better than to let go of his hold. "Masterson, you are an evil man."

"I am, and I pride myself in that fact. I've done a lot of bad in my day, but this is the one thing that has given me the greatest satisfaction. Now she's gone from both of us, and I have no idea of where she'll end up, but wherever she goes, she'll believe you dead. You think your own pain has been great, but you have no idea of what that woman has suffered."

Wallace started for Grady once again, but Bill held him fast. "Don't. You'll just get thrown in jail for killing him."

That seemed to sober Grady a bit, and he stepped back several paces. "I won't be surprised a second time. You lay a hand on me again, and I'll put an end to your life." He looked at Bill. "And yours."

"Come on, Wallace. We know where Amelia is." Bill smiled at the look of surprise that crossed Grady's face. "That's right. We know."

"That old woman told you, didn't she? I should have beaten her when she refused to tell me."

Bill shook his head. "You harm so much as a hair on her head, and we'll go to the police and let them know it was you."

Grady stared at Bill for a long moment, then shrugged. "Tell the police whatever you like. It's all been worth the effort." With that he walked away, heading down the street in the same direction the trolley went.

Bill watched him go and felt Wallace gradually relax once again. The madness of the moment was too much to fully comprehend. How could Grady have managed all of this? How could he have kept Amelia in the dark about their being alive? Bill supposed there never was all that much information given after the initial stories of a sinking. Amelia would have been very busy with the new baby and because of that probably never questioned Grady. Still, why had she trusted him?

"She thought we'd resolved our differences," Wallace said as if he'd read Bill's thoughts. "She was always praying for reconciliation with those who held something against us. She would have been delighted to know that we had made our peace, never knowing it wasn't true."

"Amelia would have been easy to deceive. She always believes the best of everyone."

Wallace nodded. "It's true. She does."

Bill put his arm around Wallace's shoulders. "We'll find her. I promise you we will. I feel certain of it."

❧

Eleanor was just starting her twentieth page when Bill finally appeared. She glanced at the clock. It had been a good six hours since she'd last seen him. She had been thinking of going to get something to eat, but she was so excited to learn the news that she had forgotten about her growing hunger.

"Did you find her? Was it a wonderful reunion?"

"No." Bill looked completely downcast. "She had gone— moved from that address."

Eleanor sighed. "I had such hopes."

"We all did." He sat down in the chair beside her. "But that's not the worst of it."

Leaning close, Eleanor put her hand atop Bill's. "What is it? What has happened?"

"It's a long story, but there was a man in Alaska who hated my brother." Bill began telling her the tale of Grady Masterson.

Eleanor listened patiently, surprised by all the underhanded actions that had taken place and the cruel deception Grady had practiced on the Reeds.

"What a terrible thing. How could anyone be so heartless?" Eleanor shook her head and squeezed Bill's hand. "I'm so sorry."

"She's lived all this time believing us dead and herself a widow. Meanwhile, Wallace thought Amelia was gone forever—lost to the sea. His baby too. And all this time we were living in the same city, just miles apart."

She sat silent for a moment, praying for guidance. "What do we do now?"

A slight smile touched his weary face. "I like that you say *we*. What do *we* do now? You are, after all, such an important part of this."

"I want very much to be a part of it. I know I'll never rest until we find Amelia and the baby and reunite them with your brother."

"Amelia's former landlady knows where she's gone but refuses to say anything. She believes Grady hired us to pose as Amelia's husband and brother-in-law. But at one point, she did say something about letting Amelia return to the land she loved. That would be Alaska. Amelia once said she had only ever been truly happy there."

"So you think she'll return to the village where you all lived?"

"I do. Apparently she's not hampered by the need of funds. Wallace is going to write to our family lawyer, but we think our father has passed away, leaving us an inheritance. When Amelia wrote to say we had drowned when the ship sank, the lawyer probably bestowed the inheritance on her. Wallace and I both had her as our beneficiary."

"Oh, Bill, I hope it's not that your father has died. That would be so terrible for you."

"I don't know how it could be anything else." He shook his head and took a tight hold on her hand.

"This is all too sad." She sat there holding his hand, happy for the connection between them.

"We need to press forward and work twice as fast. Could I impose upon you to quit your job with the Fishers and just work with me on typing the manuscript?"

"Of course. This is my work now, as well as yours. I want to do whatever I can to make things easier for you."

"If we can finish right away, then we can leave for Alaska all the sooner."

Eleanor bit her lip. Should she ask for a formal proposal? She wanted to be married before they left Seattle. She wanted her parents to be able to come to the city and see her wed. Before she could speak, Bill released her hand and got to his feet.

"I've got to get these pictures drawn, and you have more typing to do."

Eleanor held her tongue and merely nodded. She'd give him a few days, and if he said nothing, she'd bring it up. In the meantime, she'd send a letter to her folks in Kansas to put them on their guard. No sense waiting until the last minute to spring such life-changing news.

14

I've finished the letter to Mr. Potts," Wallace said. "I've told him that we're both still alive, but that Amelia was told we were dead. I've mentioned knowing about an inheritance and asked if Father passed on."

"Did you explain to him why there has been so much confusion?" Bill asked. It was late, and his mind barely registered all the details, but he knew it would be important to explain lest the poor man think himself to blame for releasing funds that shouldn't have been given to Amelia.

"Yes, I went into detail on all that has happened and that we weren't upset with him for helping Amelia. In fact, I thanked him. Then I asked if he had her address, could he please forward it to me. I told him about the address we have and that we couldn't seem to get another lead except that she hoped to return to Alaska and would have to do so relatively soon because the weather will soon turn bad and make it difficult for her to reach the village."

"That's good. She might have even discussed her plans with him," Bill said, stifling a yawn.

"I thought so too. I'll mail this in the morning, special delivery to ensure it reaches him quickly, then I intend to go to the shipping offices and see if I can share what's happened and get them to watch for Amelia and let us know if she books passage north."

"That would be difficult for them to do, I'm sure. There are an awful lot of ships sailing."

"Yes, but not that many to Alaska. Not these days."

Bill nodded. "That's true."

Wallace leaned back and rubbed his eyes. "I can't believe the way I've failed this testing."

"What do you mean?" Bill was really too tired to hear his brother's thoughts, but he could tell Wallace needed to speak.

"All of this trip south was a test. None of us wanted to leave home—not even you, if you're honest. There was the manuscript to ensure had proper mailing, but we could have posted it from Alaska. It would just have been a greater risk. Had the midwife not insisted Amelia needed better care . . . we could still be there."

"I know." Bill had already thought of these things long ago. "And I can see what you're saying about how all of this has been a test."

"A test I failed. I still can hardly believe my reaction. I always thought I would be able to face any trial. This has humbled me to the ground. I had a spirit of pride that made me believe I couldn't fail God. Now I know that I'm just as weak and human as the next man. I needed to see that, I'm ashamed to say."

Bill knew these last few months had been life altering for Wallace. He had worried his brother would never go back to preaching. But he could see now that Wallace was more suited for the task than ever before.

"God knew where my failings were—knew I needed to recognize them and grow beyond their limitations. I can't yet say that I'm thankful for the testing, but I do consider myself blessed that the outcome has been so much gentler than I feared in the beginning."

"Yes, to be sure. And had we not come to Seattle, I might not have met Eleanor."

"Do you plan to marry her?"

"You know I do," Bill replied, smiling. "She is the one God has chosen for me. I already feel that my life has only been half fulfilled without her."

Wallace looked delighted. "Have you proposed?"

"Not exactly, but after a fashion. I told her I loved her, and she admitted her feelings to be the same." Bill yawned. "I need to go to bed."

"We both do, but I think first you should settle in your heart how you will manage this situation with Eleanor. You must give her time to make her own arrangements, and if we leave right away for Alaska, that gives you only a few weeks at most—maybe less."

"I will ask her."

"Don't waste any time. I so regret all the lost time with Amelia—and God. Of course, the latter was all my fault. I still feel so guilty for all I've said and thought in my heart."

"Yes, but God forgives those thoughts. He knew the struggle you were enduring. He never left you."

Wallace's brows came together as he frowned. "But I left Him. I abandoned my faith in so many ways. I knew God was still God, but I thought Him cruel. I was convinced He no longer cared."

"That was Satan's doing, not your own. The devil is constantly whispering in the ear of believers—doing his best to get them to doubt God. He did it with Eve in the garden. He did it with Jesus, and he does it with everyone who seeks God. He wants to make us doubt God's Word and His faithfulness."

"And I did. I'm so ashamed. I never thought that would be me."

Bill took a seat opposite Wallace at the table. "But you've asked forgiveness, and you've sought reconciliation with the Lord."

"But would I have done so had Amelia and the baby really been dead?" Wallace met Bill's gaze and shook his head. "I don't know that I would have. I can't know for sure that I would have come back from the dark pit that I allowed myself to dig."

Bill couldn't help himself. He chuckled. "Do you suppose God would have let you slip away that easily? Remember the Scriptures in Psalm one hundred thirty-nine? 'If I ascend up into heaven, thou art there: if I make my bed in hell, behold, thou art there.' God never let you go for a moment, Wallace. You know that. You would have had your time of grief, then little by little you would have come back to His side—desperate because nothing else would ever feel as right."

Wallace smiled at this comment. "When did you get to be the preacher in the family?"

"I'm not, but I have a good memory. You preached on that set of Scriptures just last winter. It was powerful, and several people gave their hearts to God when you finished preaching."

"Yes, I remember that as well."

"You can't outrun God. You can't hide well enough or long enough that He will forget you. Not after accepting Jesus as your only Savior. You will be forever connected to God the Father, the Son, and the Holy Spirit. I find great comfort in that. I even thought about it when we were in the lifeboat waiting to be rescued." Bill remembered it as if it had been yesterday. "I kept worrying about us being lost in the storm. Thrown about in the ocean and lost forever. The verses from that psalm came back to me, and I recited them over and over.

'Whither shall I go from thy spirit? Or whither shall I flee from thy presence? If I ascend up into heaven, thou art there: if I make my bed in hell, behold, thou art there. If I take the wings of the morning, and dwell in the uttermost parts of the sea; even there shall thy hand lead me, and thy right hand shall hold me.'"

Bill grinned. "Even if we were settled in the uttermost parts of the sea, God would have been right there with us."

"I never even thought of those verses," Wallace admitted. "I kept thinking how foolish I'd been to abandon Amelia. I hated myself for playing the hero rather than staying at her side."

"But we couldn't have stayed at her side. It was women and children first into the lifeboats. They wouldn't have allowed you to stay with her, not unless there was room at the end, and then you could have joined her."

"Like Masterson did." Wallace shook his head. "He served the devil's purpose very well."

"He did, but now we need to forgive and forget about him.

The damage is done, and the healing must begin. We know the truth, and soon Amelia will as well."

⁂

Eleanor presented her straw boater and satchel. Both had been given to her by Mrs. Fisher for the purpose of being a Camera Girl, and now that her time was over, it was only right that they be returned.

"I am sorry to see you go, Eleanor," Mrs. Fisher said.

Addie Hanson was there as well and couldn't agree fast enough. "You have been one of our best workers. Things won't be the same without you."

"Well, I appreciate that you should say so," Eleanor replied. "I've loved this job, and the other girls have been so nice to get to know. I'll miss everyone."

"Has Mr. Reed proposed to you yet?" Addie asked.

"No, but I know he will any day now. Our marrying has definitely been implied. We have to focus on getting his manuscript to the publisher, as well as find his sister-in-law. Those things have taken precedence over everything else."

Mrs. Fisher frowned. "You don't suppose that with the circumstances having changed that he's changed his mind on marriage?"

Eleanor hadn't even considered that a possibility. "No. I can't explain why, but I know Bill and I are destined to be together. I've never been so certain of a thing in my life."

Addie nodded. "I felt that way about Isaac. There was something about the way we fit together—there was no doubt. Even when I was avoiding him and fighting against the idea."

Eleanor gave a dreamy sigh. "He's everything to me. Everything I had hoped for in a mate and more. I never dared to imagine I could find someone so well suited to my interests and life."

"What if he doesn't propose?" Mrs. Fisher asked.

Eleanor laughed and gave a little twirl. "Then I'll do it myself."

Addie smiled and looked to her friend. "Pearl, she's got it well in hand, I'd say."

Eleanor was thinking on that hours later when she walked into the apartment she shared with Rosemary. Her friend was sitting at the table, writing a letter to someone. She glanced up and seemed quite happy to see that it was Eleanor.

"I didn't know you were coming home tonight."

"I quit my job with the Camera Girls. Now I'll be working day and night to help Bill get that manuscript turned in. Then we can marry and move to Alaska."

"What? He proposed, and you didn't tell me?"

"No, but if he had proposed, you would just chide me that I haven't known him long enough." Eleanor sat and put her feet up on the ottoman. She folded her hands behind her head and leaned back to rest.

"He hasn't proposed." It wasn't really a question. "So why did you say you'd marry and move to Alaska?"

"Because that is my plan. In the next few weeks, in fact. I wrote to my folks and told them that I figure we'll be married by the end of August. I encouraged them to be prepared and said that I would very much like them to be here. I suggested they take a train and come as soon as possible."

"Oh, Eleanor, don't you think that was putting the cart before the horse?"

"Not at all. I feel quite confident of Bill's intentions. Right now, he's consumed with this manuscript and finding his sister-in-law, but I know he's still planning for the two of us."

"I think you're being wishful, my dear friend." Rosemary abandoned her letter and came to sit closer to Eleanor. "You are going to be dreadfully disappointed if all of this changes because of the situation changing."

"You sound like Mrs. Fisher. She posed the same possibility, but I feel very confident of Bill's intentions as well as my own. I won't let him slip away. I know we're destined to be together."

"But, Eleanor, his sister-in-law and baby being alive changes everything."

"For Bill's brother it does. Not for Bill."

"You can't know that for certain." Rosemary looked quite worried. "I fear it will alter the course of their plans and, in doing so, disrupt yours."

Eleanor felt only a moment of doubt, but she could see that Rosemary and the others were only trying to protect her feelings. She couldn't help them to understand how she was absolutely certain of Bill's feelings and plans. She couldn't explain her own confidence.

"You know, it occurs to me that you've never met Bill and don't really know him at all. I think we should have lunch together. If I can arrange it, would you attend?"

"We can't have a strange man here at the apartment. You know the rules."

"I wasn't suggesting we host it here. We can agree to meet at a restaurant."

Rosemary frowned. "That sounds expensive."

"I'll pay. I have my savings for school, which I'm now going to use for my needs in getting married and moving to Alaska. I'm sure I can spare a few dollars for lunch. Let me talk to Bill, and I'll arrange it. I think you'll be quite impressed with him."

"I suppose I could attend, so long as it doesn't interfere with work."

"We could make it dinner. That might be better. We'll celebrate my birthday since we couldn't do it at the time. Mother and Father sent me a check. I can definitely spare the money for a celebration, and you can hardly refuse me." Eleanor, in her newfound freedom from the Camera Girls, hadn't really considered that timing could be a problem. She didn't want to rush Rosemary's opinion of Bill.

"Very well. I will agree to meet you for dinner because of your birthday, but I'm still not convinced that this is wise."

Eleanor smiled and got to her feet. "What's wise at this moment is readying myself for bed." She yawned and patted Rosemary on the head as she passed to head toward their bedroom. "Coming?"

⁕

Dinner had been relatively silent while they ate their main courses. Eleanor had introduced Bill and Rosemary, then after a little chitchat, the waiter came and all focus went to the food. Even Eleanor had to admit it was worthy of their attention. The small eating establishment wasn't all that well known, but Eleanor and Rosemary had come to love it. They served simple fare with a bit of an upscale twist. There were fine linens on the table and for the napkins. Cut glass was used for the drinking glasses instead of crystal, but fine china graced the table.

And the food was delicious. It was said the chef was from Rome. Eleanor couldn't even begin to imagine what that place was like, but it was a city in the Bible, and that alone fascinated her.

They finished eating impeccably cooked steaks—meat so tender it nearly cut with the fork. Delicately steamed vegetables with a capers sauce and a creamed fettuccine concoction rounded out the meal. If this was Italian in nature, Eleanor found it quite delicious.

"This was a perfect way to celebrate my birthday. Thank you both for coming." Eleanor figured if anyone was going to get the conversation going, it would have to be her.

"Happy birthday, Eleanor," Rosemary said, pushing a little box toward her friend.

Eleanor opened it and found a beautiful ink pen. "Oh, thank you, Rosemary. I will cherish it."

"I'm afraid I didn't bring a gift. I've been so caught up with finding Amelia," Bill apologized. "I'm sorry."

"It's not a problem, Bill. I'm not big on celebrating my birthday anyway. I grew up feeling every day was special, and I'm just glad to finally bring you and Rosemary together."

"I must say when Eleanor first suggested this, I had my apprehensions." Bill's comment broke the tension at the table. "She told me you were quite uncertain of me."

Rosemary blushed. "I don't know you. Eleanor was talking about all these plans for Alaska, and I had concerns that she was being taken advantage of and would rue the day she had put her trust in you."

Bill chuckled, and Eleanor couldn't help but smile. Rosemary always spoke her mind. She found herself hoping that

Rosemary might discreetly ask when Bill planned to marry Eleanor.

"I assure you I care quite deeply for Eleanor and would never do anything to risk her reputation or cause her harm."

"Yes, but you have your hands quite full trying to locate your sister-in-law. Then there's the manuscript that must be completed. That doesn't really give you much time for my friend and romance."

"Ah, but that's where you're wrong. Eleanor has been with me every step of the way with the retyping of the manuscript. She has also been most beneficial in finding Amelia. In fact, had it not been for her photograph, we would never have known Amelia was alive." He smiled at Eleanor. "She has blessed me in every way possible."

"But you haven't formally proposed to her. She has no guarantee that you intend to do right by her."

Eleanor nearly spit out the water she'd just sipped. Rosemary could oftentimes be much too aggressive. She put the glass of water back on the table. She tried not to look as shocked as she felt, but no one seemed to be looking at her anyway.

"Rosemary, you needn't worry," Bill replied. "I have everything under control. Eleanor knows my heart, and there will be no missed steps where we are concerned."

"Still—"

"Still nothing." Bill interrupted whatever Rosemary was going to say. "Now, how about some dessert?"

Eleanor had wanted to hear what Bill might say to someone asking about his intentions, but now that it had happened, she felt most uncomfortable. Rosemary glanced her way with a raised brow as Bill signaled the dessert cart. Eleanor shrugged and looked away.

It was still light when Rosemary and Eleanor headed back to their apartment. The evening had seemed to go well, with exception to the question about proposing. Eleanor could tell from the conversation and remaining time eating dessert that Rosemary had liked Bill and pressed her for her thoughts. "So tell me what you're thinking. Did you like him?"

"You know I did. He's quite intelligent and charming," Rosemary said. "And, as you mentioned before, he's a man of God. I was quite interested in his thoughts on the ordeal with his sister-in-law and how God had seen him through each dark moment. I suppose I would have to say that you shouldn't let him get away." She turned and smiled at Eleanor. "Maybe see if he has another brother—one who isn't married."

15

Amelia was still in awe at the size of the little cottage. After living in one room, she found keeping up with the cleaning of the new house to be a bit daunting. Mrs. Harris had suggested bringing in someone from church to help clean. She even knew a woman and made introductions.

Helga Albright was a plump woman who had just passed her forty-ninth birthday. She had been widowed for over twenty years and had chosen not to remarry. She told Amelia she knew she could never love another man as she had her beloved Augustus and so had chosen to remain single. However, she'd never been alone. She took jobs as a housekeeper and nanny and filled her life with lovely people. Just as she was now doing with Amelia.

The two widows hit it off and seemed a perfect match for one another. Helga was more like a big sister than a housekeeper. The two women easily became friends, and Amelia found her sorrows lifted a bit as Helga shared the load.

"I have something to ask you," Amelia said as Helga arrived to work that day.

"Well, goodness let me catch my breath." She put down a bag she'd brought with her. Helga was a little thick in the waist and rather full on top, but she walked everywhere and seemed to have endless energy. "I've been carrying vegetables from my garden, and they're heavier than I thought."

"Oh here, let me help." Amelia went to take the burlap bag. It was quite heavy. "Oh my, you didn't exaggerate at all." She put the vegetables in the kitchen and returned to the living room.

Helga was all smiles. "What did you want to ask me?"

"I wondered if you might consider going with me to Alaska. You wouldn't have to stay, but it would be so nice to have the company as I travel."

"Alaska?" Helga considered this for a moment.

"Just for the trip up. Although I would love it if you wanted to stay on. However, I know that area isn't for just anyone. Alaska is vast and isolated, and although I cherish the people, there are many who would find that life appalling. It wouldn't be anything like living here."

"Tell me all about it. I feel rather adventurous."

"Well, let me see. Where to begin? The Athabaskans call themselves Dena or 'the people.' Our particular people stay near the Susitna River. They're nomadic and move around from time to time to accommodate their needs."

Amelia continued, explaining what she could. "In the winter months, they usually stay in the village, where we live. They have houses that are made from birch bark and stretched skins like moose or caribou. You might not think that sounds very warm, but we lived in one once, and it was quite cozy. Now we have a little log house. The accommodations are nothing as nice as this, and of course there is no indoor plumbing. That might be the hardest thing for you to get used to. Life there is quite primitive compared to here."

"Bah, that never worried me much," Helga replied.

They moved to the kitchen, and Helga began to sort through the vegetables as Amelia continued to talk about Alaska.

"We travel by foot on snowshoes and sometimes use dog-sleds if there are big loads. It's quite the adventure. Dogs pull the sleds for miles and miles and are quite capable of enduring the cold winter months. In the summer, we use the river for our main transportation."

"It sounds like a lot of work. I don't know that my body would be up for such a thing."

Amelia nodded. "It is a great deal of work—and dangerous too. It's not for the faint of heart to be sure. There's the weather to deal with and wild animals. You have to get used to making do with what you have or creating whatever is needed."

"What kind of wild animals?"

"Bears, moose, wolves. You have to be extremely careful. Even in just going for a walk to the outhouse, you have to bring along a firearm. Or have someone with one accompany you. Once I was picking berries and going along a dense thicket, not even realizing a bear was on the other side. Had one of the native boys not come along with us and brought a gun, we might have been attacked."

"Oh goodness." Helga's hand went to her throat. "I don't think I would be able to endure that kind of danger."

"There's also dangers with flooding when the rivers thaw and blizzards and fierce cold that could kill you if you stay out in it for too long. But along with the dangers, there are an equal number of blessings."

"It doesn't sound like a life of blessings," Helga said, pausing to look at Amelia. "Why do you want to go back?"

"It has been home for many years. We were in other places in Alaska, but this village was my favorite because the people were so good to us. I learned a great deal from them and have many good friends. I have no one down here, save Wally."

"That makes sense. A person needs to be with their people."

"Yes, and I suppose I've taken them as mine." Amelia smiled at the memory of the friends she'd left behind. "And they definitely took me as theirs."

"I don't know that I'd be any good in that world, but tell you what, I would be happy to make the trip up with you and then come back to Seattle. I have my people here since I've lived here so very long."

"That is quite reasonable. I know you would be a great help to me in the travel. I've sent a letter ahead to our village, and I am hoping they will help me coordinate transportation once the ship arrives in Alaska. It won't be an easy journey to be sure, but I will be glad to be home."

<hr />

Bill had worked since dawn on some of his drawings, and they were nearly complete. He and Eleanor had been at it until eight thirty the night before and were so focused on their work that they hardly spoke two words to each other. After having had dinner with Rosemary the night before, Bill knew he needed to formalize his arrangements with Eleanor and figure out when they could be married, especially since it was possible that Amelia had already taken a ship to Alaska.

A knock sounded on the front door, and Bill glanced up to catch Wallace's worried gaze. It was his day off, but instead of sleeping in, he was up and ready to do whatever he could to find Amelia. The knock sounded again, and Wallace hurried to the door. Bill gathered his drawings and waited to see who it might be.

"Special delivery telegram for Wallace Reed," the young man declared.

"I'm Wallace Reed."

The deliveryman nodded. "Sign here." He held up a book to Wallace and a pen.

Bill wondered who in the world had gone to such expense as to send a special telegram. He waited as the man handed Wallace the envelope. Wallace closed the door and looked to Bill.

"It's from Mr. Potts. I wasn't expecting him to go to this expense." He opened the envelope as he crossed the room to the table where Bill waited. Taking a chair, he began to read.

"He's glad to learn we're alive," Wallace said, then continued scanning the page. "He says that Father passed away the first of May. He left us both an inheritance, and Mr. Potts sent a letter to Alaska to notify us. He is mortified that he gave Amelia the inheritance despite my having told him I was glad he did."

"Poor Father. I hope he didn't suffer."

"He was a good man and will be sorely missed."

Bill nodded and smiled. "He was so enthusiastic about your missionary work. So proud of us both. A man could hardly ask for a better father."

"No," Wallace agreed. He sighed and for several long moments said nothing. "I bear guilt for not having written more often. I know Father was most enthusiastic about my work with the Athabaskan people. I should have taken more time out to write."

"He understood. Plus, there was the expense of getting the mail posted back to the States. No one else was quite as frugal as he could be, so I know that he understood the hesitancy to spend extra on postage."

"I know. I just . . . I had hoped to see him again."

Bill understood exactly what his brother was saying, but there was nothing more they could do about it now. "We can more properly mourn Father later. What else does Mr. Potts have to say?"

Wallace looked back at the telegram. "He hopes I don't see it as a breach of trust that he gave our inheritance to Amelia."

"Of course we don't. Even I am glad he saw to Amelia's needs. We can work out the details later. Does he have an address for Amelia?"

Wallace shook his head. "Just the one we had. But he does mention the bank she's using. He suggests we might go there and see if they have a new address for her. It's an excellent idea."

"I suppose you should check it out straightaway. I have some time. We could be down there when they open the doors if we hurry."

Wallace refolded the telegram and tucked it back in the envelope. "He must have spent a fortune on this."

"He knew you needed the information as soon as possible."

His brother nodded and tossed the envelope on the table. "I had asked him not to tell Amelia that we're alive. I want to tell her in person. I fear reading it in a letter would be too great a shock. She might not even believe it after all we've gone through. Had you not had her photograph, I doubt I would have believed you telling me she was alive. He assures me he'll say nothing."

"Yes, I think it will be hard on her no matter how the knowledge comes. Learning about it from afar and having no knowledge of when we might all be reunited would be maddening. We know that firsthand."

Wallace went to get his coat. "I'm ready to go to the bank. I just pray we can get some help from them."

They arrived at the bank just after the doors were opened. There were quite a few people milling about and tending to business, but Wallace didn't let that deter him. He marched straight to a man seated at an enormous mahogany desk.

"I need to speak to someone about the address of one of your customers."

The man frowned. "What seems to be the problem?"

"I am trying to locate my wife. She thinks I'm dead, but as you can clearly see, I'm not."

The man frowned. "Let me get the bank manager for you. Perhaps you can explain your story to him."

The man got up and disappeared into an office at the back of the massive lobby. Wallace looked to Bill and shrugged. "I don't know why this should have to be so difficult."

"I don't either, but try not to lose patience. I know things are going to come together in the long run."

The man soon returned and motioned for Wallace and Bill to follow him. He led them to the room where he had gone and introduced them to the bank manager. "Mr. Lowe, these are the gentlemen I mentioned."

Mr. Lowe stood behind his desk, awaiting them. He was a small man dressed impeccably in a three-piece suit. Gold-rimmed glasses were perched on his nose. Wallace stepped forward with his hand extended. "I'm Wallace Reed, and this is my brother, William."

"Please have a seat and tell me how I can help you."

Wallace gave a quick accounting of what they'd gone through when the *City of Canton* sank and how they were listed as dead in Canada.

"My wife is Amelia Reed. She was presumed to have died when her lifeboat overturned. Since then, I've learned that she survived and has given birth to my son. She believes I'm dead, and I must find her to let her know I'm alive. Our family lawyer set up an account for her here at the bank, and I'm hoping she has given you her new address because she's no longer at her former address."

"We aren't in the habit of giving out information on our customers."

"She's my wife and thinks me dead. Have a heart. I need to find her and show her I'm still alive. Please. She's the love of my life, and I haven't even seen my son."

The man frowned. "Let me see what I can find out."

Wallace waited until he'd left the room to turn to Bill. "You wouldn't think it would be this hard. A man has a right to find his wife and child."

"It is a bizarre circumstance, though. You have to allow that it must seem completely unlikely to a person hearing it for the first time."

"Yes, but they could check the newspaper archives and learn the truth. It wouldn't be that hard." Wallace twisted his hands together. "I can't bear that she's here in the city and I can't find her."

"She may already be on her way to Alaska. I think we should focus on getting our affairs in order and leaving as soon as we can. I need a week more to finish the manuscript, but after that I'll be able to leave Seattle."

"But what if we leave and then learn she's not there? It's expensive to travel and takes time. We might even arrive at the winter village and find the people haven't yet returned. Then we'd be waiting even longer trying to figure out where she is. No, I want to find her here in Seattle and take her home."

"I'm just saying she may not even be in Seattle. Her only real deterrent was Masterson and money. She's gotten rid of Masterson and has the money she needs, thanks to our inheritance."

Just then Mr. Lowe returned. He appeared to be all business, without a hint of anything personable.

"I'm sorry, but I cannot help you."

"What do you mean?" Wallace asked. "Did she not leave her latest address?"

"There is a notation on the account. The woman left word that a man who means her harm is trying to find her." He gave a tsking sound and pointed his index finger at Wallace. "You should be ashamed of yourself."

"The man she's speaking of is Grady Masterson. Not her

husband. She doesn't even know I'm alive," Wallace said, jumping to his feet. "You must hear me. She needs me. She's all alone with our son and believes me dead."

"I cannot help you, and if you aren't out of the bank in the next few minutes, I will send for the police."

Bill reached up and took hold of his brother's arm. "If you're in jail, we can hardly look for Amelia. Come on. We'll figure something out."

Wallace's expression was one of rage, and Bill knew he wasn't helping his case in the least. He all but dragged Wallace out of the building. When they were outside, Bill paused and turned Wallace to face him. "She's done a good thing by letting them know about Grady Masterson. We cannot condemn her choice just because it thwarts our efforts as well."

"I just want to find her." Wallace broke down and tears streamed from his eyes. "She needs me. I know she does."

"I know it too. And so does God. We need to pray for God to show us what to do, Wallace. He will. He's brought us this far."

❧

Eleanor realized as she typed that she was no longer really reading the manuscript as she had in the beginning. When she'd first started, she found herself caught up in the plants and all that Bill had to say about them. Now, knowing that time was of the essence, she was simply typing the letters that she saw and hoping for no mistakes.

Bill arrived around eleven with drawings in hand. He held them up like a grand prize and smiled.

"I stayed up late and got up early and got this set done. We're getting so close. I'm so excited about completing the task. My book is really going to be turned in at last."

"I'm getting faster and faster at typing. I was just momentarily sad because I'm working just to type the piece rather than read it. I guess once it's published, I'll have to sit down and read the book." She couldn't help but laugh. "Now, why are you so late today? I expected you three hours ago."

"Wallace got a lengthy telegram from our lawyer in Chicago. He didn't have a new address for Amelia, but he did tell Wallace the name of the bank in which he set her account. We went there, but they wouldn't tell us a thing. Amelia had made them note that she didn't want anyone to know her address because a man would be looking for her, and she didn't want him to find her because he meant her harm. They figured Wallace was that man and even threatened to call the police to escort him from the bank. It was heartbreaking. I have no idea if the bank manager had a new address for her or not, but Wallace is just beside himself."

Bill deposited the drawings on the table and shook his head. "I hated to leave him. He was in tears. He knows she's so close, and yet he can't be with her—can't comfort her and let her know that he's alive. Can't see his son."

He dropped his gaze and stared at the floor. "How I wish I could make it right. I've long blamed myself for the separation to begin with. If I would have just stayed with Amelia . . ."

Eleanor got up and came to where he stood. "You told me that they were only allowing women and children into the boat. They wouldn't have changed the rules for you."

"I could have told them how close she was to giving birth.

Demanded that we not be separated. I could have asserted my will."

She touched his cheek. "Bill, Amelia's disappearance was not your fault. Had she remained with the others who were picked up by that Canadian freighter, she would have been counted, but Mr. Masterson made certain that she wasn't. Then he lied and told her you were dead. You hold no blame in any of this. And while it's true that I cannot understand why God would allow such a thing to happen, I feel confident that He will make it all come round right. Just as I'm confident of my love for you."

He put his arms around her and pulled her close. Eleanor bent her head back to keep her gaze on his face. His blue eyes were intense as he watched her. She'd never seen eyes so beautiful.

His face moved just a little closer to hers, then he stopped. He seemed to search her face for the answer to an unasked question. When she said nothing, did nothing, he lowered his lips to hers and kissed her for a long and passionate moment.

Her first kiss was all that Eleanor had hoped it might be. She never wanted it to end, but it did, and he pulled away to look at her with an expression that suggested surprise and satisfaction.

Eleanor struggled for something to say to fill the silence, but there was nothing she wanted to do more than kiss him again. She wondered if he'd think her brazen if she stretched up on tiptoes and repeated the kiss. She didn't have to even try, however. He pulled her near and kissed her again.

The second kiss was just as wonderful as the first.

16

"Marry me, Eleanor, please." Bill had pulled away just enough to make his request.

"I plan to," Eleanor replied. "I can't imagine a life without you in it. You've become my whole world."

He nodded and let go of his hold on her. "I know what you mean. We've only known each other a month, and there's so much more to learn, but I don't want to face the future without you at my side."

She looked so angelic in that moment, and Bill could hardly keep himself from pulling her back in his arms. He knew without any doubt that she was the woman God had sent just for him.

"I want to marry you as soon as possible."

"I'd like that too," Eleanor agreed. "I would like my parents at the wedding, however. I've written to them and will write again to hurry them. I told them they should come right away to Seattle, but it won't hurt to stress that again. Maybe even send a special delivery letter or telegram."

"Yes, I think that would be wise. I don't know how quickly Wallace is going to want to head north. We feel confident that Amelia will be leaving soon—if she hasn't already gone. She'll know how difficult the travel will be as time wears on and cold weather moves in, especially once she reaches Alaska. Our village is a long way from the place where the ship docks. Alaska is unforgiving in its storms and getting trapped out in the wilds is quite dangerous. Thankfully she's smart enough not to risk her life or the baby's by not getting the proper help. She will contact our friends, and I have no doubt that someone will come to see her home. We'll need to have them do the same for us."

Eleanor clasped her hands together and laughed. "It's just all so exciting. I'm going to be a wife and a botanist's assistant and live in Alaska. And to think at the beginning of the summer, I was just looking forward to seeing the exposition. I had no idea God was including all these other wonderful things."

"Neither did I. It's been a series of ups and downs, heartbreak and hope, but here we are. I'm blessed beyond my ability to even comprehend."

"I know we need to get back to work so we can get this manuscript off to your publishers, but I also need you to create a shopping list for me. I have no idea what I'll need for Alaska, but I have my savings for school that I can use for the things I'll need as your wife. I want to be as wise with those funds as I can be, so if you'll tell me what to purchase, I'll do it."

"You'll definitely need warmer clothes, and we should pick up some household supplies. I was sharing Amelia and Wallace's house—they have a little room off the back where I sleep. Otherwise, I was so often out in the field that I used a tent and sleeping bag that the Athabaskans made for me.

The bag is fur lined and quite warm. I can get inside and tie it around me."

"We'll need to get them to make me one as well."

"Or make one big enough for two. Sharing body warmth is important in Alaska."

Eleanor blushed and lowered her head. "There's so much to learn."

Bill came to her and raised her chin. "It's going to be wonderful. I've never been so happy or looked more forward to the future."

"Neither have I." She gazed into his eyes for a long moment and sighed. "Come on, we have work to do."

"Yes, I know." He let her go but didn't move back. "I just want to be near you all of the time. You've been uppermost in my thoughts since I first met you. Even with all the problems I had with Wallace and then learning Amelia is alive and dealing with Grady Masterson, you were the first person I thought of when I woke up and the last on my mind when I fell asleep."

"It's the same for me, and I have no doubt it always will be."

"So you have no doubts about this despite knowing each other such a short time?"

"None." She smiled and moved away to the table. Looking back over her shoulder, she added, "I've known from the start that we belong together. I was just waiting for you to know it too. Now come on. I need to get to typing."

Bill watched her settle in at the desk and roll paper into the typewriter. She was so perfect for him. She would keep him focused and on task, yet she knew the value of enjoying herself as she performed her duties. Most of all, she shared his faith, and he knew they would be as iron sharpening iron as they studied the Bible and botany. She would learn very fast. She was smart and passionate.

He sat down and opened the case with his charcoal pencils. There were only a few more drawings to make. He pulled out one of the ruined pages. The picture wasn't all that good, but his memory served him well, and he began to redraw the image of Eskimo potato, or *Hedysarum alpinum*. The Iñupiaq called it masu, and while the seeds could be deadly, the roots were quite good. They tasted more like carrots than potatoes and could be eaten raw, boiled, baked, or fried up in grease.

Bill traced the long stems, then started the cascade of flowers starting at the top and coming down. The blossoms were a beautiful shade of pink, and he wished he could somehow portray that color. Even Eleanor's camera, with its black-and-white film, would never be able to do justice to the beautiful color.

He glanced across the table to where Eleanor's steady typing came out in sort of a rhythmic song. She was good at what she did. Good at most everything she put her hand and mind to, as far as he could see.

Without missing a beat, she spoke. "I'm not going to be able to work if you keep looking at me that way."

He chuckled and refocused on the drawing. "Sorry. I couldn't help myself."

Later that night after Bill returned home, he kept thinking of how it was all official now. He was engaged to Eleanor Bennett and would be married in a very short time. He glanced around the small apartment he shared with his brother. He certainly didn't have much to offer a wife.

"I thought I heard you come in," his brother said, coming from the bedroom.

"Yes, it's just me." Bill tossed his suit coat over the back of a nearby chair. "Congratulate me. I'm officially an engaged man."

Wallace smiled. "So you finally proposed."

"I did, and she accepted. I was just standing here thinking, however, that I have very little to offer her."

"You have more than you know. I think you're both going to be very happy. She seems perfect for you. I'm sorry that I said things to suggest you should forget about marriage."

"Given the circumstances, I completely understood. I'm just so eager to see it through and start our new life in Alaska. She's excited about it too."

"Do you have any apprehension about the ship ride to get there?"

Bill looked at his brother and frowned. "Do you?"

He sighed. "A little. I have to admit when I think of all that could go wrong . . . well, it's more than I like to imagine."

"You know, through all of this, you and I haven't spent time in prayer together as we used to," Bill said, taking a seat at the table. "I know it's late, but I think we ought to pray right now. Don't you?"

Wallace nodded and joined him at the table. "I should have suggested it myself."

⋯

Eleanor picked up around the cottage and thought of what her life in Alaska would be. Bill had talked of living in tents during his summer months of research. He hoped they would have time once they arrived to use the tents and camp before the snows came. The very idea intrigued her.

He had described his living arrangements with Wallace and Amelia in the Athabaskan dome houses that were covered with skins and then the log cabin where they stayed in the winter months.

He had also talked of the nomadic native people and how he liked traveling with them. He had told her this long before proposing, and Eleanor had thought at the time that she'd better buy herself a couple of pairs of sturdy walking boots and plenty of wool stockings. Now her mind was a whirl with thoughts of what she would need and whether or not she'd have enough money to buy it all.

She finished with her cleaning, being very quiet so as not to awaken Mary and Bertha. The two had already gone to bed, and while Eleanor knew she ought to do so as well, she really just wanted to talk and tell someone of her engagement.

Taking up pen and paper, she wrote a letter to her parents and told them. It wasn't the two-way conversation she longed for, but it was something.

She spoke in a barely audible voice as she wrote. "I hope you have been preparing for your trip here, as I need you both to come right away. I'm going to send this letter special delivery so that it reaches you faster. We plan to leave for Alaska as soon as we are married, which will be totally dependent upon how quickly you can get here.

"They still haven't found Amelia but feel confident that she will take the baby and go back to their home in Alaska. It's such a joy to know that I had a part in this still-awaited reunion. To imagine her going through life not knowing that

202

her beloved husband is alive—and for him to suffer believing she was dead—is just too awful to think of."

Eleanor still had trouble comprehending that anyone could be as evil and devious as Grady Masterson. She'd known some mean people in her short life, but he was clearly the worst of all.

She looked back to the letter and wrote of how much she missed them both, then added her love and signed it. She would mail it tomorrow from the expo. Glancing toward the bedroom that she had to herself, Eleanor sighed. Why couldn't Mary or Bertha or both be awake so she could share her news?

She dressed for bed and thought again of the life she'd have in Alaska. She imagined her room as a tent and the blankets as a fur-lined sleeping bag that she would share with her husband. A shiver went up her spine. Why did it seem like it was taking forever before they could start their new life together?

"You've only known each other a month. It hasn't taken forever," she chided herself in a whisper.

Still, it didn't matter. She wanted time to speed up and for her wedding to take place and for them to be on the ship bound for Alaska. She wanted to be in the village or in the wilderness sleeping in a tent. But most of all she wanted to be in Bill's arms. Safe and happy.

She didn't remember falling asleep, but when she awoke the next morning, it was already late. She hadn't thought to leave a note and have the girls wake her when they got up. Eleanor hurried to bathe and dress, hoping Bill wouldn't be worried as to why she wasn't at the history building yet.

When she finally arrived at the room where they worked,

she found the place quite deserted. Sunlight filtered in from the large windows across the room. There were rows of bookcases against the far wall and file cabinets tucked at the end of these. Two large tables with plenty of chairs took up the middle of the room with a set of four desks positioned along the windows. Being the only person there made it seem all the bigger.

It dawned on her that it was Saturday, and most of the faculty and staff would be at home enjoying their day off. Eleanor longed for a day off but knew that would come soon enough. She got right to work and was into her fourth page by the time Bill showed up.

"Good morning, my dear." He came to where she was typing and gently pulled her up and into his arms. Wrapping her close, he kissed her, then just held her for a long moment.

Eleanor was unused to such affection and attention but found that she longed for it. It was what had been absent in her life all along. Yet how could a person so desire something they'd never even known was missing?

"You look quite lovely this morning."

She laughed. "I look the same as I always do. You just see me differently."

"Through the eyes of love, I finally have full sight. Perhaps a person is rather dim-sighted until they find the one person who completes them."

"Perhaps." She motioned to the table. "I think you'll be pleased. I proofed and corrected everything from yesterday and have already typed another four pages. At this rate, I think I'll be done by Monday or Tuesday at the latest."

"That's perfect. I was studying the shipping schedules.

There's a ship sailing for Seward on the twenty-third. That's a Monday. What do you think?"

"It sounds fine so long as my parents can get up here and we can be married before that. I think I'd better change my letter to a telegram to make sure they have as much time as possible to make their plans."

"It gives us a little while. Not much time, but surely enough."

Eleanor nodded and reclaimed her seat. "It's all happening so fast, but you know what? I've always liked it like that. Full steam—running not walking. I suppose you should know that about me now rather than wait to learn it after we're married."

"I already know that about you and love it." He pulled off his jacket, then looked at Eleanor. "Do you mind?" He held up the coat.

"Not at all. I can't imagine that you run around in a suit and tie while studying plants in Alaska."

"No, that's true, and you should also know that I don't particularly care for dressing up."

"Noted." She grinned. "I can't say as I blame you. My father never cared for it either. Kansas is very humid, and layers of clothes just make you sweat."

He put the jacket on the back of his chair, then went to the file cabinet to retrieve his drawing supplies.

"You should probably know that I don't care much for fancy dress either," Eleanor added. "I prefer simple clothes like I've worn here. A skirt and blouse suit me far better than grand gowns with lace and beading."

"Noted. How do you think you might feel about animal-skin trousers? Winter is very cold in Alaska, and the women wear such things. You will be much warmer with them. Amelia wore them under her skirts in the early years, but over time she chose to dress as the Athabaskans do. You will probably prefer that as well."

Eleanor rolled a sheet of paper into the typewriter. "Noted."

He laughed. "I suppose we shall have to have many conversations like this."

"There will be time." Eleanor smiled. "We'll have the rest of our lives, after all."

⊷❧

Amelia had just checked on Wally when a knock sounded at the door. Helga was at the house cleaning and made her way to see who had come. Amelia joined her in the living room and was pleased when it turned out to be Pastor Harris.

"I wanted to stop by and let you know what I accomplished," he said, coming into the cottage.

Amelia welcomed him in. "Do sit down. Would you like some lemonade? Helga made some this morning after getting fresh lemons at the market. It's the best I've ever had."

"I'd love a glass."

Helga smiled and proceeded to the kitchen. Amelia took a seat in the rocking chair, which had become her favorite place to sit.

Pastor Harris chose the couch and reached forward with a couple of receipts. "I arranged everything, and the shop owners were happy to crate the supplies and have them standing by for delivery to the ship when you arrange passage. We have only to get word to them."

"Wonderful." She glanced at the handwritten receipts. "Did they have everything on my list?"

"They did. Your list made it quite easy for all of us."

"I'm glad. I suppose after nine years in Alaska, I've become quite familiar with what is useful and what isn't."

"Did you look over the shipping schedule?"

Amelia nodded. "I did. There are several possibilities. However, the baby is still getting over his summer cold, so I'm not going to rush to leave. As much as I'd like to be on my way, I won't impose that on the little guy. He's already so miserable with his stuffy nose."

"I'm sure it will pass soon enough. I think you're wise, however, to wait. It will be to your benefit as much as anyone's."

Helga returned with the drinks, and Pastor Harris was quick to sample the lemonade. He beamed her a smile after just one swallow. "This is delicious. I don't know what all you did to put it together, but it's perfect."

"Thank you. The secret is in the freshness of the fruit." She handed Amelia her glass. "If you don't mind, I'll be out back taking in the wash."

Amelia nodded. "I'll get the irons heated up."

"It's kind of warm to be ironing, isn't it?" Pastor Harris asked.

Amelia shrugged. "It has to be done, and I don't want to wait until late. Tomorrow is church, and I want to be well rested. Of course, if Wally isn't feeling good, then I'll probably stay home, but hopefully we'll both be able to attend."

"If not, I can always fill you in on the details of the sermon." He gave her a smile, then took a long drink.

Amelia sampled the drink and found it just as delicious as she'd expected. She enjoyed having Helga around and found she considerably lightened the load. Just having another woman to talk to about Wally's needs was beneficial. And Helga had such wonderful knowledge after years of working as a nanny. Amelia had always imagined how nice it would have been if Bill had married. Then she'd have a sister, and they could work together on various household projects. She imagined it all with great joy, even though it was never to be.

Another knock sounded at the front door, and this time Amelia rose to answer it. "Mrs. Harris, please come in."

"I thought you were going to call me Joanna," the woman chided and shifted the basket she carried.

"Yes, forgive me, Joanna." Amelia smiled and nodded to where the pastor sat. "He just brought me news of my supplies."

"I know. He popped into the house momentarily before coming here. I was just pulling out the last of the cookies I'd been baking. I wanted to bring you some of those and a loaf of bread as well. I've been quite busy." She extended the basket as she took a seat beside her husband.

Amelia took the basket and peeked inside. "Oh, how wonderful. We'll enjoy these."

"I hope you do."

"There's no doubt about it." Amelia looked up. "Would you like some lemonade? Helga made it fresh."

"No. I just wanted to come give you these things and to encourage my husband to get the lawn mowed. We don't want the congregants talking about us being bad caretakers of God's property."

Pastor Harris laughed and got to his feet. "She's right, as always."

Joanna stood as well. "I know you're anxious to be home. Have you decided on your ship yet and when you will depart?"

"Not yet. I was just explaining to Pastor Harris that Wally's summer cold has made him quite miserable. I want to wait until he's feeling better. The trip is a long one and will be hard enough on him, especially after we reach Alaska. There are a great many miles between Seward and our village on the Susitna River. It won't be easy for him—or me."

"That's very wise, my dear. Besides, it won't hurt to delay a few days or even a week or more. He will be well soon, and it will give you both a chance to get plenty of good food and rest."

"Yes." Amelia said nothing more. She didn't think they understood how hard it was to wait. How hard it was to live in Seattle without Wallace and Bill. Life would never be the same, but it would be most comforting in Alaska. There she would feel at home and know her surroundings and what was expected of her.

The only problem was that Wallace wouldn't be there.

17

You should get an advertisement in the newspaper right away for a roommate," Eleanor told Rosemary Sunday evening. She had decided to spend the night with her dear friend since the time was short, and soon Eleanor would be bound for Alaska.

Rosemary looked quite sad at her suggestion. "I don't want another roommate. I want you to stay."

"Even if I stayed, I couldn't be here with you because I'd be married to Bill. We could hardly all live together then." She smiled. "Maybe you can find someone at your offices. Someone who likes working inside instead of outside like me."

"Oh bother, I never really cared about that."

"I'm glad. Say, I have a favor to ask. Do you suppose you could take some time over lunch tomorrow and help me figure out something to wear for my wedding?"

"Oh yes, I'd love to." Rosemary clapped her hands. "Oh, that would be grand. There are several stores nearby that we could go to. I'll even ask to take the afternoon off. I know my boss will understand." She barely paused for breath. "You should wear blue. It makes your eyes look wonderful."

"I don't know about being able to shop all afternoon. I do have to work on the manuscript, but it's nearly done. I'm so excited for Bill to send it to the publisher. He said they are looking forward to publishing it. Just imagine, Rosemary. A book with William Reed as the author."

"I will definitely buy a copy," she promised. "We'd best get to bed. It's quite late, and we'll need our strength tomorrow for shopping."

"You're right, of course." Eleanor thought about what kind of gown she would look for. "Blue, eh?"

Rosemary nodded. "It's really your very best color."

In the morning, Eleanor stretched and yawned. She heard Rosemary moving around and decided to get up and see her off. Rosemary was just pinning her hat in place when Eleanor came out of the bedroom.

"Don't you look nice." Eleanor had always liked Rosemary's yellow sprig muslin dress with the white tulle ruching on the bodice.

"Thank you. It's one of my favorites, and this hat matches so nicely."

The wide-brim straw hat was a good choice, especially with the little white rosettes trimming the band. Eleanor would miss Rosemary's bevy of hats and her stacks of hatboxes in the bedroom.

"I'll be waiting just outside of the building at noon," Rosemary continued. "Don't be late, just in case I can't get the afternoon off."

"I won't be late."

Rosemary turned. "Is my hat on straight?"

"It is. Is that a new hat?" Eleanor asked.

Her friend smiled. "It is. I had to have something new for

the wedding. Depending on the gown you choose, I thought I might even wear this dress. If not, I have my other yellow gown, and the hat will work for that one as well."

Eleanor laughed. They'd come to be such good friends in just a few months. Funny how no one thought that friendship was uncomfortably fast. Rosemary had been full of rules and regulations when Eleanor had answered her advertisement for a roommate, but Eleanor had liked her no-nonsense style. And with her own discernment to guide her, Eleanor had felt quite comfortable agreeing to share an apartment with very little privacy. And as usual, her ability to make quick judgments about people hadn't failed her. Rosemary had been a real peach of a friend.

Rosemary hadn't been gone but twenty minutes when a knock sounded at the door. Eleanor went to answer and found a telegram delivery boy.

"Telegram for Miss Eleanor Bennett," he announced.

"I'm Eleanor Bennett." Eleanor took the offered telegram. "Oh, wait just a minute." She went and got a few pennies and handed them to the boy. He tipped his cap and went down the hall toward the front of the building.

Eleanor closed the door and opened the telegram. It was from her parents.

```
Will arrive on train on twentieth. Do not
proceed without us. Father.
```

Eleanor couldn't help giggling. They would be here Friday. They were taking the express train. No doubt they were as delighted about Eleanor's good fortune as she was. This was such wonderful news. She glanced at the clock. If she hurried, she could go to the expo and meet up with Bill and let him know. He'd be so excited to finally have a date for when they'd arrive.

She found Bill in the Alaska building just as he was about to start his second tour at ten o'clock. He was surprised to see her, but when she shared the news of her father's telegram, he was just as delighted as she'd known he'd be.

"That's wonderful. We can be married after church on Sunday and catch the ship to Seward on Monday. Will that work for you, Miss Bennett?" He took hold of her hands.

"I believe it will." She laughed. "Have you already spoken to your pastor? I could talk to mine, if not. I don't know him very well, but I'm sure a wedding is a wedding."

"I've already taken care of everything. I have him just waiting to get the final date. I'll send word to him today."

"Oh, Bill, I'm so very happy."

"As am I." He leaned forward and kissed her. "But for now, I must give a tour."

"I'll be shopping this afternoon with Rosemary. It seems I'm going to need a wedding dress. Nothing too elaborate since I'm headed for the wilds of Alaska."

"No doubt you'll look lovely no matter what you choose." He reached into his coat pocket and withdrew his wallet. "Let me give you some money."

She shook her head. "I have enough, and I still need to get some of the other things you suggested. Never fear, you'll have plenty of opportunities in the future to spend your money on me."

He chuckled and kissed her again. "I'll see you later this afternoon."

"If I get my shopping done. I might have to spend the rest

of the day shopping. You know how much I love it." She winked and headed for the exit.

She stopped by the photography shop on her way to catch the trolley. She was happy to find Addie Hanson there looking quite fit. She'd had her cast removed and was bouncing around the place like her old self.

"Oh, I'm glad to see you, Eleanor. I was going to come by the history building later. Can you please come to the shop around five?"

"I suppose so. I'll just take a break from typing. Although, I'm hoping I can finish it all by then, if shopping doesn't take too long. I don't have a lot left. And that's a good thing because my parents sent a telegram saying they'll be here Friday. I simply have to finish with my shopping and packing. Bill plans for us to marry Sunday after church."

"That's exciting. Please make sure you furnish us all with the news of the time and place. We want to be there to celebrate your big day."

A customer came into the shop and began browsing the room. Eleanor smiled and gave a nod toward the woman. "I will, and I'll be here at five."

"Good, don't be late. We're having a meeting." Addie went to greet the customer.

Eleanor didn't know why they'd want her at the meeting since she wasn't working for the Fishers anymore, but she said nothing. She supposed it would all become clear at the meeting.

She noted the time and hurried for the trolley. It was turning out to be a very busy day.

She met Rosemary at noon but found her in a foul mood.

Apparently, there was some special project going on, and they couldn't spare Rosemary for the afternoon.

"I never ask for anything. Never. Not once have I even asked for time off to go see my mother. You'd think a few hours would be acceptable."

"It's all right," Eleanor said, trying to comfort her friend. "We'll look at the closest stores, and if we find nothing, we can try another time. You know I'm not a fan of shopping, so I usually find something right away. Oh, my parents telegraphed to say they'll arrive on Friday, so we're set to be married Sunday and leave for Seward on Monday like we planned."

Rosemary's frown deepened. "But that's just days away. You can hardly plan a wedding in that short time."

"We're having a very simple ceremony and no reception. It doesn't require much in the way of planning. We just need to make sure the folks we want to be there know about it."

"Oh, I can't believe this has happened so fast. I thought you'd be here for a long time. I was looking forward to you attending college and telling me all about it. I am going to be so lonely without you," Rosemary said, tearing up.

"Now, now, don't go getting all emotional on me. We have a very short time to look for my dress."

Thankfully, they found an appropriate gown in the very first store. It was simple yet flattering—and blue.

"Durable is more important for Alaska than fashionable." Eleanor looked over every inch of the pale blue dress. She wasn't sure she'd ever have a reason to wear it in Alaska but perhaps on the boat trip north.

"Would you care to try it on so that we can see if it needs alterations?" a matronly store clerk asked.

"I suppose that would be wise," Eleanor replied. "Do you have time?" She looked to Rosemary.

"If you hurry. I'll need to get back in ten minutes."

"I feel bad because you won't have any lunch." Eleanor found the woman had already gathered the gown and was headed for a back room. "I'll make it up to you somehow." She hurried after the woman.

"Come right in here," the woman said. "Disrobe and we will see how closely this fits."

Eleanor wasted no time. She wanted Rosemary's opinion and knew she couldn't wait around. The clerk quickly helped slide the gown over Eleanor's long-line corset and Nainsook chemise.

"It is a good fit. Not too snug across the bodice nor too tight in the waist," the older woman said as she did up the back buttons.

Eleanor studied herself in the full-length mirror to the side of where she stood. The blue dress was really very simple. Long sleeves, high, unembellished neckline, and a straight, rather shapeless form, except for some pleating at the midway point.

Once the buttons were done up the back, the clerk turned Eleanor and drew a pretty beaded belt around the center and hooked it in the front. When Eleanor looked again in the mirror, she found the dress no longer without form. The little belt made all the difference in the world.

"Why, this is charming."

The clerk smiled. "It needs no alterations. Even the length is perfect."

Eleanor looked down and could see she was right. "I must show my friend."

She walked back to where she'd left Rosemary. "What do you think?"

Rosemary turned and gave her friend a quick appraisal. "It wants for a nice hat to cover up all those red curls."

The clerk nodded and went to the far end of the store, where millinery goods were displayed.

Eleanor turned one way and then the other. "I really like this. And the cotton voile will be easy to care for."

"It won't be suited to cold weather," Rosemary said, sounding apprehensive. "Goodness, what will you do for warmth up there?"

Eleanor laughed. "Bill had some rather intriguing ideas. He has a sleeping bag lined with fur, and he said his sister-in-law often wore animal-skin trousers under her skirts. But I could save this dress for warm days. You know they do have hot days in Alaska. It's not all snow and ice. Bill told me sometimes the heat can be quite a misery."

"Here we are," the clerk said, holding a fashionably large hat with plumage and large rosettes. On the side rested a white dove. Eleanor hoped it wasn't an actual bird that had been stuffed.

Eleanor tried it on and shook her head. "It isn't at all what I had in mind. I'd like something smaller."

The clerk took the hat and left once again. In a few moments, she was back with another wide-brimmed hat. This one, however, was of a less adorned nature. The straw had been tightly woven and painted white. Around the center of the band was a white ribbon with a small arrangement of blue and white flowers.

She tried on the hat and found Rosemary nodding most enthusiastically. "It's perfect," her friend declared.

"Let me go back and see it all in the mirror," Eleanor said, moving toward the dressing room. She lined up in front of the mirror. "Yes, I like this very much."

"Oh bother, I have to go back to work." Rosemary came forward and surprised Eleanor by kissing her cheek. "You look quite lovely. You'll be the perfect bride in this."

Eleanor smiled. "I think you're right." She turned to the clerk. "I'll take it."

Rosemary was long gone by the time Eleanor dressed and went to pay for her purchases. To her surprise, the price the clerk requested was quite low.

"Did you include the cost of the hat?"

"Oh, your friend paid for that. She said it was a wedding gift to you."

Eleanor shook her head. That would mean Rosemary would have to do without a new hat for a while. She was such a dear friend. Perhaps Eleanor would leave the hat with her when she headed north. After all, she couldn't imagine such a fancy hat being much use in Alaska.

Eleanor paid for the gown and waited while everything was nicely boxed. Leaving the store, Eleanor felt like she had accomplished quite a bit in a very short time. It was just the way she liked to shop.

Sunday she would be married. It was so difficult to accept the truth of it. Eleanor didn't mind things moving at a fast pace, but it did leave very little time to get used to the idea. Still, all of her life she had wanted to fall in love and marry. When she'd been younger, she'd figured her husband would be a photographer like her father, but to wind up with a botanist was even better. She could just imagine the fun she'd have learning all the new plants and flowers. To work at her husband's side was something she'd always seen herself doing. Where her friends had spoken of caring for children and grand homes, Eleanor had always thought of working with her mate at some business.

She picked up her pace, knowing she needed to get back to the university to work on the manuscript, but her thoughts were still on Sunday. She was going to become William Reed's wife. The wonder of it all was almost too much. She'd fallen in love so fast, yet it was real and it was right. She had no doubts about that.

Still, becoming a wife was a daunting thought. Eleanor had scarcely had time to think of it. She'd never really had a suitor before. There had been boys back home in Kansas who showed her interest, but none that ever appealed to her. Now she had Bill, and he was more than appealing. He was quickly becoming her entire world. How she loved him.

She sighed as she reached the apartment. She was happier than she'd ever been.

Eleanor focused on the typing at hand. It wouldn't take long to finish what was left of the manuscript. She glanced at the clock and saw that it was very close to five.

"I need to go, but I'll be back. I promised Addie Hanson I'd come for some sort of meeting at the photography shop, even though I don't know why they'd want me there."

"Could be they want to share some news about the camera. Or maybe there's a brand-new camera available." He helped her to her feet. "Just hurry back when you can. I should still be here. I have one more drawing to complete."

She nodded. "And I have about four or five pages left to type. It won't take me even an hour."

Bill smiled and pulled her into his arms. "We're nearly done. And all thanks to you."

"It's your book, and you're the one who will get all of the credit." She smiled. "I look forward to the day when I can hold the finished product in my hand. Even Rosemary plans to buy a copy."

He laughed and hugged her close. "Then we know at least one copy will be purchased."

Eleanor stretched up and kissed him. "I know a great many copies will be purchased. It's going to be a huge success because people are going to be fascinated by Alaska. After all, it's not like you can easily go there on a whim. No, your book will entice people to travel and see it for themselves. I know it will."

Bill kissed her again and let her go. "You know, I'm getting much too at ease with having you in my arms. Sunday can't get here soon enough."

Eleanor nodded. "I agree."

Hurrying along the Pay Streak, Eleanor made her way through the happy expo crowds. The place was full to capacity with people. The shops and exhibits were closing for the evening, and the band concerts and plays were soon to begin. Being suppertime, most of the folks were interested in food. The population seemed to be navigating toward the many restaurants, and Eleanor noted long lines at the YMCA's eatery. She smiled, remembering how she and Bill were going to share their dinners together. They'd hardly had a chance to do that at all.

We'll have the rest of our lives to share our meals, she

chided herself in silence. There was so much more to look forward to than to regret. She prayed it would always be that way.

She hurried to the Fishers' shop and had barely stepped through the door when she heard a loud explosion of voices.

"Surprise!"

She looked around and found that all of the Camera Girls as well as Mrs. Fisher and Addie were in attendance. On the countertop, the cameras and accessories had been replaced with packages of every shape and size.

"What's this?" she asked, looking from person to person.

"Your bridal shower," Addie announced. "I hope you don't mind, but I encouraged the girls to buy the things you'd need for Alaska."

Eleanor laughed. "What a wonderful idea."

"We have a special seat for you right over here, and Pearl arranged for there to be a cake." Addie pointed Eleanor to the chair. "So take your seat, and we'll get right to this because we know you are still working to complete that manuscript."

"We plan to finish tonight. I had hoped to see you and thank you for allowing me to use your cottage. I won't need it after this."

"It was my pleasure, and Mary and Bertha liked it so much they've asked to rent it full time—at least until after the expo."

"I like the convenience of getting up in the morning and having such a short way to come to work," Bertha said. "It surely beats having to walk to the trolley, then ride here, and then walk some more."

"I agree," Mary replied.

"I'm so glad it worked out this way." Eleanor took her chair and smiled at the circle of ladies. "I'm so blessed."

One by one the girls began bringing her their gifts. Eleanor was quite delighted with what she found. Addie had done a wonderful job of helping them to know what to purchase, from a quality set of knives that several of the girls went in together to purchase, to warm woolen stockings and gloves, to blankets and towels. Pearl had put together a wooden box of various medicines and items they might need to deal with injuries, including a suturing needle and doctor's thread, scissors, and a variety of bandages.

"This is a wonderful gift," Eleanor said, noting each item in the box. "I'm sure there will be times when this will be very needed, but I hope and pray not too soon."

"This is from me," Addie said, putting a large brown-paper-wrapped package in front of Eleanor. "You needn't unwrap it—it's better left this way. It's twenty yards of mosquito netting. You'll be happy for it, especially when you're camping out in the wilds."

"Twenty yards! Will I ever need that much?" Eleanor asked.

"Believe me, you'll be writing to have more shipped up. You can't have too much."

Perhaps the most treasured of gifts was given by May Parker. The artist had purchased a sturdy metal lantern and painted the outside in a variety of flowers, including the types Eleanor had taken photographs of on her explorations.

"Oh, May, this is wonderful. Look how pretty it is." She held it up to show the others. Everyone agreed it was a work of art.

Eleanor was so touched by the gifts, especially given that

she'd only been here since June, and none of the women knew her all that well.

"I'm very grateful for these presents. I know I shall be blessed to have them."

"Mr. Fisher has a present for you as well," Mrs. Fisher announced. "He's gifting you a camera and film. I know you planned to purchase one, but we were so delighted with how hard you worked while you were with us. You sold more cameras than anyone in that short time. It seemed only right that you should get something for your efforts besides commission."

Tears blurred Eleanor's vision. "I don't know what to say. You have all been so kind." She looked at all the wonderful stuff. "I don't know how I'll ever get it home."

"We're taken care of that too," Addie declared. "Isaac will come with the carriage. In fact, I'm surprised he's not here yet. We will take the things back to our house, and I'll see to it that they are appropriately crated for you. Then we'll see them delivered to the dock. You won't have to worry about a thing."

"Thank you. Thank you so much." Eleanor reached into her pocket for her handkerchief. She dabbed at her eyes and sniffed. "You are all so very kind." Addie came and hugged her, bringing even more tears. "My folks arrive on Friday, and Bill has arranged the wedding after church on Sunday. You're all invited, of course. It will be quite simple, and there won't be a reception or wedding breakfast. Still, I hope you'll come."

"I'll be there for certain," Addie declared.

"Me too," Mary and Bertha said in unison, while Mrs. Fisher simply nodded.

When Eleanor returned to Bill not long afterward, she told him all about their generosity and the love they had shown her. "I never expected such things."

"How smart for Mrs. Hanson to have planned such a party with things you'd need for the north. That was pure brilliance."

"I thought so too. It trims down my list considerably." She smiled and shook her head. "Especially where mosquito netting is concerned. She gave us twenty yards."

"That will definitely come in handy."

Eleanor smiled. "I'm so very blessed. None of them have known me for long at all, and yet they treat me like family. I will miss them."

She got right to work on the typing, and it wasn't long before she was typing *The End* on the final page. She proofed the page and then looked up with a smile. "All done. Your manuscript is complete, Mr. Reed."

He laughed and held up his drawing. "Indeed, it is. This is the final picture."

Eleanor sat back and shook her head. "It's truly and finally done. Now you can mail it off. I'm so excited."

"As am I. You'll also be happy to learn this bit of news. I was much too caught up to share it earlier, but I received word from the publisher that they'd like to contract my medicinal herbs and plants book. They sent me an advancement and a contract. We'll go into our married life with a cushion and a position."

Eleanor squealed and jumped to her feet. She rushed to where Bill sat and hugged him over and over. It seemed quite natural for him to pull her onto his lap and wrap her in his arms.

"We're going to be the happiest of couples," he whispered against her ear.

"I know we will," she replied with a sigh. "It can never be said we weren't meant for each other. We're perfectly suited, and no one could possibly deny that."

18

Grady Masterson had taken back his job with the city trash collections until he could figure out what to do. He hated the smelly and laborious job, but at least he didn't have to do much thinking on the task itself. Instead, he was caught up in plans to complete his revenge on Wallace and William Reed.

Walking home from work, he posed a question. "What do you think I should do, Avery?" He looked at the man walking beside him.

"*Kill 'em,*" Avery replied.

Grady nodded. Of late, Avery had appeared at important moments to guide and encourage. Grady didn't question it. "I suppose that is the only real way to even the score. They took you from me, and now I'll take them both from Amelia. Maybe then she'll see how much she needs me and not that frozen nightmare up north."

Avery smiled. *"She'll see. She'll go willingly with you and give you all of her money."*

Grady nodded. He was glad Avery had been coming around to advise him. The madness that was overtaking his mind wasn't yet complete, but with each conversation Grady held with his brother, he seemed a little closer to the precipice of insanity. Strangely enough, he didn't avoid it or dread it. Instead, it rather comforted him. Avery had always been the one with the brains. Avery had known exactly what they needed to do and when. Things would have been fine if not for the interference of Wallace Reed.

"We just need to get rid of Reed. And his brother. Maybe even that baby. End the entire Reed line and be done with it."

"Now you're thinking," Avery said with a grin.

"It's easier to do when I have your help."

Grady turned his focus back on the road. A part of him knew that Avery wasn't really there, but another part was just as certain that he was. He could feel a part of his mind slipping away, but it really didn't matter. Having his brother back was worth the price of his sanity, just as killing Wallace and William Reed would be worth any price the world might mete out. He just had to figure out how to accomplish it.

"Didn't you say that old woman told them where to find Amelia?" Avery asked. *"She's been a thorn in our side since coming here. Maybe she can tell us what we need to know, and then she can die too."*

Grady nodded. "Never liked that old woman. She always treated me like I wasn't as good as her."

"She thinks you're a lowlife, especially after Amelia told her you were making her say you were her brother. She no doubt thinks you're a criminal type. You might as well show her you can be just that. She deserves your wrath."

"She does," Grady agreed. "She was always sticking her nose where it didn't belong, and she's the one who suggested to Amelia that she go out to the exposition. That started all this. Amelia went to the fair and then came home with all sorts of grand ideas of not needing my help."

"*Yeah, it was that Becker woman's fault for sure.*"

Grady nodded and kept walking. "Yeah, for sure."

"*Maybe we should just go ahead and make our way over to her place. We can always beat the truth out of her.*"

Grady knew Avery had hit upon the answer. "I think you're right, Avery. It's time to force the truth out of that old woman."

Eleanor let out a squeal of joy at the sight of her parents disembarking the train. She ran to them and hugged them both at once. "Oh, I can hardly believe you're here. It's so good to see you again. I know I haven't been gone that long, but I've missed you."

She pulled back and let go of her hold on them. "How was the trip out? Mine was so interesting. I do love travel, and there was just so much to see that I'd never seen before. How do you feel?"

"We're just fine, Eleanor," her mother replied. "Goodness, but you are quite excited."

"Oh, I am. I'm so happy to have you here and to be marrying the man I love. You're both going to love Bill. He couldn't be here with me to meet the train, as he's working. I think I told you he is giving tours at the exposition. He's able to tell people firsthand about Alaska. Oh, and of course there's the manuscript. I told you how we were remaking it. We finished a few nights ago, and Bill was able to mail it off to the publisher. It's all just too wonderful. God has so thoroughly blessed me."

Her parents exchanged a look, but it was her father who spoke. "Perhaps we should arrange for our things and save further discussion for the hotel."

"I'm sure you're tired," Eleanor said, calming a bit. She hadn't meant to be thoughtless of their condition. "Look, there's a man with a cart."

Her father signaled the man and gave him a ticket. "We have two trunks. Please retrieve them." The man took the claim ticket and nodded.

As he disappeared into the crowd, Eleanor couldn't help herself. "I got you a very nice room at a hotel they built just for the exposition. It's called the Sorrento, and it's very nice and comes highly recommended. I think you'll really like it. The city has gone all out for the exposition. I was amazed at all the transportation that's available. There are trolleys leaving all the time for the exposition, as well as special cabs if you prefer something private. But they were particularly concerned about housing the folks who would come. I think the Sorrento was the best choice."

Her father set down the small suitcase he'd been carrying. "I'm sure it will be fine, Eleanor. You know that we don't need much to satisfy our needs. We've never been fancy folks."

"Of course not. I just wanted you to have a nice place to stay while you were here. Seattle is full to overbrimming. There are thousands and thousands of people coming for the AYP. That's what we call the expo. I do hope you get to visit. It's quite amazing, and the exhibits are beyond the imagination. They've recreated an Eskimo village, and even a village styled after those in the Philippines. There are all sorts of buildings where you can go and learn about different places. There's a Japanese exhibit. Oh, it just goes on and on.

"I've had so much fun taking pictures of folks. Father, are you selling the new Brownie camera from Kodak? It's all the rage here at the fair. You really should take time to speak with Mr. Fisher about the profit margin. I think you could make quite a bit of money if you sold them at home." She smiled. "Oh, I'm just so happy you're here."

It wasn't long until the trunks were found, and the man arranged a cab to take them to the Sorrento Hotel. Once the trunks were loaded, the driver helped Eleanor's mother and father into the carriage while Eleanor tipped the baggageman. She hurried to join her folks in the open carriage.

"I just know you'll enjoy the new hotel. People have been saying wonderful things about it. I was so excited to be able to get you a reservation there."

"You've already mentioned the hotel," her mother said, shaking her head. "I'm sure it will be fine. You must calm yourself."

"I know I keep repeating myself, but I want to make sure I tell you everything." Eleanor thought for a moment. "A special trolley comes to the hotel to pick folks up for the exposition. I really think you should try to see it before you leave. Oh! I never even thought to ask you when you were leaving. We'll have to make sure you can have the room for the full length of your stay."

Eleanor took the seat across from her parents and arranged her dark green skirt. The driver was quick to get them on their way, and something about the speed in which he drove caused laughter to bubble up from inside Eleanor. Life was just too good, and everything was so perfect.

"I was already happier than I thought possible, but having you here makes everything even better. Coming to Seattle was absolutely the best thing that ever happened to me. And I know that God has been in the middle of everything. I know He was the one who arranged for me to meet Bill. We just have so much in common, and while I know we've only known each other a short time, he's the perfect man for me. You'll see." She barely drew a breath before continuing. "My discernment hasn't failed me. Just as I knew Rosemary was the perfect roommate—and she has been—I know that Bill and I are destined to be man and wife.

"Oh, and you won't have to do a thing. Bill has arranged everything. We'll be married Sunday after church and then board the ship for Seward, Alaska, the very next day." She glanced out at the passing traffic.

"No, you won't," her father said in a firm voice.

Eleanor immediately sobered and turned to face him. "What?"

Her father exchanged a look with her mother. "I said, no, you won't."

"I don't understand. Everything is already planned out." It dawned on her that they probably didn't understand the urgency of the situation. She smiled and relaxed back into the seat. "We sped things up because of Amelia. We think it's possible she's already gone ahead to Alaska. Amelia is Bill's sister-in-law, if you remember from my letter. Besides that, the weather is very unpredictable. They could have a cold snap blanket everything in snow by September. We need to get up there so that we can journey to the area where they live and minister. It's a considerable distance—over two hundred miles. We can take the train a little way north of Seward. I think Bill said it runs about sixty miles or so, but after that we'll be on foot and use mules to pack our supplies. If it snows, we'll use dog sleds. The weather is a strong consideration, and that's why the wedding is taking place on Sunday."

"We haven't made ourselves clear," her father said, shaking his head. "We aren't here to attend the wedding. We're here to stop it."

Amelia looked at the tickets in her hand and then raised her gaze to Pastor Harris and his wife. "Thank you. This makes it seem real now."

"We tried to find a ship that was leaving later in the month, but the twenty-third was the best choice. The only other means of transportation didn't have staterooms. It was more of a freighter than a passenger service, although it did offer both."

"I don't mind leaving on the twenty-third. I'm sure it will be just fine. Wally is feeling better, and Helga and I already discussed leaving sooner rather than later. I do so appreciate you managing this for me."

"It wasn't any trouble at all," the pastor assured her. "Your tickets entitle you to a large stateroom with every comfort and a smaller adjoining room for Helga. We even put in a request for a cradle, and they assured me it wouldn't be a problem. Oh, and of course, meals are included."

"That's wonderful. I'm sure to enjoy the luxury. There'll

be none of that once I reach Alaska." She smiled. "Not that I really mind. I have a lovely little house about two hundred and forty miles northwest of Seward. It's quite the trip."

"It sounds most arduous from what you described to me the other day," Joanna admitted.

"Yes, it isn't easy. That's for sure. It was awfully hard making it from our village to Seward with me expecting a baby. They arranged for me to ride in the sled part of the way and later on a donkey. It wasn't at all comfortable, and I feared I might go into labor at any moment given all the bouncing around."

Pastor Harris shook his head in amazement. "That's quite impressive. I can't imagine Joanna having to endure such a thing while being with child."

"No, you would never have seen me even attempt such a thing," the woman agreed. "I'm not meant for such difficulties. I would give it my best try, but I know my limitations."

"You might be surprised. Sometimes you can do amazing things," Amelia said, remembering her first encounter with Alaska. She hadn't believed herself capable of enduring the hardships, but God had other plans for her.

She smiled. "Now I'll be carrying a baby with me, but the Athabaskans have all sorts of ways to make that easier, and I know they'll help me." She looked at the tickets again. "So I shall make every effort to enjoy my luxuries while I have them."

"I know you have to go, but a part of me does wish you could stay longer," Joanna said with a sigh. "I've truly come to enjoy having you here. I love seeing the baby, and it's been wonderful to make things for you."

"And we've definitely appreciated it," Amelia replied. "I

have felt so cared for and loved. Since losing my husband, I've known nothing but sorrow, but here at least I knew I wasn't alone."

"And it had to be a relief to get away from that terrible man who wanted to force you to marry him." Joanna frowned. "To imagine such a thing just makes me angry."

"Well, it's behind her now, my dear." The pastor patted his wife's hand.

"Yes." Amelia thought very little of Grady these days. "Oh, Pastor Harris, would you be able to do me one more favor? I'll need someone to go to the stores where you purchased my supplies and let them know to have them delivered to the ship."

He nodded and gave her a smile. "Yes, I will handle that yet today. I just wanted to make sure the tickets were acceptable to you first."

"They are quite acceptable."

"I'll also make sure you have a ride to the ship on Monday," he added. "We can discuss when you might wish to leave later." He got to his feet. "For now, it's nearly lunchtime, and I'm half starved."

"You will come to the house and eat with us, won't you?" Joanna asked. "I have a casserole in the oven warmer and blackberry cobbler."

"Sounds wonderful. I'll let Helga know. She's out back hanging out diapers. She has been such a great help to me. I tried to talk her into staying with me in Alaska, but she figured it would be too difficult. I must agree it would probably be too much, but it would have been nice to have her with me. I'll miss her greatly."

"Well, just enjoy her along with the luxury stateroom,"

the pastor suggested. "Count your many blessings and relish them while you can. And just know this: God will always provide more."

Amelia nodded, but her thoughts went to Wallace and William. How she wished they were making this trip together. How she longed for them to still be among the blessings that she counted.

⚬❧⚬

Grady stood looking down at the dead woman's bloodied face. Mrs. Becker had been more than a little difficult to deal with, but he'd finally gotten her to talk about the Reed men. She'd had the audacity to accuse him of having hired them to begin with and scoffed when he asked where he might find them.

Eventually, the conversation came around his way, and the old woman remembered a card that William had given her. She retrieved it, nursing what Grady figured was a broken arm. He was fairly certain he'd heard the bone snap when he'd twisted it behind her.

"*You did a good job, Grady,*" his brother told him.

Grady looked up and found Avery smiling. Of late he'd come more often, and Grady found life more tolerable with his brother at his side. "I did what had to be done. If she'd cooperated with me, it might not have had to be so painful."

"*She didn't deserve an easy death,*" his brother declared. "*It wasn't right of her to keep that information from you regarding Amelia. I'm sure that she knew where the woman went.*"

"I am too, but she was bound and determined to protect

her. I don't think she would have ever said a word about Amelia, no matter how much pain I caused her."

"No, probably not," Avery agreed.

Grady looked at the card he'd taken from Mrs. Becker's bloodied hands. "Don't you think it's strange that she thought they were working for me yet she told them where Amelia had gone?"

"Maybe they just said that, Grady. You can't think she'd go through a beating like you dished out and just give the information without a fuss to men she thought were working for you."

"Yeah, it doesn't make sense." He looked at the card again, then tucked it in his trouser pocket. "But I know where this address is. It's not all that far. Let's go pay a visit to this place and see if we can pin down the Reed brothers."

19

Eleanor could hardly register her father's words. It was impossible to believe that her parents had come to Seattle to stop the wedding instead of celebrate it. What in the world did it all mean? How could they be against it?

At the Sorrento Hotel, the clerk checked them in and asked how long they'd be staying. Eleanor said nothing and let her parents handle the entire matter. She tried to figure out what she would say once they were in the privacy of the hotel room. She had to somehow convince them that their thoughts on her wedding were wrong. She had to appeal to them to rethink their thoughts on the matter.

What in the world had ever brought them to such a conclusion? Eleanor followed obediently as the bellboy directed them to their room. He opened the door for them, then handed her father the key and promised to return shortly with their trunks.

She watched as her father tipped the young man and then closed the door to the hotel room. Mother moved to the far side of the room and took off her gloves. Next, she unpinned her hat and removed it as well. It all seemed surreal, as if a dream.

Eleanor looked around the room and found it quite lovely. A little sitting area was arranged near the window, and it was here that she went. She thought about sitting but decided against it and began to pace.

Her father and mother joined her. They each took a seat, and Father began to speak. "You must understand, Eleanor, we were completely taken off guard when we received your letter declaring your intention to marry. You have only known this man a month. Can you think for just a moment what a shock this was to us?"

Eleanor slowed her pacing but continued to walk back and forth by the bed. "You don't know Bill, and you're making a false judgment of the situation."

"What do you expect us to do, Eleanor? You leave home for the first time, and we have barely adjusted to that when news comes that you intend to marry a man you hardly know and move to Alaska," her mother replied.

Eleanor stopped and faced her folks. "I know it seems impossibly fast. I agree. It wasn't what I was expecting. However, it is real, and it is what I believe God has brought me to. I've prayed about this and have complete peace about it."

"We too have prayed and do not have peace about it," her father said, shaking his head. "Not at all. It might, I suppose, be different if not for your plans to leave for Alaska. Perhaps if you and Bill returned to Salina where we could get to know him and learn of his character, then we might feel differently."

"You raised me to have good sense. I've always been a fair judge of character. You even told me you were impressed in the people I chose for friends. Before I left for Seattle, Father, you told Mother that my judgments regarding other people were particularly keen. That you trusted my abilities to see danger. Now I find a man whom I believe without any doubt is meant to be my husband and suddenly that trust in my ability to see a person for who they are is . . . gone."

"Yes, well, we women are easily deceived by our emotions. It's easy to get caught up in thoughts of romance and love, especially in a foreign setting," Mother said.

"Foreign setting? This is still America, and just because there is the excitement of the fair, do not think that caused me to suddenly let go of my senses."

"Eleanor, please try to understand. Your mother and I are not trying to be harsh. We want to protect you from what might turn out to be a very bad situation. You hardly know this man or his background."

"That's where you're wrong. I know him very well. First of all, he loves the Lord, and that is the most important thing to me. Second, he loves me, which makes it all the better." She smiled and took a seat on the edge of the bed. "He's a good man, and I hate that you aren't even giving him a chance."

"We aren't opposed to giving him a chance. Perhaps if we could get to know him over time—say a year or so—then we'd feel good about giving our blessing," her father replied.

"A year? No, that won't work. We are meant to be together now. Bill is a botanist who has been given approval to move ahead on a new book. This one will be about medicinal herbs and plants in Alaska, and I intend to help him research that book. I have plans to take photographs and help with compiling the information. We have a future together that is already taking shape, and I won't let you deny me that."

She frowned. "I am twenty-one. As you'll recall, I just had a birthday. Thank you, by the way, for the card and money. My point is, I don't need your permission." She had never taken such a tone with her parents and immediately felt guilty for it. "However, I do want your blessing. I never expected this attitude from you."

"Nor did we expect this attitude from you," her father countered.

Her mother raised her gaze to meet Eleanor's. "All of your life, we've given in to whatever whim you had. We've spoiled you to be sure, but you were our only child. Try to understand that this isn't like those other times. The things you've asked for in the past weren't going to change your life the way this will."

"Your mother is right. I blame myself for giving in to you all those times, but I cannot give in on this. You don't know the dangers that some men present. You're innocent of the world and the way some people take advantage of others."

"But I'm not." Eleanor fought to keep her tone even. She didn't want to sound like a rebellious child. "Bill's sister-in-law was taken advantage of by such a man. Addie Hanson, my supervisor, was nearly killed by her oldest brother because she wouldn't give him all her money. I know what dangers can be presented to innocent women and children. I'm not naïve. Mr. Fisher even checked Bill out and learned he was a responsible worker and faithfully attended church. Two things that I know are important to you. Or at least they used to be."

"They should be important to you as well," her father replied.

"And they are." She knew she was getting nowhere. "Look,

why don't you wait to pass judgment on Bill until after you've met him and have a chance to talk to him? We had planned to take you out to dinner tonight. Come with us and get to know Bill. I am confident that you will love him, just as I do."

Her father and mother exchanged a look, and Mother nodded her approval. "Very well," Father said. "We will meet your young man, but please don't think this changes my mind. It is my duty to keep you safe, and I take that quite seriously. I wasn't too excited to have you come here by yourself and stay on to work and live in Seattle, but I knew you were happy. And despite what you might believe at this moment, I do want you to be happy."

"Then try to look at this with an open heart and mind. Pray about it while you rest this afternoon. Bill and I will come to the hotel at just before six. The restaurant is close, and we'll walk to it." She got to her feet. "I do hope you will pray. I feel so certain this is God's will for my life, and I know He can help you to see the same. Just know that nothing has ever been more important to me."

Her father got up and came to her. "I know this is hard for you to hear, Eleanor. It wasn't our intention to cause you pain, but you must look at it from our point of view. A month isn't long enough to know a man you intend to spend the rest of your life with."

"But you taught me that with God all things are possible." Eleanor couldn't help but remind them. "Don't find fault with me for believing what you swore was true."

Eleanor returned to her apartment and wished that Rosemary was home. Then again, Rosemary might have agreed with her parents. She liked Bill well enough and had gotten used to the notion of Eleanor marrying the man, but she'd been of the same mindset. Everyone had the same thoughts. It was too little time to know that Bill was the right man for her.

"But it isn't too little time. I feel absolutely certain. I would die for him, and I believe he would do the same for me." She paced the apartment and wrung her hands. This wasn't at all anything she had expected. She had figured her folks would arrive and be just as happy for her as she was for herself. But to instead find them so adamant that she must not marry Bill . . . It was just too much to think about.

"But I have to think about it. I only have until the day after tomorrow."

She went to the window and looked out. Would she marry even if her parents disapproved? Would it be wrong to stand up for her own heart? She had prayed and prayed about this matter. She had felt at peace in deciding to marry Bill and move with him to Alaska. What more did she need? She didn't want to defy her father and mother, but she was fully of age. She didn't need their permission to marry. She didn't need their approval. She knew that in time they would adjust to the situation and love her despite the choices she made.

"But I've never defied them," she whispered against the glass.

Would it be a sin to marry Bill without her father's blessing? *I'm an adult and fully responsible for myself.* She shook her head as a dozen thoughts played out in her mind. If she married Bill in defiance—in a desire to hurt her folks—then that would be sinful. But she didn't feel that way. She wanted to marry Bill because she loved him. She didn't want to hurt her parents because she loved them as well.

Oh, God, please help me.

She stood there for a long while contemplating the situation and wondering how she could convince her parents that this was the right decision. She knew that without God to intercede for them, her parents would never approve of the wedding.

Bill knocked on Eleanor's apartment at exactly three o'clock. They were taking her parents out to dinner tonight, and he wanted to make sure they'd arrived safely.

Eleanor opened the door a minute later, and when their gazes met, she shocked him by bursting into tears. Bill did what seemed right and took her in his arms. He entered the apartment with her sobbing and closed the door behind him.

"What's wrong?"

She pulled back and tried to speak, but a moaning sob was all she could manage. He held her close as she cried and wondered what tragedy had struck. Had her parents been unable to come? Was she ill?

"Eleanor, please tell me what's happened. Were your parents unable to come?"

She shook her head and pulled away. "No, they're here. They're the problem." She sniffed back her tears and wiped her face with the back of her sleeve. "They are forbidding me to marry you."

Bill frowned. "But why?"

She shook her head. "The same excuse as others gave me. It's too soon. I don't know you well enough. They don't understand that I do know you—I feel I've always known you. You're the part of me that was missing. You're the husband that God intends for me."

He smiled. "You don't have to convince me. I feel that way too."

"I've been trying to pray. I told them to pray and ask God to show them how wonderful you are and how we are meant to be together. But, Bill . . . what if they don't pray? What if they don't see the truth?"

He crossed his arms. "I don't know. I suppose you must answer that question for yourself. I intend to marry you. I cannot imagine my life without you."

"They want us to wait a year and let them get to know you. I told them we can't wait—that you're writing another book and that I'm helping you with it." This brought a new barrage of tears, and Eleanor buried her face in her hands.

Bill's heart hurt for her. He went to her and put his arm around her. "Come, let's sit down and reason through this. There must be an answer."

She nodded with her face still hidden in her hands. Bill guided her to the table and pulled out a chair. Eleanor sat down and again wiped her face against the back of her sleeve. He pulled out his handkerchief and handed it to her. "This might make it easier for you."

She took the offering. "Thank you. I don't know why this must happen. I was so happy. Happy to see them. Happy to tell them all our plans. Now that happiness is ruined."

He drew the other chair close and sat beside her. "You'll be happy again. Are you folks willing to go with us to dinner?"

"Yes, they said they would meet you."

"Good. We have tonight and all day tomorrow and even

part of Sunday to convince them that they have nothing to fear in our union."

"You don't know my father. He's stubborn, and when he puts his foot down about something, it doesn't usually move."

"But I know our heavenly Father, and He can change hearts and minds. I know God can make this right, Eleanor. We know we're meant to be together. We've both prayed about it and feel strongly that we belong to each other. I know God can change their minds."

She sniffed and nodded. "I know that too. I do."

Bill could see how much she was hurting. She was afraid— fearful for the future. "No matter what, I love you, and I know this will work out."

She gave a sort of half smile. "I love you too. More than I can even say. I know it happened all at once—that day you kept me from falling into the lake. That's when I fell in love with you. I know it was fast, but I do things that way all the time. Not fall in love. You were the first one I've ever had those kinds of feelings for. But I do things quickly. You might as well get used to it."

He chuckled. "I've always liked that about you. And just for the record, I fell in love with you when I saw you sprawled out on the grass, hanging over the edge of the lake bank. So I've loved you even longer."

Eleanor leaned against him. "I'm going to marry you no matter what. I've already decided that. I want my parents to love you and approve, but it's not a sin to love someone. It's not like I want to marry you in order to make my parents unhappy. I'm not seeking to hurt them. I love you. You're stuck with me."

"That's all right with me. I like being stuck with you." He kissed the top of her head. "I'm going to go home and change my clothes. I want to look my best for dinner. I'll be back to get you about five-thirty."

She drew a deep breath and nodded. "I'll be ready."

They got to their feet, and Bill took hold of her hand. "Remember, you're their only child. Imagine how you'd feel if our daughter came home after knowing someone just a month and told us she was going to marry him and run off to the wilds of Alaska. We'd fret too."

Eleanor lifted her gaze to his face. "I hadn't really thought about us having children, but I suppose we will."

"Yes, it seems likely." Bill smiled. "You do want children, don't you?"

"If they're yours, I certainly do. We can have a dozen or more, and I'd welcome each one."

Bill's eyes widened. He hadn't quite considered a dozen children as a possibility, but if they were Eleanor's and his, then that would be just fine. He had a lot of love to give, and he knew that whatever family God gave them, they'd find great happiness.

Wallace was at the apartment when Bill arrived whistling. He wasn't daunted by Eleanor's news. He couldn't really explain it, but he knew God would make all this work together for good.

"We need to pray," he announced to his brother. "Right here. Right now."

"What seems to be the problem?" Wallace asked.

"Eleanor's folks don't want us to marry. They think it's too soon—that we are moving too fast."

"Well, it's hard to argue with that concern."

Bill shook his head. "But God has ordained this. I know He has. I've prayed over it and have had such great peace. But they need to have the same peace and understanding, so we need to pray."

Wallace came to where Bill stood. "And what happens if they don't give their approval? Will you marry her anyway?"

"I don't want to dishonor them or pretend their feelings don't matter, but, Wallace, I feel God would have me marry Eleanor no matter what. I know that may sound pretentious, but I feel that strongly about her—about us."

Wallace seemed to consider that a moment. "There must be a purpose even in this, so let us pray for understanding and wisdom. You don't want to go into marriage striking out against her folks. That will make for difficulties between you for a long time."

Bill had already considered that. He sighed. "I know. I just love her so much."

"Then like you said, we need to pray." Wallace knelt down, and Bill quickly followed suit. When his brother bowed his head, Bill did likewise. "Father," Wallace began, "we thank You that You've already heard this prayer and have made provision for our needs. We are grateful that You brought Bill and Eleanor together and pray You will always guide their steps.

"But You know the problem they are up against. Father, we ask that You open the eyes and hearts of Eleanor's father and mother—that they would see who Bill is and understand the love he holds for Eleanor. We ask that You change their hearts, Lord. That they would give their approval for the wedding to take place on Sunday. We trust You to make the path straight because we believe that Your hand brought Eleanor and Bill together in the first place. Help Bill, no matter what happens, handle the situation with respect and godly wisdom. In Jesus's name, amen."

Bill looked up and smiled. "Thank you. You have always been able to calm my fears with your prayers. Even when I was a little boy, I remember you praying with me when I was afraid."

"You prayed for me when I was afraid," Wallace replied. "Throughout this entire nightmare you never once faltered. You encouraged me and never gave up on me."

"That's what brothers do for each other—whether blood related or joined in God's family. You taught me that." Bill drew in a deep breath and let it go. "Everything's going to be fine. I know that God is in control."

20

E leanor dressed in a summery pale green gown with a high rounded neckline and sleeves that came to the elbow. She had worn this one to church many times, and while it wasn't all that current a fashion, it would do. Not only that, but her mother made it for her. Perhaps seeing it again would soften her heart toward Eleanor.

But she wasn't hard-hearted toward Eleanor, just the idea of her marrying. Mother was very practical, and Eleanor was certain she found it difficult to process the idea of a rapid wedding.

God, please help Mother to understand my love for Bill and my reasons for rushing forward to marry. She had prayed off and on since Bill left. Sadly, she didn't feel any more at ease than when she'd started.

Eleanor arranged her red curls high atop her head and secured the coiffure with pins and a ribbon of dark green. She thought momentarily of borrowing one of Rosemary's large, fashionable hats, but it truly wasn't Eleanor's style. If she wore one of those grand millinery concoctions, her parents might think she was putting on airs.

She adjusted the ribbon a couple of different ways and finally settled on simply tying it around her head with the bow in the back. It was something she'd done many times, and her parents would see it as normal.

Once she was satisfied with the arrangement, she went in search of her gloves. She would be very properly attired, she had decided, proving to her parents that she was paying heed to her responsibilities of upkeep and proper etiquette. She hated wearing gloves but knew her mother would expect it. At least Eleanor could rid herself of them at dinner.

Bill arrived at precisely five-thirty as he'd promised. He just stared at her for several long minutes. Eleanor couldn't help but smile at the approval she saw in his expression.

"You're so beautiful, and I am truly blessed."

"As am I." Eleanor nodded toward him. "You look quite dashing in that navy suit."

"I bought it secondhand. I hope that doesn't matter."

"My mother made this gown. I hope that doesn't matter."

Bill laughed. "You know it doesn't. In fact, it gives me even higher regard for your mother. She's very talented."

"She is. I thought I'd wear this and tell her how many times I'm complimented on it and how much I still love it."

"Try to win her over to your side, eh?"

Eleanor shrugged. "I didn't figure it could hurt."

"No, not at all. Tell me about your father as we make our way to the hotel. What are the kinds of things he enjoys? He must love photography."

"Yes, he's been involved with that all his life. He also likes to fish. He often goes to the river to sit and think and cast a line."

"I can talk about fishing. I often fish in Alaska. I'll tell him about the salmon run and how the fish are so thick you can't even see the bed of the river. Added to that, the bears and eagles are fighting you for their share. The danger is quite exciting."

"Oh, I wouldn't stress the dangers. You know they are already against my going to Alaska. If they know about how dangerous it is . . . well, I'm sure that won't help our case."

He surprised her by laughing. "Don't be so downcast, my love. This is going to work out. Wallace and I prayed the moment I returned to our apartment. I feel confident that God is at work in the hearts of your folks."

"I've been praying too, but I don't feel as confident as you do. I hate that this should even be an issue. I never expected them to disapprove, yet here we are."

"They love you and want you to be safe and well-cared for in life. You are precious to them, just as you are to me. I simply must convince them that I want the best for you as much as they do. They'll see it. I know they will."

"I certainly hope so." She reached for her little purse and shawl. "I'm ready. Shall we go?"

He held out his arm, and she took hold. "I'm so nervous about tonight. I just can't help feeling overwhelmed by not knowing what they will say or do. I don't want to hurt them by defying them, but I cannot alter the course of a future I feel confident God has ordained."

"If He has ordained it, do you suppose anyone can alter it? Have faith, Eleanor. Just rest in Him and trust that His will is going to be done."

She locked the door behind her, then reclaimed her hold on Bill. "You are so reassuring and positive in spirit. Are you always this way?"

"What do you suppose?"

"You've been like this since I first met you. I'm guessing this is your regular demeanor."

Bill chuckled and patted her arm. "I'm an eternal optimist. Even after the ship's sinking—before the lists of the dead were printed—I held out hope that Amelia was alive. When we learned her lifeboat sank, we were both lost in sorrow. I won't make that mistake again."

"But it could have just as easily been true. There were those who lost their lives," Eleanor countered.

"Yes, but this situation has taught me God can do anything—even bring the seemingly dead back to life. We both feel certain it's His will that we marry, right?"

"Right."

"And we believe God can do anything—even change a person's mind?"

Eleanor thought for a moment. "He can, but will He?"

"I believe He will. I don't feel we've been defeated in our plans for marriage." He gazed overhead at the trees. "There's just something God has put within my spirit that tells me it will be all right."

"Does it always work out that way?"

Bill looked at her and nodded. "Seems to. I cannot honestly say there was ever a time when I felt this certain and it didn't come around right."

She smiled, feeling further bolstered by his words. If this was a gift God had given him, who was she to say otherwise? Perhaps the smart thing to do was just to trust that God had it all under His control.

They arrived at the hotel and found Father and Mother waiting in the lobby. Bill removed his hat and dropped his hold on Eleanor. She immediately missed his touch but knew it was as it had to be. She went to her parents and hugged them, determined to keep a smile on her face.

"Mother and Father, I want you to meet William Reed, my intended."

Bill stepped forward and gave a little bow toward Eleanor's mother, then he extended his hand to Eleanor's father. "Mr. Bennett, this is a pleasure. I've heard so much about you both." They shook hands, and then Bill looked to Mother. "Please call me Bill."

"I'm glad to finally meet you . . . Bill." Eleanor's father looked Bill over from top to bottom. Eleanor knew he could find no fault in Bill's attire nor in his etiquette.

"We shouldn't dally here," Eleanor said, still smiling. "We have a six o'clock reservation."

"The restaurant is just across the street and down a block," Bill said. "If that's too far to walk, I will have the doorman get us a cab."

"No, the walk will be fine. It's such a pleasant evening," Father replied.

Eleanor was pleased Bill had offered the idea of a cab. They certainly couldn't find fault with that either. As they headed outside, Eleanor was glad to once again be on Bill's arm. She felt more confident at his side. Not that she'd ever really been one who lacked confidence, but there was something about this situation that had completely altered her disposition. At least for the time being.

The short walk consisted of Bill pointing out a few flowering bushes and talking about the abundance of blackberries. Mother seemed impressed by his comments, but Father looked bored. Eleanor hoped that Bill would remember that her father loved to fish. She almost brought up the topic, but then remained silent.

"I see you wore the dress I made you for your high school graduation," Mother said. "I always liked that shade on you."

"I love this dress," Eleanor replied. "I get so many compliments on it, and I'm always so delighted to tell them that you made it."

"You're very talented, Mrs. Bennett," Bill offered.

"Eleanor is just as talented. She might not have told you, but she can sew quite well."

"But not as good as you, Mother." Eleanor didn't want Bill to mention that he knew nothing about her talents. It would only be one more sign that they didn't know each other well enough to marry.

When they reached the restaurant, they were ushered inside and immediately seated at a corner table. The atmosphere was one of fine dining yet had a sort of casualness to it that allowed for families. The restaurant was another addition that had come about because of the exposition.

"I've heard the food here is excellent. It came highly recommended by the staff at the Sorrento," Eleanor said as they glanced over the menus.

"It seems quite nice," her mother replied. "Linen tablecloths and napkins are always a good sign."

Eleanor wasn't sure what to say next, so she said nothing. She'd never felt this way around her parents. They'd always been able to talk about anything and everything, but now they felt like strangers. Eleanor silently prayed for wisdom and strength to endure the evening.

The waiter arrived and took their orders. Mother and Father ordered the creamed onion soup and fresh-caught king salmon with steamed asparagus. Eleanor did likewise, and Bill followed suit.

"The salmon is sure to be excellent," Bill began the conversation after the waiter departed. "They're coming to the end of their season down here, but silvers and pinks should be plentiful. Have you had salmon before?"

"Only canned," Father replied. "I have been told of the amazing quality when fresh."

"It is a very good fish. And the fight that they give you to catch them can be quite exciting."

"Truly?" Father posed it like a question and looked to Bill for an answer. "So you fish?"

"Indeed. The salmon run at different times depending on the variety, but each one can be quite exciting to catch. I've been able to try my hand at each type but must say that the king salmon is my favorite. They put up an amazing fight."

Eleanor saw her father's eyes light up. "What is the general size?"

"On average about twenty to fifty pounds, and twenty-four to forty inches long."

"Oh, that is quite impressive."

Bill smiled. "Yes, and they can get even bigger. My brother once caught one that weighed in at seventy-five pounds. He was told they have recorded even bigger ones than that."

"I'll be. Sounds like quite the adventure."

Eleanor could see her father was happy with the conversation and leaned over to her mother. "I hope you had a nice rest this afternoon."

Mother nodded. "It did much to restore my spirits."

Eleanor didn't want to press and learn if her spirits only needed restoring from the long journey or if Eleanor herself was the cause. She toyed with her linen napkin as the men continued talking. Father was now telling Bill about fishing in the Smoky Hill River.

By the time the soup was served, the two men were laughing like old buddies and sharing tales of the "one that got away."

Eleanor waited for her father to offer grace, but when he didn't, Bill did. "Would you mind if we prayed to bless the meal?" he asked. "I know some folks don't care to do that in public places, but I don't mind at all."

"That would be fine, Bill," Eleanor's father replied, then bowed his head.

Bill offered a short prayer and finished just as the waiter returned to offer pepper for the soup. They declined and sampled the soup just as it was. Eleanor thought it quite delicious. It was rich and full of flavor.

"Oh, this is good," Mother declared.

"It is," Father agreed.

At least they found no fault in the food. Throughout the meal, Eleanor checked and rechecked her attitude. She watched her parents closely. She tried to examine each word that was said and figure out what her parents were thinking as they conversed with Bill. Bill seemed completely at ease. He spoke of his education and interest in botany. He talked about the way he had researched his first book and the plans he had for researching the second. There was nothing in the conversation that appeared to distress or bore her parents, so Eleanor said very little. However, this didn't go unnoticed.

"Eleanor, you've hardly spoken this evening. Are you feeling all right?" her mother asked.

"I'm fine. I just wanted you and Father to get to know Bill. I want you to see him for the same wonderful man that I know him to be."

Father lost no time picking up the thread. "Bill seems to be quite a nice gentleman. There's no doubt about that. However, one evening can hardly tell the quality of a man's character."

"I beg to differ," Bill said, surprising everyone at the table.

Eleanor wanted to melt into the floor. He had contradicted her father. That would never go over well. Just then the waiter arrived with their salmon. She breathed a sigh of relief, hoping the matter might be dropped in lieu of eating.

"This looks wonderful," she said as a plate was deposited in front of her. She picked up her fork and dove right in.

The salmon had been fixed with some sort of sauce on top of it. It was creamy with a lemony flavor. Eleanor found it delighted her tongue.

For a few moments they ate, and no one spoke. The hum of conversation all around them, along with the occasional clanking of utensils on china, was all that Eleanor heard. That and the rapid pounding of her heart.

"This is quite good," her father announced after several moments. "I think I can say I like the flavor better than catfish."

Bill chuckled. "I thought you would approve."

Father took another bite. "Yes, it's exceptional." He wiped his mouth with the napkin and looked at Bill. "But you were about to speak to my point on a man's character being impossible to tell in one setting."

Bill nodded and dabbed his own napkin to his lips. He took a sip of iced tea and nodded again. "I was going to say that I believe as Christians, God can give us the ability to discern a man's character upon a moment's notice. There have been many times when that ability was critical to situations in which I found myself needing guidance."

Father looked quite thoughtful at this. Eleanor took the opportunity to take another bite of salmon. She saw that her mother was quite happily devouring her meal and found some relief in that.

"I do believe you make a valid point, young man. I suppose I discounted the possibility of divine intervention."

"It is a blessing to be certain, and I believe one can only attain that through a close walk with the Almighty," Bill continued. "As a businessman, I'm sure there have been times when you've had to rely on such discernment."

"To be sure." Father appeared deep in thought on the matter. "It has perhaps even saved my life at one time or another."

"Yes," Bill agreed. "It has done that for me to be certain. But even in meeting you and your wife, I can fully understand your hesitancy to rush in with your blessing on our marriage. You want to be certain that you guide your only child into wise choices. I would expect nothing less. If I were in your shoes, I would have my fears for her. Fears of her being duped. Of leaving this area and never returning. Of being misled by someone with false intentions. As I told Eleanor, your concerns are legitimate. I can only pray that God will give you that discernment to recognize me for who I really am. A man of God who has fallen deeply in love with your daughter. A man who would give his life for her."

"It's easy enough to say such a thing," her father countered.

"That is true, but as a man of God, doesn't your heart confirm my sincerity?"

Eleanor looked at her father and could see his expression as he considered this. He wasn't angry at Bill's comment nor dismayed. He didn't say it, but Eleanor knew without a doubt that her father recognized the truth of Bill's statement. She wanted to jump up and give a shout but knew that wouldn't help matters. God was clearly at work, and she needed to remain silent and let Him do what was necessary. The entire situation was teaching her an important lesson that sometimes it was better to listen than to speak.

⁙

"I'm sorry to be the bearer of bad news," Pastor Harris said, looking with great sorrow at Amelia Reed. "But I knew you'd want to hear about it right away."

He had just shared with her that Mrs. Becker was dead—murdered. One of the girls who rented from the older woman was also a member of the church, and she'd come straightaway to Pastor Harris to tell him what had happened. The poor girl had been inconsolable and was even now being calmed by Joanna Harris.

"What happened?" Amelia forced herself to ask.

"They aren't sure. They found her beaten in her own living room."

"It was Grady Masterson." She looked at the pastor and shook her head. "This is all my fault."

"Nonsense. This was the fault of a depraved mind. If it was Mr. Masterson, then we should go to the police and let them know your thoughts on the matter."

"I know it was him. I feel it deep in my soul. He was determined to find me." She tried to ignore the feeling of icy fingers at her throat. Would Grady beat her to death if he found her?

"What if she told him that I'm here? The poor woman could hardly be expected to remain silent when her very life was being taken from her."

"That's a good point. We need to see to it that you and Wally are given ample protection." He thought for a moment. "I know. You should move into the house with Joanna and me. I'll see about getting a couple of the young men from church to come and stay here in this house. If she told Grady of your being here, you'll be safe with us."

"But you could end up being his next victims. I can't put you at risk."

"Nonsense. There is safety in numbers, my dear. We'll set this place up like a fortress. It's just until Monday. But in the meanwhile, we need to talk to the police. Are you up for a trip to the police station?"

"Of course." She thought of the baby and Helga. "But we must get Wally and Helga out of danger. Let's move them into your house first."

"Absolutely. One of the young men I know who can help us lives just two doors down with his parents. I'll go see if he might come and provide extra protection. Get your things together, and I'll be back momentarily to move you in. Lock the door behind me, and do not open the door to anyone but me. Understand?"

"Yes."

Amelia lingered for a moment after he'd gone. This was all too much. Grady had surely lost his mind if he'd murdered an innocent woman.

"Helga?" she called, getting to her feet. "Helga, come quickly."

An hour later, Amelia sat in front of a uniformed police officer and a rather nicely dressed older man who wore a three-piece suit. He was the detective who'd been placed in charge of Mrs. Becker's case.

"And you feel confident that this man would commit murder to get what he wanted?" he asked Amelia.

"I do. He has always been determined to have his own way. When we first arrived and he arranged for me to stay in Mrs. Becker's apartment, he absolutely insisted I never leave the place. The one time I did, he was livid. He barely contained his anger with me, and I'm sure that was only because he knew it would scare me away. Which it did. That was one of the reasons I was happy to move into the pastor's cottage."

The man nodded. "Do you know where we can find this man, Mrs. Reed?"

"He lives in a rooming house down by Skid Row. There are eight or nine other men who share the place." She gave him the address. "Grady wanted to make sure I knew where he was so that if need be, I could send him a message."

The detective nodded. "Why do you think he would kill Mrs. Becker?"

"She knew where I had gone," Amelia barely whispered. The truth of it was just too much to bear. "She was his only connection to finding me."

21

Wallace waited in the lobby of the Sorrento Hotel for Mr. Bennett. The bellboy had taken up a handwritten note, and Wallace hoped Mr. Bennett might join him shortly. He knew the man and his wife were against Bill marrying Eleanor, and he hoped to help allay their fears.

When he saw the older gentleman approach, Wallace got to his feet. "Mr. Bennett?"

"Yes, and you are Mr. Reed, William's brother?"

"Yes. Glad to meet you." They shook hands, and Wallace pointed to a corner of the lobby where there were two empty chairs and no one else around. "I wonder if you would join me there for a little discussion?"

"Of course."

They took their seats, and Wallace immediately began the conversation. "I'm sure you must know that I've come to help persuade you to allow Bill and Eleanor to marry. I have prayed considerably about this and about coming to see you. I hope you don't think me wrong to get involved."

"I don't," Mr. Bennett replied. "I'm sure you love your brother and want to do whatever you can to see him happy."

"That's true, but it is more than that. I've been praying for my brother to find a wife for a long time. There were a great many women who tried to get Bill's attention, but he wanted the right woman. The woman God had for him. He isn't at all the type to just go willy-nilly into a relationship.

"When we lived in Chicago, there was no shortage of unmarried females, especially at our church. I found Amelia, my wife, almost immediately. We were just perfect for one another, and when I mentioned wanting to serve God in Alaska, Amelia was in complete agreement that this was a worthy cause. Yet even after we wed, there was no one that seemed right for Bill. When our mother and father teased that he was too picky, he just encouraged them to pray about it."

"I can't fault that idea," Mr. Bennett said. "I've long prayed for a mate for Eleanor."

"So you do understand. We were all praying for Bill to find a mate. Instead, when I left for Alaska with Amelia, Bill decided to come along and study the vegetation. A few years after we arrived in Alaska, he arranged with a publisher back east to write a book on the topic. While traveling for research, he met a great many women who found him to be quite handsome. But, again, none of them were right. Bill knew that they weren't who God intended him to marry."

Wallace shifted his weight and leaned toward Mr. Bennett. "Everywhere Bill goes, there's always an interested female. He's handsome, some might even say dashingly so. He's educated, kindhearted, and hardworking. Bill is a godly man who carefully considers the various aspects of his life in the reflection of God's Word. If you haven't already figured that out about him, I hope you will reconsider. Bill does nothing without a great deal of prayer."

"I'm impressed that you would come here to tell me all of this," Mr. Bennett said with a hint of a smile on his lips. "It's quite admirable that you would make such a stand for your brother."

Wallace shrugged. "I felt compelled after praying this morning to come to you on his behalf. Although he doesn't know I'm here, and I'd rather he not. I realize it's difficult to imagine a month being long enough to make a lifelong commitment, but when God calls you to a thing, how can you say no?" He smiled and shrugged again. "I've never seen Bill in love until now. Eleanor is all he thinks about, even while he was trying to get the work done to turn in his manuscript to the publisher. Eleanor's needs are uppermost in his mind. He talked to me for hours about what she would need for comfort in Alaska. I just want you to understand that my brother didn't enter this without great consideration. He truly loves your daughter."

"I think I saw that when we met with him last night," Mr. Bennett replied. "I can even say that many of my concerns were assuaged. My wife and I sent word to meet them for lunch. I still have questions, but I am seeing God's hand in all of this."

"I'm glad. I hope that you will be able to put aside all of your fears and approve tomorrow's wedding. I know it means so much to Bill and Eleanor. They want to start out their new life in a manner that will please God."

◈

"I'm quite nervous," Eleanor told Bill as they approached the restaurant for lunch.

"I see this as good, my dear. Your folks want to see us again—together. I think that's very positive."

"I hope you're right. We've only this one day to convince them."

"We don't need to do anything. God is already at work, Eleanor. Have faith."

She grimaced. "I do, but I suppose when it comes to something that is so very important to me, I feel overwhelmed. It's hard to have faith because . . . well, maybe I'm not worthy of you, and God is interceding to protect you."

Bill surprised her by laughing out loud. He pulled her a little closer as they walked and shook his head. "What if I'm not worthy of you?"

"You're perfect," she countered.

"Just as I think you're perfect. Honestly, Eleanor, have faith. This is a very good thing." Just then Bill spied Mr. and Mrs. Bennett. "There are your folks." He gave a wave.

As they approached the older couple, Bill could feel Eleanor stiffen. She was so worried about her parents approving their marriage. Bill wished he could calm her fears, but she would learn in time to just rest in the Lord. It had taken him time to learn that too.

"Hello, Mother, Father." Eleanor broke away from Bill and gave them each a kiss on the cheek. "How did you sleep?"

"Quite well," her father replied.

"The room was perfect," her mother added. "We've arranged to stay until Tuesday."

Eleanor's father offered his arm to his wife, and they led the way into the restaurant. Bill and Eleanor followed. Once they were seated, the waiter immediately began to discuss the three specials they were offering.

"We have clam chowder with toasted garlic bread and a fresh vegetable salad. We also have a fried fish special: two pieces of battered fish with toasted garlic bread and a fresh vegetable salad. And lastly, we have a seafood casserole that consists of crab meat, shrimp, clams, and cod. It's served with toasted garlic bread and a fresh vegetable salad."

Bill had to smile. No matter what you chose, you were getting garlic toast and salad. They placed their orders with everyone settling on the fried fish and iced tea. The day was getting warm, and the tea would serve them well.

"I suppose you're both surprised by this invitation," Eleanor's father began, "but we didn't want to put off speaking with you." He looked at Eleanor and smiled. "We've had a change of heart regarding your marriage."

Eleanor looked at Bill, who couldn't help giving her an *I told you so* raise of his brow. He might have laughed at her expression had it not been such a serious situation.

"Please . . . please go on," she finally managed to say.

The waiter interrupted with their iced tea and bowls of sliced lemon and sugar. "Will you need anything else?"

"No," Eleanor's father replied before anyone else could speak up. "We're just fine. Thank you." The man nodded and left them to their discussion.

All gazes turned to Mr. Bennett, causing him to smile. "I know you're quite anxious that I continue. We did as you suggested, Bill. We prayed, and I must say the peace that came over us both was quite amazing. I woke up several times in the night to ponder the subject of you marrying our only child and taking her off to the isolated wilds of a dangerous land. And each time I tried to think negatively of it, I couldn't. God had altered my reasoning."

"Does this mean you'll stand with me tomorrow?" Eleanor questioned.

"It does. Your mother and I are in agreement. You may marry."

Bill couldn't contain his excitement. "Thank you. Thank you so much Mr. Bennett, Mrs. Bennett. I felt confident God would make a way in this."

"And your confidence was something I could see." Mr. Bennett sobered. "I have to say, when you spoke of God giving discernment to lend understanding to a man or situation, I was thoroughly chastised. You didn't mean it as such, I know, but God did. I came to realize I was not allowing for God's influence but rather relying on my own feelings. For that, I apologize."

Eleanor was dabbing at tears, and her mother reached out to hand her a handkerchief. "You were never good at keeping one of these handy."

Bill chuckled. "That's for sure."

"I don't generally need one. Until recently, I was not given to tears." She shook her head. "I'm just so happy. I am grateful that you listened to God. Grateful that Bill encouraged me to pray and listen to Him as well."

"I think you're going to be a wonderful influence on my daughter. You seem like the kind of man who will keep her grounded and fixed on the truth of God's Word." Her father's expression was one of confidence.

"I will do my best," Bill said. "I love her very much. But I want to say something more as a pledge to you. I know that you'll miss her very much, and I'd like for us to travel to Kansas to see you in one year. Of course, this is all if God wills it. I'm not trying to dictate our future to Him. However, I know that it will ease your mind and hearts to be able to look forward to us returning so that you can see for yourselves that Eleanor is happy."

"That would be so wonderful," her mother replied. "I hate the thought of her going away and never returning."

"Yes, we even discussed that," Mr. Bennett said. "It was hard to give that one over to God's will."

Bill smiled. "I can understand. I wouldn't want a life of never seeing Eleanor again, and I am certain that you wouldn't. That's why I feel compelled to give you this promise."

"Thank you . . . son." Eleanor's father reached out to touch Bill's shoulder. "I'm confident that you'll take good care of her."

Grady Masterson was just returning to the run-down house where he shared a room with his coworkers. The hair on the back of his neck prickled, and he paused before peeking around the corner. The sound of men talking could be heard but not understood. Grady slipped behind an over-grown bush and peered carefully toward the front door. There were two policemen exiting the place, still talking to several of his roommates.

It was difficult to hear, but Grady knew why they were there. Mrs. Becker must have been found, and someone had pointed to him as the responsible party. It was always the kind of luck he had.

He edged away from the bush and hurried along the alleyway and back the direction he'd come. Now they would be looking for him, and the dangers he faced had doubled.

"*It's time to leave this city,*" his brother said once they were well away from Skid Row.

"Don't I know it. But we can't leave things undone. I have to take care of those Reed brothers. They're the reason my life is a mess."

"*Mine too,*" Avery replied.

Grady looked at his brother and nodded. "Sorry, I didn't mean to say that my situation was worse than yours."

"*No bother. We must figure out how to deal with William and Wallace. We have their address. I'm thinking we go over tonight and break in. We can end their lives and be done with it once and for all.*"

It made complete sense to Grady, but there was still the question of Amelia and the baby. What was he supposed to do about them? She would have all that money, and it could come in handy for him and Avery as they relocated.

As if reading his mind, Avery spoke up. "*I don't think you should worry about Amelia. We would have to spend way too long looking for her, and once you kill her husband and brother, the police will tie it all together with the old lady's death, and you won't stand a chance. No sense in you getting hanged—like I did.*"

Grady nodded. "I suppose you're right. You always knew better. But what about the money?"

"*We'll take what we can off the men and leave. That will have to be enough.*"

"I just think it would be nice if we had the inheritance too."

"*But you're not using your head, Grady.*" Avery stood his ground. "*We haven't been able to find Amelia.*"

"Yeah, but Wallace said he knew where she'd gone. Maybe I can cause him enough pain that he'll confess the details."

Avery laughed. *"You're more dim-witted than I knew if you think that's gonna work. That man ain't gonna let you know anything. Even with his dying breath."*

Grady nodded. "I suppose you're right. He's always been stubborn. Ever since I first met him, he's been a hard nut to crack. Guess we'll just have to forget about the inheritance."

"Now you're thinking clearly," Avery told him. *"Say, let's go have a drink or two before we commence to killing."*

Eleanor had never known such happiness. She had enjoyed their time together at lunch, and afterward when her parents mentioned the exposition, Bill had suggested they all go together and spend the afternoon there.

At the fair, Eleanor pointed out the Camera Girls and took her parents by the photography shop to meet the Fishers. Father was quite impressed with the setup, and he talked for some time with Otis Fisher as the man led him from room to room.

"I'm very pleased to meet you," Mrs. Fisher told Eleanor's mother. "Your daughter was one of our very best workers."

"That doesn't surprise me. She's always done everything she puts her hand to with great enthusiasm."

"That she does. She sold more Brownie cameras than anyone else in our employ."

"The Fishers gave us a camera and film as a wedding gift," Eleanor told her mother. "And Mr. Fisher helped me to purchase the right chemicals to develop the film in Alaska. It's going to be so wonderful to set up our own darkroom and be able to take lots of photographs. I'll be sending some to you so that you can see how we're living."

"That would be nice," her mother said. She turned her attention back to Mrs. Fisher. "I see you're going to have a little one."

"Yes, our first. We've waited years and years for this blessed event."

"We had some difficulty ourselves, and Eleanor is an only child. But she was worth ten children. Yours will be too, I'm certain."

"I am too," Mrs. Fisher said, putting her hand atop her rounded abdomen. "I'm just happy to have one, but if God chooses to send more, that will be fine too."

Mother nodded. Father returned with Mr. Fisher. The two were still deep in discussion, but Eleanor wanted to move them along. Bill was waiting for them at the Alaska building, where he planned to explain as much as possible about the new life Eleanor would have in that far-away district.

"We really should be going. Bill is waiting for us," she reminded them.

"Of course," her father replied. "It was a pleasure to meet you, Mr. and Mrs. Fisher. And I plan to take your advice on these cameras and see if I can't get folks in Salina excited about them."

"I don't think you can go wrong with them." Mr. Fisher put his arm around his wife. "We've been able to purchase a new location for our business because of their sales. I have no reason to believe they won't go on being just as popular."

"We will see you at church tomorrow," Eleanor said, waving good-bye to her former boss.

Mr. Fisher smiled and gave her a wave. "We will be there."

Eleanor led her folks outside and into the growing crowds. "I'm glad you were able to meet the Fishers. They've been so good to me. Addie Hanson has been good too. She and her husband are the ones who plan to pick us up in their carriage tomorrow. They'll take us to the church and be there for the ceremony. And they promised to take us to the hotel afterward."

"This is quite the place," her father said, looking all around. "Reminds me of the Chicago fair in some ways."

"It's terribly noisy. I don't know how you endured this day after day," her mother added.

Eleanor smiled. "It is noisy, but there was something so alive and amazing about it. I found it quite enjoyable, and I think I shall miss it. Oh, here we are." The sign outside read *Alaska* in bold black lettering.

Eleanor linked her arms with her mother and father. "This is where you can learn all about the life that is soon to be mine."

Bill was in the corner talking to someone. Eleanor wondered if it was his supervisor. She waited until he excused himself and came to join them before saying anything.

"That was Mr. Bradley. He's come to see this building every day since the fair opened. They gave him a pass to get in after the first couple of weeks. He's planning a trip to Alaska, and I was telling him that we were headed up on Monday."

"Is he going to join you?" Father asked.

"No, he said it was too quick to get his life in order." Bill leaned closer and lowered his voice. "Between you and me, I don't think he'll ever come north, but he likes to dream, and I don't mind encouraging him."

"That's very kind of you," Mother said. "I'm sure he appreciates the stories you share."

Bill put his arm around Eleanor. "He seems to. He always sought me out."

"It's so sad though that you think he'll never go." Eleanor knew her own excitement and hated to think of not being able to fulfill that desire.

Bill gave her shoulder a squeeze. "For some, the dream is enough. For others, it only counts if it comes to fruition. I think Mr. Bradley is quite happy just dreaming. Now, if you'll come with me, I have some special photographs to show you. The photographer is the one in charge of photographing the exposition. His name is Frank Nowell, and he once lived in Alaska."

That evening after seeing Eleanor's parents safely back to the hotel, Bill escorted Eleanor back to the apartment she shared with Rosemary.

"Just think, this time tomorrow we'll be married," he said as they said goodnight.

"I know. I'm so excited. I have everything packed, and I withdrew all my money from the bank yesterday. Addie and Isaac Hanson are picking me and Rosemary up in their carriage tomorrow, then we'll go pick up Mother and Father and come to the church."

"It'll be hard not to be with you until after the services," Bill said, pulling her into his arms. "But I suppose it will be all right. After all, I'll have you for the rest of our lives." He kissed her for a long and tender moment. It was hard to leave her here and go home alone.

He abruptly released her and pushed her toward the door. "Go now. I'll see you tomorrow after church."

"I'll be the one with the red curls," Eleanor said, smiling over her shoulder.

Bill laughed. "And I'll be the one with the gold band."

22

Grady Masterson had no idea where he was when he first woke up. He and Avery had put away a lot of drinks the night before, and his mouth was more than a little sour. His stomach too. He moaned as he rolled over. Apparently, he had found a place to hole up in and slept through the night rather than make his way to the Reed brothers' apartment.

He stretched and got to his feet. Wherever he was, it looked to be a gardening shed. There were rakes and shovels, as well as a wheelbarrow beside him and coils of rope and wire hanging on the wall. Along one side there was a table with clay pots and a mound of dark soil.

Moving as quietly as possible, Grady tried to remember where he was, but nothing came to mind. He opened the shed door just a bit and looked out. He winced. The day was far too sunny. Wasn't Seattle supposed to be fraught with rain and clouds?

The scenery around him meant nothing. Maybe this was a place Avery knew. Speaking of his brother, where was he? Grady looked back in the shed but didn't find him there. He supposed Avery had something to do and would catch up with him later.

His stomach churned, and without warning, Grady lost its contents. That would be an unpleasant surprise for the gardener. He wiped his mouth with the back of his hand and straightened. There was nothing more to be done about it.

Hearing no one around, Grady pushed the door open and stepped outside to further survey the area. It was clearly residential. He was in the backyard of a large brick house. Moving away from the house, he found himself at the property line, where a row of flowering bushes acted as a fence.

He looked for a way through the brush but found no openings. There didn't seem to be a way out except to go back the way he'd come and exit through the front yard. This didn't sit well with him at all. Avery would think him lacking good judgment for sure.

"Well, Avery's not here," Grady said to no one. He headed across the yard as bold as if he owned the place. He had a knife in his boot. The knife he planned to use to kill Wallace and William Reed. Just let someone try to stop him.

By the time he reached the street, Grady was cursing himself for having gotten too drunk the night before to take care of the Reeds. It was Sunday now and knowing them they'd be at church. He'd have to wait until this evening to do the job. Avery was sure to be displeased.

Eleanor found it hard to sit still through the sermon. She was sandwiched between her mother and father. Mary and Bertha and the Fishers sat beyond Father to the right, and

Addie and Isaac Hanson, as well as Rosemary, were seated to Mother's left.

Eleanor's new clothes fit perfectly, and even the fancy hat didn't feel as uncomfortable as Eleanor had feared. She twisted her gloved hands together and tried to force her stomach to relax. Now was certainly not the time to have an upset tummy.

She'd seen nothing of Bill, and it was nearly time for the benediction. She blew out a breath and drew her mother's attention. Mother reached over and took hold of Eleanor's hand and gave it a squeeze. Eleanor forced a smile as she glanced into her mother's eyes. The older woman smiled and nodded, giving Eleanor a great sense that all was well.

The pastor offered a prayer and then announced that there was to be a wedding. Eleanor tried not to squirm as she waited for the pastor to bid the wedding party forward. Finally, he called for Bill and Wallace to take their places. After the men came to stand beside the pastor, he did the same for Eleanor and her father. Rosemary came as well since she was Eleanor's maid of honor.

When Eleanor caught sight of Bill for the first time that morning, she was almost overcome. She felt weak in the knees, and a wave of dizziness threatened to send her to the floor. Father gripped her hand, and she knew he'd never let her fall. She drew in a deep breath and settled her nerves. After all, this was what she had dreamed of. This was exactly what she wanted.

She met Bill's gaze and found him smiling. She returned the smile and immediately felt better. There was just something about this man that made her feel that all would be well.

"We are here today to celebrate the joining together of Eleanor Bennett and William Reed. Who giveth this woman to be married?" the pastor asked.

Eleanor looked at her father and realized how happy she was that he had agreed to the wedding. Could she have said yes knowing it would go against him? She had thought so, but now she wasn't so sure. Her deep love and respect for the man she called Father was a binding thing. She would have hated to hurt him and Mother for any reason.

"Her mother and I do," he said and then handed her over to Bill.

Bill's warm grasp furthered her confidence. He was so strong and capable. She loved him more and more each day. It was true they didn't know everything about each other, but it would be a grand adventure to learn.

"Marriage is a big responsibility," the pastor began. "It will require great strength and the ability to endure all kinds of trials and temptations. You will make a promise to one another today, but remember, you are also making a promise to God. Do not enter this commitment lightly, or there will be dire consequences that will affect the rest of your lives."

He spoke for a few more minutes, and then they exchanged their vows. Eleanor felt dizziness wash over her again when Bill slipped the ring on her finger. She felt the gravity of her decision as the minister spoke the words "till death do you part."

And then the ceremony was over, and everyone was circling around to congratulate them and give them best wishes. Eleanor clung to Bill, wishing they could just leave the church and get away from everyone. She needed to sit down and let the importance of the moment sink in. She was now a married woman. A married woman who would start a new adventure away from all she knew and everyone she loved. Save one.

The thought of her life with Bill calmed her nerves and gave her a bit of strength. She was always one to run headlong into action. She was the one who pursued her desires at full speed. This was no different, and she wasn't going to regret it before it even started. She had made the right choice. Bill was the man God had given her, and he was perfect for the job.

"We've arranged for our driver to take you to the hotel and then come back for the rest of us," Addie said in a whisper as she hugged Eleanor.

"Thank you. I was so wanting to get away." Eleanor looked to her husband. "Did you hear what Addie said?"

"I did, and I heartily approve."

Eleanor kissed her mother and father good-bye. The thought of being alone with her husband left Eleanor feeling a little shy, but at the same time, she was so excited to start her new life. Tomorrow they would head for the docks and bid everyone good-bye for a very long time, but she and Bill would be together. Nothing else mattered as much as that. For once in her life Eleanor felt complete.

"Ready?" Bill asked.

Eleanor met his eyes and noted the love reflected there. "I am."

 ❧

By the time Grady reached Bill and Wallace Reed's apartment building, he was limping. He had a hole in the sole of his shoe, and a rock had bruised his foot. He was of a single mind, however. He was going to wait until it was late in the night, then sneak into the building and make his way to the Reed place. That would be his only opportunity. Avery had been certain he needed to leave town before being caught for the murder of Mrs. Becker.

The weather had given them a lovely evening and had beckoned many of the men who lived in the building to come outside for discussion. Wallace sat in the midst of several men who seemed quite caught up in whatever it was he was saying.

Grady stayed back and tried to blend into the shadows and shrubbery. He moved around the perimeter of the building to see what was what and make sure he could get away at a moment's notice. It was as he made his way back that he ran into Avery.

"Where have you been all day?"

"Had things to do. We're leaving, remember?"

"Of course I remember. I just thought you were going to help me with the Reeds. After all, there's two of 'em and just me unless you help."

"You don't need anyone to help. You'll get this done without breakin' a sweat. What have you figured out?"

"I don't know exactly. There are too many people millin' around. Wallace is out there sittin' with a few other men."

"Maybe you should try to hear what they're saying. Maybe that will give you an idea of how to get this job done."

"That's a good idea. I just can't risk having Wallace see me."

Avery nodded. *"It's dark enough now. If you slip up behind where they're sittin', no one will be the wiser. Just keep to thick evergreen bushes. They'll hide you and disguise your stench.*"

"My stench?"

Avery laughed. *"Yeah, you need a bath."*

Grady ignored his insult and made his way around the building to where Wallace was laughing and telling a story. The evergreens were rather prickly, but Grady paid it no mind and hugged in to hide himself in the shadows.

"We're leaving tomorrow. Taking the *Star of the North* to Seward," Wallace was telling the men. "Bill and Eleanor got married today and are staying at a hotel tonight." A couple of the men made crude comments, but Wallace ignored them. "They will join me on the ship, and hopefully when we arrive in Alaska, we'll find my wife and son."

"That's a long way to go. What if they aren't there?"

"I thought long and hard about that. If they aren't there, then I'll come back. Bill and Eleanor are going to our village, and if Amelia shows up, they'll be able to send me word. Meanwhile, I'll come to Seattle and get them to put a big story in the newspaper. We didn't think of that in time. It might have helped us find her before she left, but something tells me she's already arranged to go north. I think we'll find her already in Alaska when we dock in Seward."

"Will she still be there?"

"There or just to the north. There's a train line that runs north out of Seward about sixty miles. She'll have to wait for someone she trusts to escort her back to the village. The Athabaskan tribe we live with will be returning soon, but there may not be anyone readily available. It takes time and effort to travel the two hundred miles from the winter village to Seward. Bill worked on arrangements in advance to meet us at the rail's northern terminus, but I don't know if Amelia would have thought to do that."

Grady frowned. So Wallace didn't know where Amelia had gone. Maybe that meant the old woman didn't know either. Maybe he had killed her for no good reason. She had given him this address, and that did allow him to know where Wallace and Bill had gotten off to, but maybe she didn't know where Amelia was and hadn't lied to him. For some reason, that idea bothered him. He wasn't of a mind to kill for no good reason.

He tried to figure out what to do next. Bill wasn't here and would stay somewhere else tonight with his new bride. Wallace was here, but would it be wise to kill only one and not the other? Bill would know Grady was the guilty party and put the police on his trail. Just as someone had done with Mrs. Becker's killing.

"Do you have any apprehension about taking the *Star of the North* . . . since you know . . . the ship coming down sank?" the man beside Wallace asked.

He shook his head. "No, I thought about it but realized no matter what, God is in control of my life. If I'm meant to die at sea . . . well, I'll die at sea. I've put my trust solidly back in the hands of God. I was such a fool to ever doubt His love and protection. I'll spend the rest of my life remembering my doubt and working to teach others about the way Satan deceives to get us to disbelieve God's Word."

Grady hated it when Wallace talked about God. The man seemed ever so keen on the matter and knew exactly what to say to cause second thoughts. Even now, it made Grady uncomfortable, and he backed out of the evergreens and retraced his steps around the building.

"*Where are you going?*" his brother asked as he caught up with him.

"Bill won't be here. He's with his new bride somewhere. But he and Wallace intend to leave on the *Star of the North* tomorrow. I'll be down at the docks and find a way to kill them both when they show up there. If you'll just help me, we can get it done quick and easy before anyone knows we're even there."

"*All right. I'll help you, but then we leave this godforsaken city,*" Avery said, fixing Grady with a stern look. "*Agreed?*"

Grady nodded. "Agreed."

Pastor Harris finished taking Amelia's things to the carriage while she told Joanna good-bye. There was something bittersweet in the leaving, but Amelia looked forward to heading back to Alaska.

"Are you sure you have everything you need?" Joanna asked as Amelia securely tied her hat.

"I have everything and more," Amelia admitted. "You have packed us a goody basket of food in case the ship's meals don't agree, and you and the church ladies provided some wonderful blankets and diapers for the baby. How can I ever thank you enough?"

"Ready?" Pastor Harris asked. "The *Star of the North* won't wait for you, you know." He grinned. There was plenty of time, but Amelia wanted to board the ship as soon as possible.

"I am ready. I was just saying as much to Joanna. You've both been so kind, and I will miss you. Mrs. Becker too. Poor woman." Amelia frowned. "The ending to this adventure is not one I would have written had I been the one telling this tale."

"But there is good to be had," Joanna replied. "Wally is doing so well, and you're going home. Perhaps not in perfect order, but in good shape. Now promise you'll write often."

"I will." Amelia smiled and reached for her gloves. "Of course, remember it will be hard to get mail out during the winter. Not impossible. Just hard." She pulled on her gloves and glanced around the room. "I believe I have everything."

Joanna leaned forward and hugged Amelia close. She kissed the younger woman's cheek, then turned to Helga, who held the baby. "I hope you have an easy time of it and suffer no sea-motion sickness."

"I'm sure to be fine, and I'll be back before you know it."

Amelia still wished Helga would accompany her all the way home, but it was all right. The woman had to do what was right for herself, just as Amelia was doing what was right for her and Wally.

She turned and smiled at Pastor Harris. "We're ready. Take us to the *Star of the North*, please."

<hr />

"I'm going to miss you," Eleanor told her parents. The day had turned chilly with overcast skies, causing her to pull her shawl closer. "But hopefully I will see you next summer."

They embraced, and Eleanor pulled away, glancing around for her husband. He and Wallace had gone to check on all the crates of supplies that were to accompany them back to Seward.

Addie and Isaac Hanson had already bid her farewell and were waiting in their carriage until Eleanor's parents were ready to leave. They had been so sweet to afford them all the privacy they needed to say good-bye.

"I will write to you and send photographs when I can," Eleanor promised.

Her mother sniffed back tears and dabbed at her eyes. "Oh, I do hope we can see you again."

Eleanor smiled. "I know we will. I feel confident of it."

Father put his arm around Mother. "We shouldn't keep the Hansons waiting, my dear."

Glancing around, Eleanor shook her head. "I don't know where Bill and Wallace got off to, but I had hoped they'd return before you had to leave. I know Bill—"

The raised voices of a man and woman reached Eleanor's ears, causing her to stop in midsentence. What in the world was going on? She wasn't the only one who paused to figure out what was happening. Even Mother and Father were concerned.

Moving across the dock, Eleanor gave no thought to what kind of trouble she might be getting into. When she rounded the building, she saw a scruffy-looking man accosting a young woman dressed in black. There was something familiar about her.

"You're coming with me," the man demanded. He took hold of her arm. "You owe me, and you owe Avery."

"I owe you nothing. I paid my debt to you." She glanced over her shoulder as if looking for someone.

The man started dragging her toward the street. Eleanor didn't know if she could prevent his leaving with the woman, but she intended to try.

"Let her go!"

Eleanor had opened her mouth to call out that very thing, but it wasn't her voice. It was the voice of a man. She glanced behind the struggling couple and spotted Wallace.

"Let my wife go, Masterson!" He rushed toward the couple and took hold of the man around his neck.

It was then Eleanor recognized Amelia Reed.

The two men began to fight in earnest. Wallace knocked the man to the ground. Eleanor realized it must be Grady Masterson—the man who had caused all of their trouble. Masterson threw a punch that narrowly missed Wallace's face, glancing off his shoulder instead. Wallace countered with a strike that squarely hit Masterson in the nose. The man flew backward and landed on the wooden planks of the dock.

Masterson jumped to his feet and shouted something about Avery helping him as he raced toward Wallace. Eleanor wondered who that might be. Didn't Bill mention something about a brother named Avery? But wasn't he dead?

Wallace avoided the charging figure. As he swept aside, Wallace kicked Masterson in the backside, sending him again to the ground. The man rolled over and hopped up. He paused only a moment to refocus his attention.

"I'm going to kill you, Wallace. Amelia is going with me. She owes me. I kept her and that brat of yours alive. She's mine." A small crowd had begun to gather.

"She'll never be yours." Wallace somehow managed to keep his temper and stand his ground.

Eleanor was surprised Wallace didn't advance the attack but instead waited for Masterson to make his move. He didn't wait long. Masterson charged again, but this time he was careful to grab hold of Wallace rather than just try to knock him down. The two men held each other fast while trying to also throw punches. It was unlike anything Eleanor had ever witnessed.

Wallace managed to get Masterson off balance and gave him a solid hit to his midsection. Eleanor heard the wind go out of the man in an "oof." He landed on the ground and rolled to his side gasping for air. He wasn't done, however, and managed to get to his feet.

"Enough is enough," Wallace declared. "I'm taking you to the police."

"I ain't going." Masterson got his wind back. "Me and Avery intend to make you pay."

"Avery's dead."

"Not as dead as you're gonna be," Masterson said, charging again.

The two men continued to fight, and Masterson got in a solid hit that sent Wallace backward—blood spurting from his nose. With Wallace down, Masterson pulled out his knife. "I'm going to end this now."

Eleanor wondered why no one else interceded. Amelia screamed, and a uniformed policeman came running with a plump woman and baby following. Upon seeing the police officer and feeling certain he'd take charge, Eleanor hurried to Amelia. "Amelia Reed. Oh, we've looked all over for you."

Amelia looked at Eleanor with a confused expression, then fixed her gaze back on the two men, who were both once again on their feet—but not for long. Eleanor turned and saw Masterson swipe the knife in Wallace's direction. He jumped back and lost his footing. Wallace went down, and Masterson went after him.

That's when the policeman stepped in. "Stop in the name of the law." Masterson looked up and realized the situation. He wasted no time in leaving the scene.

"Stop him!" Amelia yelled out. "He killed a woman."

The policeman went running after the man, while Wallace got to his feet and came to his wife's side.

Amelia stared at him as if he were a ghost. "They told me you were dead."

"Grady told you that. He made sure we thought you were dead too." Wallace stopped directly in front of her and reached up his hand to touch her face. Amelia didn't shy away.

She pressed her hand to the back of his and closed her eyes. "If this is a dream, then don't let me wake up."

"Open your eyes, Amelia. It's no dream. I'm really here." Wallace pulled Amelia into his arms and hugged her close.

Eleanor knew the moment Bill arrived. He stood directly behind her like a protective shield. She had prayed for this reunion, as she knew her husband had. It was even better than she had hoped for.

The woman with a babe in her arms stepped out of the shadows. Another police officer showed up, as did Eleanor's parents and Addie and Isaac Hanson.

"Where did the attacker go?" the officer asked.

"That way. Another policeman ran after him," Eleanor said, pointing.

The officer went running in the same direction. While the older woman looked at Eleanor as if to question her part in all of this. Eleanor smiled. "I'm Amelia's sister-in-law."

The woman frowned and drew the baby a little closer. Eleanor could see doubt in her expression. Bill stepped out from behind Eleanor.

"I'm Bill, her brother-in-law. That's Wallace, my brother and her husband, embracing Amelia."

"But he's dead," the woman replied.

Bill nodded. "I know that's what Grady Masterson told her. We thought Amelia was lost to us as well." He looked down at the baby. "Is that my nephew, Wally?"

The woman nodded. Just then Amelia pulled away from Wallace and drew him over to the woman and child. She took the baby from the woman and handed him to Wallace.

"Our son. I named him for you because I thought you were forever lost to me."

Wallace took the baby in his arms. His eyes were already wet with tears, but now those tears ran freely down his cheeks. "My son."

Eleanor felt her eyes dampen. She hadn't figured to put a handkerchief in her purse, but she needn't have worried. Bill handed her his, then whispered in her ear. "You'll have to share that with me."

She could see that his eyes were wet as well and smiled. "Of course."

23

The police returned with Grady struggling between them. They paused to speak with Amelia and Wallace. Bill waited long enough to get the story of what had happened, then took Eleanor by the hand and went to explain the situation to the others.

"We have no idea how he found her here," Bill told the Hansons and the Bennetts. "Somehow, he learned she was to leave on the ship. He approached her and tried to drag her away, but she argued with him and eventually started screaming.

"Wallace only knew that someone was in distress," Bill continued, "although I have a feeling he subconsciously recognized his wife's voice and went to the rescue. He and Grady fought, and Amelia's traveling companion went to find an officer to help."

"Before Wallace arrived, I saw a man trying to drag a woman to the street and figured to try and stop him," Eleanor threw in. "I was never so happy in my life to see Wallace show up to take the man in hand."

Just then Wallace and Amelia came to join them. Wallace

was still holding his son, and the sight of them filled Bill with wonder. He knew there was nothing better that God could have given his brother than the return of his wife and son. He silently praised God for His mercy and love.

"We have to remain in town a few days at least. Maybe a couple of weeks. They want to be sure they can close the books on Grady Masterson," Wallace said. He looked at Amelia and shook his head. "Grady is babbling on and on about having killed Mrs. Becker and that he came to the docks to kill me and Bill."

Eleanor grabbed at Bill's arm and held it tightly against her side. Bill hadn't even considered Grady might have wanted to kill him as well as Wallace.

His brother continued. "He is clearly insane. He talks as if Avery is still alive. Said that Avery was going to help him. He tried several times to lunge at me, but the police kept him under control. They've placed him under arrest for Mrs. Becker's murder."

"Goodness," Addie Hanson said, looking to Isaac. "This is terribly reminiscent of my brothers' antics. Are there so few good people left in the world that I know them all?"

Isaac put his arm around her shoulder and hugged her close. "There is a lot of evil, my dear. But rejoice, there is good as well. Just look at what God has wrought today."

Wallace smiled. "The lost has been found. I could not be happier."

"Nor I," Amelia replied, looking directly at her husband. "I was so certain you were dead. I still can't believe you're here."

"Well, believe it," Bill threw in. "We have Eleanor to thank for even knowing you are alive. If she hadn't taken that picture of you at the exposition and kept a copy because of her fascination with you, we would have never known you were alive. Grady would have gone on deceiving you."

Amelia stepped away from her husband's side and took hold of Eleanor's hands. "I'm so glad you asked to take my picture that day. When I look back on all of this and see God's part in it, I am overcome with awe. He prompted you to bother a poor widow with her babe so that in time my brother-in-law would see the picture you took and know I lived. It's all so amazing."

"I know," Eleanor said, giving Amelia's hands a squeeze. "I'm in awe of it too."

Amelia smiled. "And now you are my sister-in-law, and I shall have the privilege of getting to know you better in Alaska. It's all too wonderful."

"I agree." The two women embraced.

"This is all such an ordeal to even imagine, much less experience." Eleanor's mother dabbed her brow with a handkerchief. "I've never in my life even read about something more complicated."

"I'll agree with that." Mr. Bennett put his arm around his wife. "We have truly seen the work of God this day."

Addie had been speaking quietly to her husband, but now she stepped forward. "Since you folks have to stick around for a few days, Isaac and I want you to come stay in our new house. We have plenty of rooms and furnishings. There's no sense in you having to pay for a hotel."

"That's quite generous of you both," Wallace said, looking to Amelia. "What do you think?"

"I think it would be quite acceptable and welcome. I know I'm completely worn out."

"Then we accept," Wallace declared.

Eleanor came back to stand with Bill. "I'm happy to do whatever you like," she told him.

Bill looked to Isaac and Addie. "Thank you. I believe we'll take you up on the offer as well."

"Then let us leave this place," Isaac said, shaking his head. "I will arrange for an extra cab to take us all to our house."

"We can just return to the hotel," Eleanor's father said. "We're quite tired and have a room already waiting." He stepped to where Bill and Eleanor stood. "Why don't we meet in the morning at the hotel?"

"That would work for us," Bill said, looking to Eleanor, who nodded her approval.

Mr. Bennett kissed his daughter on the cheek and then put his hand on Bill's arm. "Until morning."

The ship's whistle sounded, and for just a moment, Bill regretted that they weren't on board. He resented the way Grady had changed their plans, but had he not, they might not have found Amelia. Although she and the baby were scheduled to be on the same ship. He could imagine the shock of running into each other on the trip north.

"All of our things are on the ship." Eleanor put her hand to her mouth.

"It's all right," Bill assured her. "We'll go speak to the freight office and arrange for everything. It'll be awaiting us in Seward."

"But I sent all of my clothes." Eleanor looked to Bill and then the others. "I didn't think to keep a bag with me."

They laughed, and Bill put his arm around her. "We'll buy you what you need. I received an advance, remember? We'll celebrate a little while we wait to go home."

Amelia glanced toward the ship and then to her husband. "I wish we were on that boat and headed home. I am weary of this place."

"I am too, but it won't be for long, my dear. I promise I will get you home as soon as I can."

❦

Eleanor remembered everything Bill had told her about Alaska as they docked two weeks later in Seward. The magnificence of the coast and all that she'd seen during their sailing was overwhelming. Bill had tried to describe the beauty, and photographs had depicted it, but it wasn't the same. The enormity of this land and its features were almost more than her mind could take in.

"What do you think?" Bill asked her as they stood at the rail waiting to debark. "You're blessed to see Seward at its best. Seems they've managed a lingering summer. The sea breeze feels so wonderful against the sun's warmth."

"It's everything you promised and more."

"And this is just a tiny part of it." He pulled her close to his side, and Eleanor went without hesitation. Bill turned her in his arms to face him. "And it's made so much better because you're here with me. Finding us was the biggest blessing of my life." He gave her a quick kiss, then released her so as not to make a huge public display. Eleanor made no attempt to move away. Instead, she turned to the scenery once again and leaned back against Bill.

"I can hardly believe we're here and that all of this is to be my home." She shook her head and continued to try to take it all in at once. "It's too wonderful. Just look at all God has done."

"I think about how terrible my life was just a few months ago. I was lost in sorrow and mourning. I couldn't see how God was going to set things right. I have to admit that as brave of a face as I put on, I wasn't anywhere near so strong."

"You had gone through a great deal." Eleanor considered his trials. "You had lost so much—not just Amelia and the baby, but in so many ways your brother. Then there was the manuscript you'd worked on so long and hard. Maybe this next one will go faster with me by your side."

"Everything seems to go faster with you by my side," Bill said, chuckling. "It will be quite a challenge for you up here. Things go at a different pace. Alaska time isn't the same as what the rest of the world knows."

Eleanor considered that a moment. "I'm sure I can adjust. That's another thing you'll have to learn about me. I can be quite flexible when I learn a better way. You should keep that in mind."

"Noted," he said in a most serious tone.

Eleanor glanced back at him and saw the twinkle in his eyes. She smiled and turned back to gaze across the docks. "It's so glorious here. I'll be happy to adjust to Alaska time."

Bill put his arms around her. "I sometimes imagine the Garden of Eden being like this, only without the harsh cold and—" He slapped at a mosquito that had landed on his cheek. "And the insects."

Eleanor laughed. "Oh, they aren't so bad. I'm sure we'll get along." A mosquito landed on her bare arm, and she followed Bill's example.

"I see you've met the welcoming committee." Wallace chuckled as he and Amelia joined them. The baby was sound asleep in Amelia's arms, and she had carefully covered him with netting.

Bill nudged his brother. "My wife was just saying she was sure she'd be able to get along just fine with the pests."

Wallace laughed all the more. "Tell me that in a week."

"Exactly my thought," Bill replied.

Eleanor turned and smiled at both of the men. "No matter what problems may come, I am fully prepared to be happy here. God has given me all that my heart desired. How could I not find contentment and joy?"

"Well said." Wallace looked at Amelia. "Who cares about those pesky little problems when God's blessings stand before us in abundance."

"All ashore for Seward," one of the ship's officers announced.

Eleanor looked at her husband, eyes wide and heart pounding. "This is really happening."

"It is," he agreed. He took her by the arm. "Shall we go forward?"

She nodded. "With you, my dearest love, I would go anywhere."

Tracie Peterson is the award-winning author of over one hundred novels, both historical and contemporary. She is often referred to as the "Queen of Historical Christian Fiction," and her avid research resonates in her stories, as seen in her bestselling HEIRS OF MONTANA and ALASKAN QUEST series. Tracie considers her writing a ministry for God to share the Gospel and biblical application. She and her family make their home in Montana. Visit her website at traciepeterson.com or on Facebook at facebook.com/AuthorTraciePeterson.

Sign Up for Tracie's Newsletter

Keep up to date with Tracie's latest news on book releases and events by signing up for her email list at the link below.

FOLLOW TRACIE ON SOCIAL MEDIA!

Tracie Peterson   @authortraciepeterson

TraciePeterson.com

More from Tracie Peterson

 Haunted by heartbreak and betrayal, Addie Bryant escapes her terrible circumstances with the hope she can forever hide her past and with the belief she will never have the future she's always dreamed of. When she's reunited with her lost love, Addie must decide whether to run or to face her wounds to embrace her life, her future, and her hope in God.

Remember Me
PICTURES OF THE HEART #1

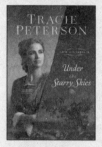 When an accident leaves Cassandra Barton incapacitated, she spends her time compiling a book of stories about the men working on the Santa Fe Railroad. But worry grows as revolutionaries set out to destroy the railroad. As the danger intensifies, Cassie and her longtime friend Brandon must rely on their faith to overcome the obstacles that stand in the way.

Under the Starry Skies
LOVE ON THE SANTA FE

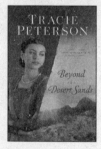 After living an opulent life with her aunt, the last thing Isabella Garcia wants is to celebrate Christmas in a small mining town with her parents. But she's surprised to see how much the town—and an old rival—has changed and how fragile her father's health has become. Faced with many changes, can she sort through her future and decide who she wants to be?

Beyond the Desert Sands
LOVE ON THE SANTA FE

◊ BETHANYHOUSE

Bethany House Fiction   @bethanyhousefiction   @bethany_house   @bethanyhousefiction

OB Free exclusive resources for your book group at bethanyhouseopenbook.com

 Sign up for our fiction newsletter today at bethanyhouse.com